THE REBOUND PLAN

AINSLEY BOOTH

Cover design, Ainsley Booth.

Copyright Ainsley Booth, 2024.

All Rights Reserved.

www.ainsleybooth.com

This one is for the readers who are love a slow burn, because there is a lot of stuff to burn in this book. A marriage, first. We're going to burn it to the ground because it isn't right. And then all the shackles that hold us back from everything we've ever dreamed of.

ABOUT THIS BOOK

I've got one week to get my head in the game and forget about my inconvenient attraction to my teammate's wife.

A relaxing retreat to cottage country with my teammates is the perfect way to prep for the upcoming hockey season.

Or so I thought.

Now I'm trapped in my cabin with my crush–and her jerk of a husband–where it's impossible to get space or clarity. Or get over her. And that mission becomes even harder when I learn that Shannon's marriage is failing.

With the lines of loyalty and friendship becoming blurred, and relationships being tested in all directions, I know I need to tap the brakes hard.

Until one night when everyone else is at a party down the lake, and the team captain makes me an offer I can't refuse…to share his wife, and have a taste of the forbidden I always assumed was forever out of reach.

GLOSSARY

*aka let's talk about how Ontario may or may not be the centre of
the universe*

The Rebound Plan takes place in Ontario, Canada, and so even though one of the main characters is American (and the other was born in Scotland!), it is written in Canadian English! For example, "centre of the universe" is spelt with the -re spelling instead of -er on centre!

Now, don't worry, there are a lot of characters who do *not* think that Ontario is the centre of the universe. (This note is primarily for readers from Western Canada)

But I get this specific in my glossary terms because just like other geographically vast countries, Canada has a lot of regionalisms!

I've also highlighted a hockey term you may not have heard of before. For more Canadianisms, check out the glossaries in the other novels in this series, *The Playing Game* and *The Scoring Secret*. The complete glossary is also posted on my website.

Muskoka Chair - an Adirondack chair, basically, but located outside a cottage in the Muskoka region of Ontario, aka where hockey players go in the summer when they aren't at weddings in Banff

Golden Horseshoe - the dense string of cities around the western curve of Lake Ontario, stretching out in all directions from Toronto, where 25% of Canada's population lives; a creative writer might look at the map and think Hamilton is actually at the centre of the horseshoe, and they would be correct. For hockey context in this series, the Golden Horseshoe teams would be Toronto, Hamilton, and Buffalo

Kinloss - a hamlet in Scotland; also a hamlet in Canada, close to where I grew up! Much of Southwestern Ontario was named by Scottish settlers.

Shoresy - the main character in a Canadian comedy series about a small-town hockey player; a spin off from the TV show *Letterkenny* from the same creators. Worth checking out clips of both of them on YouTube! NSFW humour, FYI

Waivers - the process through which a hockey team makes a player available to other teams to claim, for a twenty-four hour period, before sending them down to a lower league for assignment; this prevents a team from sticking a player in the minors who would otherwise be wanted by another team; but because of the hard salary cap in hockey, good players do clear waivers regularly, but fans have to hold their breath for those 24 hours

CHAPTER 1
SHANNON

"I'm sorry, I don't know where Max is," I say apologetically. That part is true. But my expression carefully also conveys that my husband's absence is a strange mystery, and that part is a complete lie.

I know exactly why he hasn't shown up to this photo shoot—it's a punishment.

Until a month ago, he would never have done anything this blatant. For the first eight years of our marriage, I always wondered if the occasional edge of anger that I saw was just in my imagination. That's how good he was at masking.

And then I ruined everything.

The nearest door to the small banquet hall where the photographers and videographers are set up swings open, and in strides a hockey player in full gear except for his skates, which are slung over his shoulder—but not the one we're expecting.

Instead of Max Tilman, captain of the Hamilton Highlanders (and my husband for at least a few more months), it's a third line forward named Russ Armstrong.

A big, tall, brooding Scottish distraction. My husband's teammate.

His gaze slices across the room, immediately locking on my face for a second that feels like a lifetime. His expression tells me that he knows I've been abandoned, that Max meant for this to be embarrassing, and Russ isn't going to let that happen.

Damn them both.

I don't need to be rescued. And if anyone is going to be embarrassed by a no-show, it's going to be the narcissistic asshole whose number is unfortunately plastered all over the custom WAG jersey I've been wearing for the last hour. It's a feminine version of Max's jersey, cut to my proportions.

Maybe Russ knows that I'm not the person to convince that he's being a hero right now. Instead, he beelines to Mabel, who is the head of public relations for the Highlanders. "Seems like there was a mixup. I'm not exactly a pretty face, but I can fill in."

"You're perfect," she says with the kind of bright enthusiasm I used to channel with ease. "Shannon, we might not..."

I nod and wave my hand at the same time. Of course they won't need me in the photo anymore.

While Mabel murmurs with the photographer about rearranging the kids who will be in the promo material for our winter Highlanders Ball, Russ and I pretend not to look at each other, which doesn't really work.

He grunts something imperceptible and crosses to the pile of toys on the black cloth photo backdrop. "Hey, kids," he says in his slight Scottish burr, moderated by living his entire teen and adult life in Canada. He drops down to an easy squat and holds out his hand to the first child.

I spin around and busy myself with examining the storyboard the photographer has sketched out that won't be used, Max and me, wearing matching jerseys, surrounded by children in formal suits and tiny ballgowns.

Behind me, there's a ripple of giggles, and another grunt. Then murmurs.

Suddenly a small child is beside me, tugging at my jersey. "Can I wear your shirt?"

I glance down at her. "This one?"

She nods, pointing back at Russ. "He says it would be funny if I'm wearing a grownup jersey."

I follow her finger and meet his gaze. "Maybe we can get her one—"

"The others are all too big," he says, cutting me off. "Yours is just right to puddle on the floor at her feet."

Mabel holds up a spare jersey, but Russ is right. They're all bigger than this little girl. But the one they made for me might just look like a long, slouchy dress on her.

He stands, murmuring a joking apology to the kids who had crowded in around him, and crosses to me in a few long strides. His gaze never wavers from my face, and by the time he stops in front of me, my cheeks are blazing. He lowers his voice. "If you need another jersey to wear instead, you can have mine."

And suddenly I'm breathless.

I tug the custom jersey over my head, and when it clears my face and I can see Russ again, his gaze has shifted. There's a primal sharpness to his expression now, something I haven't seen quite exactly before. Something that feels much more dangerous than anything else we've shared over the last five weeks.

It's not the softness he showed me when he discovered me crying outside a family law office, or the confused awareness that zinged between us that night by his pool.

This look is one of a hunter.

Maybe this is how his opponents feel when he eyes them from across the ice and decides they aren't going to win a puck battle.

He takes the jersey that has Max's number on the back, the number I always wear at team events, and he drapes it over the little girl who is bouncing excitedly next to us. "There you go, princess. Fits you perfectly. You can keep that one."

I gape at him, but he doesn't look back at me. He's not interested in debating whether my jersey is his to give away or not. He just reaches past me and grabs one of the others Mabel is holding out.

"Don't want you to get cold," he says, turning back.

It's his own jersey, just like the one he's wearing. He floats it over my head, the heavy fabric settling on my shoulders with a weight that feels heavier than just a hockey sweater.

Against my will, I feel myself pushing my arms through the sleeves, and his hungry gaze drops down to his number there.

If I turn around and stalk away from him, he'll see it branded on my back.

"We're ready to start," the photographer says.

"This won't take long," he says. "Wait for me."

And I want to, so much, but I can't.

As Russ is pulled back to the children, I flee, racing out

the side door and across the hall to another room that's being used for anything. I'm not needed for this photo shoot anymore.

I'm not needed for anything to do with this team anymore, and it breaks my heart.

In the quiet, I yank off his jersey.

It doesn't take him long to follow, though.

When the door behind me opens, I nearly jump out of my skin.

Russ raises his hands. "It's just me."

I laugh weakly. "That was fast."

He winces. "You waved at a reporter I know on your way in here."

The anxiety explodes in my brain, like an oncoming car turning on their high beams. "A reporter?"

"It's okay." He comes closer. "Aaron's a good guy, and you wearing my jersey isn't sports news. There are some weirdos on Twitter who might find it interesting, and I really liked it, but it's your personal business."

I throw his jersey at him. "Not funny."

"I'm not laughing."

He closes the gap between us.

"Russ, we can't…" I trail off as he lifts his hand.

His fingers hover just above my bare shoulder. "Can't do what?"

"Anything."

"But we already have." His hand lowers, those fingers making contact with my shoulder.

I shudder at the deep, profound ache that spirals through me from that warm press. I miss being wanted.

I miss being desired. That's all that this is. I'm vulnerable to his attention because I haven't been a good enough wife and—

He drags his fingers up my neck and tips my chin up. "I'm not going to kiss another man's wife, don't worry."

I gasp and jerk away from him.

Russ catches me and spins me around, pressing me against the wall. Crowding against me.

He murmurs secrets in my ear.

I choke on a sob, and he just holds me tight, pressing me against the wall, until the fight leaves my body and I sag.

Then he turns me around and pulls me into his chest, hugging me even tighter than he pressed me against the wall.

"Why did you..." The words clog in my throat. I hope he can read my mind with the rest of the unspoken question. *Why did you get physical like that?*

After a long pause, he grates out, "You looked like you needed it."

I have to fight against this, because I hate what it would mean if he's right. "You don't know what I need."

"Maybe I don't. But neither does your husband."

CHAPTER 2
RUSS

Five weeks earlier

The hockey season is measured in games, and if you're lucky, wins. If you aren't, then injuries. Eighty-two games in the regular season. One stint on the injured reserve list for an upper body injury. Sixteen wins in the playoffs to make it all the way to hoisting the Cup over your head.

The hockey off-season, on the other hand, is measured in weddings. And if you're single and lucky, phone numbers.

Luck has not been on my side this summer. Or last season. Or any season in the sixteen years I've been playing professional hockey.

And yet I still believe, deep down, what I learned from my juniors coach—if you're really stuck into it, if you're competitive enough, and you've got your teammates' backs, eventually the luck will turn your way. "It's hard work, boys," he would say. "Hard work and teamwork. Never give up on that. Be fucking relentless."

Last year, we came really fucking close.

Not close to getting the Cup. Not *that* close.

We shat ourselves in the first round, unfortunately. Our playoffs were measured in four losses, and then we were kicked to the curb for wedding season to start earlier than we wanted it to.

But in the regular season, we had the right combination. We worked so fucking hard. We pulled ourselves together as a team, climbing the standings and finishing on a hot streak. And in that streak, at the end of the season, that's where we got really close.

That's also where it ended.

But we had the right combination. We could taste it.

All summer, in between the inevitable weddings, all we've talked about is getting that energy back for this coming season.

And now everyone else is finished with social events.

Me? I have one more wedding. It's in progress, actually, and I'm the big dummy paying more attention to his phone and the group chat than I am to the party around me.

But dancing has started and I don't feel like it.

I've been miserably in love with someone off-limits for a year, so I'm not yet ready to browse the singles table. Also, nobody wants to dance with a six-foot-five enforcer. I wear a neon sign that screams *this guy has no rhythm*.

So I've succumbed to the team group chat.

The vast majority of us keep training pretty hard in the off-season, but there's "stay fit and keep skating" and then there's "training camp is around the corner and we want vengeance for how last year ended."

Two different modes, and our captain is officially shifting gears. He starts with the smaller group chat for the older players, those of us who aren't going to get waived out of training camp.

> **MAX**
>
> Marshie, are you back from your honeymoon yet?
>
> **KIERAN**
>
> Just flew back this morning. What's up?
>
> **MAX**
>
> We need to start training
>
> **KIERAN**
>
> Did you ever stop?
>
> **MAX**
>
> Never
>
> **KIERAN**
>
> I'm getting back to it, don't worry - Rusty's booked us some ice time next week up at his new cottage
>
> **MAX**
>
> New cottage? Armstrong, WTF, you holding out on us? You secured some real estate?

I groan and shoot Kieran a private WTF message of my own. I did buy a cottage, a right place, right time opportunity that landed in my lap right after Kieran's wedding, when I was having a personal crisis of confidence in some of my choices over the last year. The property is my commitment to myself, that I'm going to earn the performance bonuses due to come my way if we are better this year.

If I'm not distracted.

KIERAN

Sorry, bud, jet lag got the better of me

But Max is already going full steam in the group chat.

MAX

Dude, we need to have a team retreat immediately.

How many people can this place sleep?

Even as I'm sighing, I have to admit Max has the right idea. And my cottage *is* big enough for this.

RUSS

At least fifteen.

MAX

Excellent

The girls, too? You know Marshie's not going to be separated from his new bride. I'd be down for guys only, of course.

RUSS

Better halves are welcome.

And then a string of individual texts come in as he spreads the word. Some I like, like an earnest one from last year's best rookie, Hayden Calhoun.

HAYDEN

Congrats on the new cottage, man! Tiller says I need to work with you on my defense, so count me in on a retreat.

And some I don't know how to respond to.

SHANNON

Hey, so... Max says you bought a new place and everyone in town is invited? That's really generous of you.

Dots appear on the screen, then disappear. A minute goes by and I just grip my phone. Other text messages from teammates come in and I ignore them, waiting for those dots again.

This is exactly the problem. I need to move on from these feelings that trap me in moments exactly like this.

SHANNON

Whatever you need, I'm yours.

Fuck. Me.

I drop my phone on the flower-laden table in front of me. I'm ready for the hockey wedding season to be over.

I need a far less romantic setting for my first attempt to get back into the dating space. Because I *do* need to get back on that horse.

Can you call it a rebound relationship if there wasn't a break up before it? I need an emotionless, physical fling to get over my nothing-but-one-sided-feelings obsession.

"What's wrong, Rusty?"

The groom's sister drops into the seat beside me. I haven't seen her in a couple of years, but that doesn't stop her from immediately inserting herself into my private misery.

Once upon a time, Emery "Buzz" Granger was a tomboy teenager who geeked out on getting to play hockey with pro athletes because her older brothers are all in the league.

Today, she's a bridesmaid at her oldest brother's third wedding. She's still a bit of a tomboy, because she's got

Converse sneakers on under her champagne-coloured satin dress. Earlier, she won an arm-wrestling competition against a D-man twice her size.

Grangers have always been fiercely competitive. And nosy.

"Who said anything's wrong?" The open bar has thickened my usually mild Scottish accent. Twenty-four years of living in Canada undone by top shelf liquor.

"Your face."

An observant tomboy, then.

I narrow my eyes at her. If the universe thought this was the woman to put in my path, there's no hope for me.

But all I see staring back at me is friendly curiosity.

And fuck it, I need to talk this out with someone. Might as well be someone who doesn't know anyone on the Highlanders. Emery speaks hockey, but she lives three states and a province away from all my problems. I'm not likely to see her again for another three years after tonight—or ever.

"I bought a house two weeks ago." I leave out the fact that it was a rash purchase, a reaction after another wedding just like this one, teaming with hockey players and their wives and girlfriends.

The girls, too?

I walked right into that one.

The worst part is that he doesn't even want her there—but I can't resist the temptation of making him bring her along.

"My condolences," Emery says dryly.

"It's a huge compound in cottage country."

"Even worse."

"And my team captain just found out. He's, uh, demanding I host something for the team next weekend."

"Oooooh." Now her sympathy seems sincere. "You got volun-told."

"I sure did."

"A team-only retreat before training camp? Getting everyone on the same page about coming back even tougher than last year?"

"You really were raised in the NHL, weren't you?"

"The hype speech pumps through my veins, yeah." She lowers her voice and does a bang-on imitation of her father, a legendary player and now a part of the Chicago front office. "You have to dial in and really find a focus together."

I laugh despite myself.

She sighs melodramatically. "How are you going to survive?"

"Shut up."

"Okay." She swirls the ice in her glass, then shoves it at me.

I take a swig, expecting it to be whiskey.

It's ginger ale, and the sweet carbonated bubbles make me choke in surprise.

She laughs, burying her face in her hand.

I swear under my breath, and she wipes her eyes. "Oh, man. Your face right now. I've missed you, Rusty."

"Same, kiddo." I make a face and down the rest of her drink. "What's new with you?"

"I went to culinary school. But let's not change the subject so fast. What's the problem with hosting what you know is probably a good idea?"

Because it's getting harder and harder to lie to myself about what I really want. "It's complicated."

"Try me."

"It's private."

"I'm good with secrets."

"Buzz—"

"Do you know why my nickname is Buzz?"

I try to remember, but I've had a lot of whiskey and her childhood was a long time ago. "No."

"My brothers told me to buzz off all the time, and I refused to leave them alone."

I laugh, because the way she delivers it is funny. And then I stop, because it's not really funny. "Ach."

"I'm persistent," she says.

"I got it. That's pretty clear."

"Is this a midlife crisis?" She tips her head to the side. "How old are you?"

I sigh. "I'm thirty-six."

She pretends to do math on her fingers. "So…it could be. Like Camden marrying a divorce attorney."

Aye, that was a weird choice for his third wife. Hopefully she's his forever person, but the odds aren't in his favour and I bet that prenup is weighted nicely in hers. "Fuck off."

She smiles. "Is it a nice cottage?"

Sighing, I pull out my phone and show her the photos. She whistles as she scrolls through them. "Straight out of a fancy magazine, Mr. Armstrong."

"I've never bought a house before. Turns out, I can afford a pretty nice one."

She snorts. "You think?"

"Hey, have some sympathy for those of us in the bottom six, okay? Being relatively rich but also having constant job security concerns is more stressful than you might think."

She purses her lips together and nods mockingly. "Tell the girl skater more about how hard your hockey career is, bro."

Fuck. "Sorry."

"It's all right." Her eyes twinkle. "All of my brothers have full no-move clauses, so I wouldn't actually know what this stress is that you talk about."

"You. Brat." I swat in the air. "Fully earned your nickname."

"Won't it be nice to show off your place to your teammates?"

"It's not just the guys." I swallow thickly. "The attached ones are bringing wives and girlfriends."

Her brows knit together. "And?"

And it fucking hurts. "I feel like a damned fifth wheel. I'm the only older guy who's single, and I'm over that. I bought this place to put down roots and tell the universe I was ready for more. By more, I didn't mean a dozen overeager young hockey players."

"Ah." She nods.

"What, *ah?*"

"This was supposed to be a house to feel your feelings in, and now your teammates are going to crash that party."

I grunt. "I wouldn't say it like that. It's the first step in a rebound plan."

"Rebound from what?"

"Never mind."

She carries on as if I've said more than that. "Most people just hook up with a stranger. Real estate is an interesting choice." She waves across the tent at her brother. "Camden bought a lake house after his first divorce. A word to the wise, though—he slept with the stranger, too, *at the lake house,* and she became his second wife."

I remember. It didn't last long. "Did she get the lake house in the divorce?"

"Oh yeah." She twirls her finger in the air to refocus the conversation. "Okay, so this retreat is a good idea, yes?"

"Yes."

"But you don't want all the happy relationships rubbed in your face in your last week of summer."

A heavy weight presses down on my shoulders. I hate how easily she got all of that out of me. I need to deal with this shit once and for all so I can focus on hockey properly this upcoming season. "Get to the point, Buzz. And don't be too wise. I'm not humble enough to take advice from a twenty-one-year-old."

"I'm twenty-four," she says blithely. "Is that too young for you to date?"

I jolt upright, too fast, and my chair topples sideways, dumping me onto the floor.

Everyone turns and looks.

Emery waves her hands. "It's okay, folks! He's just had too much ginger ale."

I stare at her sneakers, then at the swish of her satin gown as she stands and leans over to give me a hand up. I avoid making eye contact with her cleavage as the world tilts around me and I heave to my feet. Because twenty-four or not, she's still my buddy's little sister, and I'm in love with someone else.

"Is the idea of dating me that awful?" She's teasing.

I glare down at her now that we're both standing. "You're teasing, right?"

Because I need to be sure, and I've had a lot to drink.

She pats my chest with the confidence of someone who hasn't been drinking at all. "Relax."

"Look, Emery, you're very pretty and smart and—"

"You don't need to let me down gently, Rusty. I'm not

into you. Ew, please be serious. You're the same age as my thrice-married brother, and you literally just bought your first house. No offence, but my standards are higher than that. I'm offering you my help." She looks at me like I'm an idiot, which is very possible given that I didn't consider the obvious fact that, of course, the youngest Granger would be above dating *me*, a third-line journeyman player. A nobody.

"Can you take pity on an old man and spell out what exactly this help you're offering might be?"

She gives me her cutest, most deadly smile. "You don't like that this was thrust upon you. You don't want to feel like an outsider at your own housewarming party."

"I wouldn't call it a party."

She rolls her eyes. "Yes, but you *should*. And to make it a proper party, you need a hostess." She flutters her hands down her satin-covered body and back up to her now-innocent expression. "Me."

CHAPTER 3
SHANNON

"Shan!" My husband's voice rings through the lovely house we bought a year ago when he was named the captain of the NHL's latest franchise team. A house I made a home, because that's my job, and I'm very good at it. "Where are you?"

"I'm in the kitchen," I sing out, proud of how my voice doesn't tremble.

I don't mention the fact that while I waited for Russ to get back to me, I spent twenty minutes deleting tags and mentions of both of us on Instagram. Max doesn't check his own account very often because fan comments get in his head, so I have his account on my phone, too. And this afternoon, we were both tagged in another picture of me from a lifetime ago.

A photo where I'm only wearing other people's hands.

At least it wasn't one where I'm on the arm of a billionaire. Max hates those the most.

There are a couple of troll hockey gossip accounts that are fixated on my modelling career and who I was photographed with in New York before I met Max. It's petty and uninteresting to the vast majority of hockey fans, right up there with the rumoured penis piercings of certain players and the weirder stories from around the league like the cute but dumb himbo centre who married his own stalker. Off-season interest only.

During the hockey season, there's enough current gossip that old news sinks. But every summer, little whispers circulate, and Max hates them, so I do my best to stay on top of both of us being untagged, and blocking any new accounts that pop up so he never sees it.

When I do it well, it's something he's completely unaware of—and so it's hard to expect him to appreciate me for that work.

The smoothie makings being set out on the counter when he gets back from a workout, however, he can see—and is appreciative about. He steps into the kitchen and grins. He's a creature of habit, and I like making him happy.

"How was your workout?" It's a safe question to ask because he's in a good mood. If he was cranky when he came home, I'd ask him about something that might mollify him, like what he wants for dinner, or remind him of a movie he wanted to watch.

"Good." He pops a frozen raspberry into his mouth, then carefully measures out everything he wants in his smoothie. As he finishes with each ingredient, I put it away.

At this point in the off-season, he's starting to shift from bulking up to cutting fat. We're just a few weeks away from him reporting to training camp, although enough of his teammates live here in Hamilton year-round that it still feels like he's pretty dialled in to the team training over the summer.

When he's got his smoothie in hand and the kitchen is pristine again, I remind him that I'm heading out. "I'm going to a Paint and Sip night with Ani."

Unexpectedly, he catches my wrist as I turn to leave.

I glance back, and he has a funny look on his face. There's a shard of uncertainty that I recognize—deep down, Max needs a lot of petting—but there's something else less familiar.

"You know I appreciate you, right?"

"Of course." I let him pull me in close.

We're not the most affectionate of couples, especially when alone, unless Max wants sex, and he never wants sex after a workout.

So for him to just hug me is...unusual. And he's holding a smoothie, so most of my attention is on the cool condensation being pressed against my back.

I wind my arms around his neck, giving him whatever he needs, even if I don't understand it. That's my job because I'm his wife, and I'm so good at this.

Everyone says so, and Max so rarely seems to share that sentiment.

"Everything okay?" I whisper into his hair.

It's a tricky question. If the answer is no, then he'll find a way to take it out on me.

"Everything's great." He swallows hard, his throat working against my upper arm. "Contract talks are heating up. I think they want to announce something before the start of training camp, which puts us in a great position."

"Oh!" I exhale in relief. "That is great news."

Max is going into the final season of an eight-year deal he signed in New York, a contract that Hamilton picked up last year when they named him the first captain of the new team. He's the marquee player, so of course they'll want to renew his contract, but the way it works in hockey is that players in their thirties take less money on subsequent contracts—eating a bit of a discount to stay in a place where they are beloved—to allow salary cap space for the next generation to get their once-in-a-lifetime big deal contracts.

Max has had his. We are set for life with the money he has already made, and anything else will be gravy. It grates on him that he'll be expected to take a pay cut, and he doesn't like it pointed out that at thirty-four, his best playing years are behind him now.

It's not like he's alone on the team in this position, but he hates that being pointed out, too.

And he's weird about me and his money. Maybe because of the company I used to keep, and the wild life I once had—he's convinced I was more into drugs than I ever was—but our marriage contract and prenup are both *tight*.

So, I never say anything. It's none of my business. His career is his career. My role is charity support and being the pretty, cheering face in the stands.

"Yeah, I'm relieved that we finally have some good leverage. This new agent is earning his cut, that's for sure." He releases me and takes a big, slurping sip of his smoothie even before I pull away from him.

And I guess the sweet intimacy part of our day is over.

I pat his arm. "Russ hasn't texted me back. Are you sure he wants the wives and girlfriends to come up, too?"

"That's what he said." Max wipes his mouth with the back of his hand. "Apparently this place is huge. Big enough for a good party, with separate accommodations for couples." Max waggles his eyebrows at me.

And now the pervy suggestions part of the evening begins. My husband is a teenage boy when it comes to sex—mostly a lot of hot air and promises that don't materialize, which is for the best because his idea of what is *super hot* is often super not. He never believes me that I'm happy with the standard vanilla basics, but the way he tries to fancy it up can be a mood-wrecker.

Add beer into the mix and…a weekend with his teammates sounds like a lot of feelings to manage. His, mine, and outside observers.

"I don't know," I say, but then his expression drops.

Trap, trap, trap.

I resign myself to the inevitable. "I'll get on the group chat, then."

He gives me a cocky grin that tells me I negotiated the mine field well. "You're the best, hun."

SHANNON

Have you guys all heard about this mini team retreat Russ is hosting next week? We're invited, too. Let me know if you have any questions.

While I wait for the other wives and girlfriends to reply, I walk over to Ani Hale's house, just a few blocks away. She and her husband Jenson are a decade younger than Max and me. Jenson wears an A on his jersey as an alternate captain for the team, the hometown boy who will be the face of the franchise for the next decade or more. Right now he's in Vail at a skating camp with a few other Black professional hockey players, both from the NHL and the new women's pro league, and some other minor pro leagues, too.

Since she's alone for the week, and our other friends aren't in town—Harper in Italy on her honeymoon, Becca up north in Pine Harbour, Kiley in Miami—it's been my pleasure to distract her.

The fun little painting adventure we're going on tonight is exactly what I need to take my mind off the strange, unsettled feeling that looms whenever I'm alone.

She's outside when I get there, talking to her neighbour, a middle-aged white hippie chick who I recognize from previous visits but I can't remember her name. She smells like patchouli and weed, and reminds me of my first landlady in NYC. She's also a fan of Ani's art, if maybe slightly too enthusiastic.

Today she seems to have questions about an Indigenous banner Ani has hung out front to represent her Six Nations heritage.

"No, but Ani, I *love it*. Name your price."

"Here's my friend," Ani says brightly, excusing herself from the conversation. "We're running late for a Paint and Sip night!"

"What was that all about?" I ask once we're safely in Ani's car.

"She wants me to make her a matching banner for *solidarity*," Ani says. "And wasn't picking up on my clues that I made that for myself, not to sell."

"That's awkward."

"A little bit. But she'll have forgotten by tomorrow. Or when she's not high, she'll hear my no more clearly. Anyway, are you ready to get your paint on?"

"For a professional artist, you are very into this idea." I narrow my eyes as she innocently stares straight ahead.

"Wait a second. Are we doing professional reconnaissance here?"

"Maaaaaybe." She winks at me. "But not for profit. I was thinking of hosting a fundraising paint night for the team foundation. I didn't want to put the idea forward until we'd actually gone and done one of these things, to have a proper feel for it. What do you think?"

"I love it. Truly, a genius idea. And if you wanted to make it a series of events, we could probably have a goalie helmet artist lead a night, too?"

She bounces in the driver's seat. "Yes! And maybe…"

We pinball ideas back and forth until we get to the shopping centre where the studio is located. Inside, we're shown to our reserved easels, and then a waitress comes around with a menu.

I order a glass of red wine, and Ani asks for the featured mocktail.

I don't ask if that's only because she's driving, or if it's related to the fact that her and Jenson are trying to get pregnant.

She reads my mind anyway. "My period arrived this morning. This is only because I'm being a responsible driver."

"Oh, honey, I'm sorry." I squeeze her hand.

"Oh no, we were trying *not* to do it this month. Nine months from now would be right in the middle of…" She knocks on her easel. "*Playoffs*," she mouths.

"Do you know how many babies show up between April and June every year? I swear, NHL players get all their sperm out of their system in the summer. But you're smart. Another month, and you'll pretty safely be past that and into a darling summer baby for next year."

Giggling, she glances around. "It looks like there's a good crowd tonight."

I nod. It's quite a mix of people. While there are a couple of clusters of who I'd expect—women our age, out for girls' nights—there are also a few older people, and a couple of college-age kids who look like they might be on a date.

Immediately to my left, there is a good-looking guy sitting on his own who looks uncertain, which makes him stand out.

"Welcome to Paint and Sip," our instructor says, drawing our attention forward. "Tonight we're painting a Harvest Sunset. When we finish, there will be a chance to mingle and chat as your paintings dry. If you have to leave before they are ready to travel, we'll keep them safe for you and you can come back any time this week to pick them up."

"That's a bit of a logistical consideration for us," Ani whispers. She makes a note on her phone.

It's a pretty straightforward experience once we get into it. First, we paint the background, and then we take a break so that can dry before we add the sunflowers to the foreground.

I order another glass of wine and examine the differences between my painting and Ani's. Hers is even better than the finished example at the front of the room. No surprise, given her training and talent. And mine...

"What do you do with the paintings if they aren't good at the end?" That question comes from the solo guy next to me.

I laugh and look over at his painting. He's clearly compared ours and decided we are in the same boat, and he's not wrong. "I was just thinking the same thing."

"I'm Jake," he says, holding out his hand.

I put my wine glass down and shake it. "Shannon. And this is my friend Ani."

"Nice to meet you both."

Our break ends before we can talk any further. The next hour races by with a good amount of swearing under my breath, which Ani finds deeply entertaining.

At one point, Jake gets so frustrated he gets up and paces away. Ani immediately leans over. "He keeps checking you out."

"Because we're both so bad at this." I sigh. "Why is yours so pretty?"

"Not my first rodeo. Want to bet he offers to buy you a drink when we finish?"

"I'm wearing a wedding ring!"

She smirks. "Some men like married women."

"They're barking up the wrong tree with me."

But just to make that clear, when Jake stalks back and takes a deep breath before sitting back down, I lean over slightly. "So what you're saying is, I shouldn't bring my husband here on our next date night?"

He laughs. "It would be more fun with someone else."

"You have us now," Ani says.

He glances at her canvas and his eyebrows shoot up.

"She's a professional artist," I explain.

"Do you want to finish mine?" he asks her. "I'll get you ladies another round of drinks if you do."

"No can do," she says sweetly. "Now shhh, this is an important part of the lesson."

And then she flashes an *I told you* look at me, but he didn't offer to buy *me* a drink. He was willing to barter drinks for Ani's incredible skill.

When we finish, I get up and stretch, my shoulders stiff and aching from holding my brush too tightly, apparently.

As I lift my arms over my head, Jake glances at my chest for a split second before beelining to the bar for another beer.

From across the room, he mimes lifting a glass at me, but I shake my head.

Ani is deeply enjoying all of this far too much.

"Stop it," I whisper under my breath. "How long until these will dry?"

"Another hour, maybe."

When Jake returns, though, he only has his own drink, and he's clearly accepted that flirting isn't going to happen tonight.

He makes the rounds of the other paintings, encouraging everyone to look at his if they want to feel better about their own, and he admits to the women next to us that he came out tonight because his fourteen-year-old daughter told him there would be lots of single ladies.

That gets a big laugh from everyone within hearing range.

"It really is more of a date thing than a single mingle," he mutters as he returns to his easel. He looks at me with an easy, *don't worry I didn't forget you're married* look. "Your husband might have fun after all."

The odds that Max would have fun at a place like this are negative ten million.

Jake frowns a little and looks at my face again. "You look familiar. Have we met before?"

Now that he's given up on my boobs, he recognizes me. I give him my public smile. "Are you a hockey fan? It's possible you recognize me because of my husband. He plays for the Highlanders."

"That's it." He snaps his fingers. "Both of you are WAGs, right? I'm a big fan. Of hockey, I mean. Not WAGs, although you guys are great, I'm sure." He's tripping over his words now, but in a fun kind of way. He really does seem like a fan. "I really like the big Scottish guy, Russ Armstrong. He came out to my kid's school last year. He was amazing. Who are you married to?"

"Max Tilman, the captain. Ani's husband is Jensen—"

"Hale, of course." Jake cuts me off, his attention now all on Ani. "He went to the same high school that my daughter's at now."

"I went there, too," Ani says. "Graduated five years ago."

"Okay, way to make me feel old," he chuckles.

I've lost them to a conversation about life on the Mountain, what locals call the suburban stretch of city up on top of the escarpment that divides the city. The hockey arena is right downtown, in the heart of the grittier, more urban part of Hamilton wedged between the bay off Lake Ontario and the cliff-like ridge of the endless Niagara Escarpment.

I think about his reaction to us being wives and girlfriends—the WAGs—and also how interesting it is that a journeyman like Russ has had the biggest impact on him out of all the hockey players, because he took the time to do community outreach that felt personal.

I find the community and business parts of professional hockey endlessly fascinating.

Jake mentioning Russ also reminds me of my text that I sent him earlier, so I pull out my phone. Still no reply.

I don't text any of Max's teammates that often. I introduce myself to all newcomers, of course, but Russ is like us, one of the original expansion draft members. I think our entire chat history is maybe ten messages stretching over the last year.

But he's never left me on read before. Maybe I overstepped by offering to help. I'm pretty sure my husband has bullied him into having a team retreat at his brand-new-to-him cottage, and I just want to smooth that over as much as possible.

"I think our paintings are dry enough now we can head out if you want," Ani says.

I put my phone away immediately and she laughs.

We say goodbye to Jake and everyone else, and hit the road.

"I think I'm going to give mine to my neighbour," she says as we pull into her driveway.

"Oh great," I say, straight faced. "That means I can gift you mine, and you won't have two identical paintings."

She giggle snorts. "Can I tell Jenson I painted it and see how long he goes before asking me if I was drunk?"

I clutch my chest. "You wound me, friend."

She pats my shoulder. "You'll survive."

I'm about to ask her if she wants me to hang out for a bit when her phone rings. The car tells her it's *Handsome Husband* calling, and she gets such a lovesick look on her face, I immediately say goodnight, leaving my painting behind on her back seat.

As I walk home, dozens of discordant thoughts bombard my brain. I'm usually very good at flicking away anything that threatens to plant a little seed of doubt, but it's been a long, lonely summer, and today was a weird day.

Maybe it's good that the team is getting together in Muskoka for a cottage retreat. I'm always on more confident footing during the season, so yes, let's start all of that sooner.

I know people like Ani are less eager for the season to start, because it'll mean seeing their husbands less, but I like the routine we have. If anything, I find too much time with Max in the summer is stressful, because he's a lot to manage.

During the season, he has a whole front office who helps with that.

My role sharpens to making our home life as easy as possible for him. My goal is always to smooth out any wrinkles in my husband's life that stand between him and his team getting the cup the next season. I don't kid myself on how much of a role I have to play in that. It's more about *not* playing too much of a role, not being a distraction, not being in the way. It is about being as easy as humanly possible, and the reward for that is a life of leisure, is a life of ease, a life of safety.

But there are trade-offs.

Truthfully, the problem with settling for safety, security, and decent sex a few times a month when the stars all align is that it leaves a lot of room for inappropriate thoughts. I manage to ignore most of them, but the odd one slips through.

I'll never act on them, of course. I sowed my wild oats early on, before my marriage, and I know exactly how mediocre an experience it is to spread my legs for a fantasy.

But as I inch into my thirties, my libido is getting harder to ignore. Louder in its demand for a good, hard release. Or a few releases, over and over again, a favourite middle-of-the-night idea I indulge in…and then feel guilty for.

Most of the time, I exhaust my body with long runs and I busy my mind with exciting projects, like Ani's fundraiser idea. And I'm thinking about starting a podcast, although I keep spinning my wheels on the direction I want it to go in.

I'm almost home when my phone vibrates.

Finally, Russ has texted me back.

> **RUSS**
>
> Thanks.

I stop and laugh at the brevity. I start typing back, eager to get going on whatever he needs me to do. But before I can hit send, another message comes in, making mine unnecessary.

> **RUSS**
>
> I'm at Camden Granger's wedding right now, so couldn't respond right away. We've got a plan, and it's going to be great. Heading there tomorrow and will get everything organized. Just come and enjoy yourself. One last taste of summer before things get real.

I frown at the *we*. Who is we?

A spasm of something I can't name zaps through me.

Pushing it away, I flip over to the group chat with the girls. Dots tell me that Harper is currently typing, everyone finally checking in at the end of the night.

> **HARPER**
>
> Can't wait to see you all. I'm so tan from the Italy. The sun is just different there? Hopefully I'll be over my jet lag, too. Just woke up from a five-hour nap.

> **KILEY**
>
> That's not a nap. That's a short overnight sleep. Your brain thinks it's morning now.

HARPER

Oh, shit. Noooo.

SHANNON

So happy you're home. Let's catch up this
week.

ANI

Can we do coordinated outfits for the
retreat?

I exhale happily. Yes, yes we can.

All I need is a weekend in the country with my husband
and his teammates and all of these weird little threads of
summer loneliness and worry will fade away. My happy
place is the hockey season. And that is around the corner,
and then everything will get back to normal.

CHAPTER 4
RUSS

Over the next week, Emery proves herself deeply useful and very annoying at the same time. Peak little sister vibes, although I'm going out of my way to not treat her like that. It's the least I can do when she's embraced this party as if she truly is the hostess for it.

She's the first guest to arrive, with a beat up national team hockey bag and a rental car full of groceries, even though I already did a big food order.

After I introduce her to the off-season trainer who will be working with the team this weekend, Foster Howard, he heads out to the converted garage gym and I help Emery with her groceries.

"How many kinds of peppers did you buy?"

"One can never have too many food platter options, Russell. And you're going to be working these boys hard, right?"

"Don't call me Russell when they get here," I say absently, leading her into the kitchen.

"Just trying things other than Rusty on."

"Rusty is fine."

She gives me a look that reminds me of her insane plan. That I agreed to, of course, because I'm desperate.

"Or Russ. Russ is great." I clear my throat. "Let me show you to your room."

I have four separate guest spaces in this compound. And we need all of them, because it's a packed house.

I list a bunch of names for Emery, and we joke that she won't remember them all, so she records the list on her phone so she has a reference.

Above the garage is a double suite, which is where I've put my best friend on the team, future Hall of Fame first rounder Kieran Marsh, along with his new wife Harper, freshly returned from their honeymoon in Italy. In the same suite will be her best friend Kiley Forge—because where Kiley goes, so goes our hotshot centre, Ty Connor, who fell hard for her as soon as he was traded to our team at the end of last season, and their relationship spilled out into being public knowledge at Marshie's wedding.

The walkout basement bedroom will be for one of last year's rookies, Hayden Calhoun, and his fiancé, Becca Kincaid.

Our alternate captain, Jenson Hale, and his wife, Ani, are down at the boathouse.

And everyone else will be in the main part of the house, which has two primary suites. I've got one of them at one end of the upstairs hallway, and Emery pokes her head into that as I give her the run down of where the couples will all be sleeping.

"Our team captain and his wife will be at the far end of the hall, in the so-called Primary Suite No. 2."

"Is it exactly the same as this one?" She whistles at the size of my en suite, making me grin.

"Pretty much, yeah. It has a different seating arrangement in front of the fireplace, but otherwise furnished exactly the same."

"And all of this came with the house?"

"Totally turnkey. The only thing I've added is hockey memorabilia."

"Nice."

I guide her back out into the main hallway.

In between the two deluxe rooms are a string of regular bedrooms, for the single, younger guys on the team, and Emery is in the room closest to mine.

She's nodding along as I give her the run down of all of those names, but then she gets a little wrinkle between her brows. "Hiro Watanabe, Roan Dodaj, Gregor Sokolov, Malik Zondi, me... what about Mason?"

"Jamie Mason?" I shake my head. "He's not coming."

She pulls out her phone and taps into Instagram, showing me an update from an hour ago where Zondi, one of our incoming rookies, lists the other guys in a story visible to close friends only about being on their best behaviour for the weekend.

"First of all, since when are you on a close friends loop with these guys?"

She looks delighted at my suspicion. "Jealous, Russell?"

"Overprotective. And I—"

"Don't be like that. I just followed a few people. And we might have DMed about training and food."

"Well, the kid can sleep on a couch downstairs, because he didn't RSVP."

"No, don't make him do that. That's so close to rookie hazing."

"Hazing? It's a perfectly nice couch!"

"He can have my room."

"You're not sleeping on a *couch*."

"You just told me it's a perfectly nice couch."

"For a rookie. Not my guest of honour."

"Awww, that's sweet." She pulls on her lower lip, thinking. "These guys already think we're together, so maybe I should just sleep in your room."

"They *what?*" I agreed that she could host a party with me. We never agreed on actually pretending she was my *date.*

I can't tell her why that feels so fucking wrong, my skin wants to turn itself inside out.

"I wasn't going to tell them that you're suffering from mid-life crisis ennui, Russell."

"Russ." I feel the start of a headache coming on. "What did you tell them, exactly?"

"Who can remember?"

I give her a murderous look. "You. You can remember. Now."

She has the good graces to look slightly embarrassed, at least. "Ummm…" She taps on her phone, then hands over a DM chain between her and some of the rookies.

EMERY

Hi all! Just wanted to introduce myself since we're all going to Rusty's cottage this weekend and I've self-appointed myself the Queen of the Charcuterie Boards. Any food sensitivities I should know about?

MALIK

Granger...any relation to Camden or Wyatt?

EMERY

And Forrest, too, yes, I'm their little sister

And I'm bringing my skates, btw

MALIK

Nice. Looking forward to meeting you

I stop reading and scowl at Emery. "I'm not sure I like how he says, *looking forward to meeting you.*"

"Good, that's good. Channel that energy into pretending to be jealous."

I skim past Hiro and Roan answering her questions about food, and then stop again when I get to the part where Malik assumes she's my girlfriend.

MALIK

Rusty's been keeping you a hot secret this summer, huh?

EMERY

Maybe you're just not on the need to know list yet, rookie!

ROAN

LOL Malik got told

HIRO

Real

ROAN

See you this weekend, Emery...keep that blade sharp!

"So…" Emery takes her phone back from me. "Maybe it would be for the best if I shared your room."

It's not the rebound plan I wanted. But if anyone else were in my shoes, I'd tell them to grab the girl and make the most of it.

But I don't want to.

Outside, there's a crunch of wheels on gravel.

Fuck.

Time's up.

I take a deep breath. "You sure about this? I can take the floor, or maybe I can head to the outfitters later and grab a cot."

She follows me to the front door, stopping me as I open it. "I have four older brothers," she says. "I know how to construct an impenetrable pillow barrier on a king-sized bed."

Great. Just… excellent.

"And during the day?" I gesture at the door, and my teammates on the other side of it. "How are we supposed to act during the day?"

She smiles, far too bright and bold and confident for my liking. "It wouldn't be a hardship to pretend I'm your rebound girl, would it, Russell?"

Ah, fuck me. "This can't get back to your brothers."

"They aren't on Instagram," she scoffs. "And I don't want your tongue down my throat. You can just hold my hand and be respectful."

To prove her point, she weaves her fingers through mine and squeezes.

I take a deep breath. "All right. On one condition, though."

"Anything."

I try to ignore the stab in my chest. "Don't call me Russell."

———

Being in love with another man's wife used to be a sharp, agonizing pain, a self-inflicted injury of the worst sort—preventable.

More recently, it has often felt mundane. A fact of life.

Today, though, it feels pretty fucking dangerous.

It doesn't help that Max and Shannon are running late. It's like a countdown to running a gauntlet. Everyone else has arrived, the spouses setting up by the pool, my team-mates and Emery already in the gym with Foster.

All the young guys are eager for Max to arrive, giving him all the credit for this coming together. And I have to give him the nod for the original idea, but the rest of it? Ensuring that Foster could come up to cottage country as well, kitting out the gym with everything we need...hell, I even hired a skills coach Foster recommended, a former Olympian named Thea Brown who lives up in this area in the summer and runs clinics for all the NHL players who flood Muskoka in the off-season.

Foster is even staying with her since I'm so full up.

There has been a lot of thought and effort that has gone into this being everything we need to start the season right, and Max Fucking Tilman didn't do anything beyond the initial decree to make it happen.

Ever since I arrived in Canada at the age of twelve, it has been drummed into me that hockey is a fraternity, a brother-hood. Being a part of a team is doing something bigger than one's self. All wins are team wins. All losses are team losses.

And no matter what, differences are left outside the dressing room.

The higher I went with competitive hockey, the more intense that code got. By the time I was drafted into the NHL, it was a rule I felt in my soul: whatever team I was on, that was my family.

And some people might say, but families don't trade you away for business reasons.

Mine did, though, so that part was never a problem for me.

All of these connections are temporary and transactional, but when we're in, we're all the way in.

Right now, Max Tilman is my captain. My brother.

Coveting his wife is an easy ticket to being traded away faster than I can say *third line nobody*, and the thought of never seeing Shannon ever again is a hundred times worse than seeing her regularly but never getting to call her mine. So...I mostly lock it down.

But deep down, I have to admit I'm not inspired by him the way my younger teammates are. And that's my own damn fault. By every observable metric, Max Tilman is one of the league's best players. Dangerously fast, he's a sniper from afar and a bully in the blue paint. But he's also calm and cool under pressure. He's the guy you want to talk to the refs when they keep calling penalties against your side and your side only.

When I'm being uncharitable, he can be manipulative. It's like he's constantly assessing the balance of power, trying to keep it on his side.

But again, even at my most uncharitable, I have to admit that's a great characteristic in a hockey captain.

I don't always love being on his team, but I never liked playing against him, either.

A roar of an engine through the trees tells me my uncomfortable wait is over—and that Max has decided today is not a day for subtlety or respect.

I open the front door as he brakes sharply in the driveway, then take a deep breath in and square my shoulders just in time for the woman who glides from the passenger side to give me a bright, effortless smile.

The last time I saw Shannon was at Kieran and Harper's wedding last month. I watched as she asked her husband to dance, as he brushed her off and made her face fall, and wished desperately that I could take her in my arms instead.

She's changed her hair since then. Her long blonde waves are darker now, as if the bottom layers have been painted with caramel and chocolate. And she's traded the glitzy summer gown from that night for skinny jeans and a loose plaid shirt that flows over her willowy body. Even though it's still August, she looks ready for fall and the return of hockey. The return of her cheering on my team while wearing another man's number.

"Thanks for inviting us for the weekend," she says with more warmth than I deserve, given that I wake up most mornings hard as a rock for her.

"Glad you could make it," I grind out.

Max comes around from the driver's side and extends his hand. "Buddy," he says. His grip is too tight for a teammate, and his smile is too hard. "You had to buy a place in the middle of fucking nowhere, didn't you?"

I don't bother to point out that this is a popular lake with hockey players and the only reason he is here is because he invited himself.

He wants to get the jab in, and since I'm going to covet his wife all weekend, it seems fair to let him.

Not that I always play fair.

I thump his bad shoulder and give him a big grin. "You seem cranky, Tiller. You need a nap? I saved the best room for you."

He grins back. "I don't need a fucking nap. I just sat on my ass for three hours in the car. I want to see the gym you've got set up here. Who else is here? Maybe we can make it competitive."

Oh, we're going to make it competitive. My return smile to him is as genuine as can fucking be. "Foster has everyone working in the gym already."

"And just like that, the day's agenda has been set," Shannon says lightly. I make an apologetic face in her direction, but she waves me off. "It's fine. I'm used to it. Where am I going to find my girls?"

I grin. "Let me tell you about the pool…"

"You've got a pool?" Her expression brightens immediately. "Point me to the lanai, Russell. I know what I'll be doing while you boys get sweaty."

CHAPTER 5
SHANNON

After Russ shows us to our room and I get changed, I head downstairs again.

I find Ani first, in the kitchen. Like me, she's wearing a black bathing suit under a white coverup.

We coordinated that on our group chat, because that's just how blessed life is for hockey wives and girlfriends—matching outfits are our biggest problem. I love it with my whole heart.

"You made it!" She throws her arms around me, wrapping me in joy that more than makes up for the grumpy drive here. "We're all out at the pool. I was just refreshing drinks. What can I get you?"

"Is there white wine open?"

"There sure is." She pours me a glass, to my usual amount.

"More."

She laughs and tops it up to the emergency level that we break out as needed. "Long drive?"

"We left too late and hit traffic." I close my eyes and

exhale. "But now I'm here, and I'm so ready for some pool time."

Outside, I find the rest of our squad. At the start of last season, which was the debut for the Hamilton Highlanders as the NHL's newest expansion team, we were a trio: Ani, a local girl who married her high school sweetheart and then he got picked to play for the hometown team; me, the experienced American hockey wife transplanted north with a slick elite player to Canada for the new team; and Becca Kincaid, the youngest of us all, but the only one of us who is a mother.

Her now-fiancé, Hayden Calhoun, skipped the hockey draft after Becca found out she was pregnant in high school, and then he was scouted by a minor league team and worked his way up to having his first full rookie year last season.

Ani and I took Becca under our wings, although she's got such a bright light personality that it's not like we need to give her much guidance. She's a natural at being a hockey better half. Effortlessly pretty, sparkling energy, and a clever wit, too.

Then the season got started, and something unexpected happened—Kieran Marsh, a confirmed hockey bachelor, fell head over heels in love with a woman he saw in the stands. A nurse, who was sitting next to one of our team doctors.

What followed was a bit of a mystery, because Harper Roberts is a private person, but everyone found out Kieran was in a pretty serious relationship when he got a concussion and refused to go home, wanting to go to Harper's apartment instead.

Which led Kieran to asking me to take Harper under my wing, too.

I pride myself on being the go-to person for smoothing everything over for the team, but something funny has happened in the last year—all of these women, including the most recent addition, Kiley Forge—have bloomed in their relationships in ways that makes me feel...

Well...

Not jealous.

That wouldn't be fair, or right.

By most measures, I have so much to be grateful for. I need to remember what my life could have turned into if I hadn't met Max when I did.

I've been Mrs. Max Tilman for almost eight years, and most days I never think about who I was before—a model, principally. And like a lot of pretty girls who want to be actresses and models, I found out the hard way that being a dazzling star in one's hometown is not a guarantee of even being noticed in New York City.

So I quickly learned how to make ends meet. I was sometimes a girlfriend for a night. A weekend. A full week on a yacht in the Mediterranean could pay my rent for a year.

And I was suited to it. I liked the intense sex that was part of the lifestyle. I liked being wild. It felt like I was giving the middle finger to everyone back home who told me I wouldn't amount to anything because I was too slutty —a horrible thing for a fourteen-year-old to have thrown at them. Especially because it turned out later on, I learned what *actually* being slutty was, and my teen self had no clue.

It was never anything as formal as actually being an escort. At the level I socialized at, the men don't need to hire sex workers. There are always young women like me willing to do it "for free", knowing that we'll get a new wardrobe out of an adventurous romp in a private dressing room, that our rent will be covered discreetly if we're good enough.

I was very good.

Still made me disposable, of course. Every pretty girl has an expiration date.

One night, a billionaire took me to a gala for the New York Rangers, and a handsome young hockey player wanted what that billionaire had: me.

Max paying my bills felt different. It wasn't as temporary or disposable, especially when he got me added to the WAG group text chat and I started going to games.

Then he proposed, and I felt such a rush of relief that I thought I could never be happier than in that moment.

Our life together in New York was insanely busy. We lived in the city, and most of his married teammates didn't, so while I liked the other wives and girlfriends, I mostly socialized with them in formal settings, for charity events and game nights.

Ironically, after marrying Max, my modelling career took off a little, and I even did some guest hosting on morning TV in the summer months, mostly to give some visibility to the charity foundations the team spouses supported.

So it wasn't until we moved to Hamilton last year, and Max was named the captain of the NHL's latest franchise team, that I noticed the foundation of our marriage might not be as solid as I thought it was.

We bought our dream house in the suburbs, on the most exclusive street in the same neighbourhood that his teammates were settling in. But a big, empty house has a lot of room for loneliness to echo through. Bedrooms I thought we might decorate for children stand empty, and Max is rarely home. I never minded his travel schedule when we lived in New York, but it's been harder since we moved.

"Shannon!" Harper calls out my name with such delight —and then it's echoed by the others like a chorus of angels— that I feel like an absolute bitch for the pang of misplaced longing I just felt.

Because it's not their fault that their lovely, open friendship has sent me spiralling on the inside.

That's all on me, and the choices I made once upon a time.

"I see this is where the real party is," I say, toasting them all with my glass of wine. It's crisp on the tongue and sharp sliding down, which is exactly what I need right now as my husband couldn't wait to get away from me and get a workout in. "Welcome back from your honeymoon, Harper."

She beams at me. "Thank you. Don't say a word about how married life is going to change once the season starts up again."

"I would never," I promise, taking the seat beside her. "And it'll be fine."

It always has been for me. If anything, I find the summers more stressful with the non-stop travel schedule and adjusting to full-time husband management. But I keep that to myself, too.

"Isn't this place incredible?" Harper waves a hand at the expansive terrace that flows out from the house and around the long, rectangular pool. Beyond it is a lush green lawn that spills to a border of trees and a wide wooden staircase that leads down to the lake. "I can't believe Russ of all people splashed out for *this*. But I mean, good for him. He deserves to put down some roots."

Getting traded is part of the life of a hockey player, and Russ Armstrong has been moved around more than most of them. He's a bottom six journeyman, not a star, and it's a toss up whether his best value to a team will be on the ice or as a trading piece at the deadline.

"Do you think this might be his last year playing?" Kiley asks. "Is that why he's finally making a big real estate investment?"

"Yeah, I don't know," Harper says thoughtfully. "It definitely feels like something has changed for him, though, doesn't it? New house, new girl."

"New girl?" I twist so quickly, white wine splashes onto my hand. "What girl?"

"Emery Granger," Ani answers.

I give her a blank look.

"She's nice! And cute," Harper adds. "They were holding hands when we arrived. She's young, but they have a lot in common, apparently. She's a hockey player. Youngest sister of three NHL brothers, in fact. She's training with them right now."

My stomach twists with anxiety. My husband likes the young, athletic type a lot. What are the chances we get through the weekend without him saying something inappropriate to Russ's new girlfriend?

I take a big gulp of wine. There's an annoying wobble in my belly that I hate. These women look to me for cues, and if Russ has a girlfriend, that's great. I can't wait to meet her.

Ani waves her phone. "I've got her profile here."

"Oh God, no, that's not—" I shake my head. "We shouldn't—"

"Too late." She winks. "One of her brothers played with Russ in Minnesota, it sounds like. So she probably trained with them then, and he was just waiting for her to grow up?"

Becca throws a foam ball at Ani. "She's older than the two of us."

"But we're not dating the oldest player on the team."

"So she's a bit younger than him," I say smoothly. That's better. "Maybe that explains his new energy with this place. Young girlfriend, thinking of starting a family..." Hard to picture Russ with kids, but it's the trend on the team. Ani and Jenson are trying, and I'm sure Harper and Kieran won't be far behind them.

"Maybe as a thank you for the weekend, you can give Russ the name of your couple's therapist," Harper says to Ani.

"Couple's therapy?" My head snaps to my friend. "What?"

Ani beams, unbothered. "We're doing some counselling around the whole trying to have a baby thing. Especially because it's taking us longer than expected. But mostly it's preventative, because we were raised in very different ways, and we want to be on the same page about our parenting styles."

"I'm surprised. And impressed! That's so cool that Jenson was on board with that," I say.

Ani gets a soft, dreamy expression on her face. "Honestly, at first I think he just agreed to do it for me. But it's actually the best thing they ever did for our relationship. It's really..." Her cheeks turn red. "It's really, really good."

"I'll cheers to that," Kiley says, lifting her glass. "I bet Ty would do it if it was *really, really* good, too."

Ani squeals and covers her face with her hands.

"Can I get the name of the therapist, too?" Becca asks, her eyes twinkling. "Hayden also—"

"Stop," Ani gasps as the rest of them dissolve into giggles. Then she grins. "Don't we have the best husbands?"

I force a smile onto my face.

They sure do. Their husbands care about being good partners.

One of the most painful lessons I've secretly learned over the last year is that people who are in healthy, happy relationships don't see a limit on how good their relationship can be. They only want it to get better. They find ways to be softer together, they find ways to be happier, to laugh more, to turn each other on more.

It's my greatest shame that I don't have that kind of marriage.

I set my wine glass down and shrug off my wrap. "Who wants to swim?"

CHAPTER 6
RUSS

"Okay, boys, gather round." Max claps his hands together, grabbing everyone's attention. We've gathered in the massive garage, which already was partially set up as a gym—part of what I liked about this compound—but as soon as Max invited the team here, I got on the phone and called in favours to get everything we might want delivered and set up for today.

Red light therapy. Cold plunge pools. A second weight rack. Tether points installed for bands and suspension training.

I even rented a couple extra bikes and treadmills.

"Last year was a roller coaster. Nobody expected us to make the playoffs in our first season, but we beat those expectations and finished the regular season on a real high." Max's expression tightens. "Going out in the first round after finishing the regular season on a high note was honestly fucking brutal. I never want to do that again. We had momentum on our side and we squandered it."

The rookies exchange nervous looks. Hayden Calhoun,

who was in their shoes last year, slumps. He got a lot of pointed criticism from the press for mistakes he made, but at the end of the day, hockey games are won and lost with team systems, not individual errors.

Jenson bumps shoulders with him. "None of us were happy with that, right? That's why we're here. We know we're capable of it."

"Here's the thing," Max continues. "We're not going to do another post mortem on last season. We're not even going to think about next season. Not yet. That's coming. But right now, I want us to take a deep breath and be in this moment, together. All of us have spent the summer working on our fitness. I can see that. You all look like beasts. You look hungry. So let's dial in now and find our focus."

"Amen," Jenson says.

"I third that," Kieran says.

And the rookies—and Hayden—let out a sigh of relief.

I can't deny that the man is good at saying what they need to hear.

Foster takes over again, and Max comes over to me—and Emery, who is standing at my side. "We haven't had the pleasure," he says, giving her a once over that makes me grunt to get his attention.

"Buzz Granger," she says, wrapping her hand around my arm. Presumably so he can't try to shake it. "But now I'm Emery to Russ."

Max's eyebrows shoot up.

Right, that's my cue to wrap my arm around her. "She also has the most Olympic medals in her family," I say dryly.

"Those Grangers." Max nods. "Cool."

"The first and last time I underestimated her fierceness in the gym, she was seventeen years old and kicked my arse."

"And that was when he was a much younger man," she teases.

"Watch it, kiddo," I growl.

She blows me a kiss.

I push her past Max. "Let's go listen to Foster, you brat."

The trainer is just finishing up his explanation. "We're going to warm up with some dynamic movements that will help us find our edges, and I want us to do this in pairs. Max and Ty, let's start with the two of you."

He goes through the group, pairing everyone up with someone who will push them. No buddies.

And the group responds to it, turning the warm up into a push or be pushed contest. By the time we're all limber and starting to sweat, Foster has their full attention.

Once he explains the stations he's set up next, and the scoreboard for the workout—because of course he's scoring us—the next hour and a half flies by.

Emery is right in it with my teammates, posting really competitive scores, and they love her for it. Some of them a little too much.

"Is that all you got?" Emery scoffs as Max drops off the chin up bar.

"You're the devil," he growls.

I'm laughing, enjoying myself at his expense, but the grin slides away when she turns around and his gaze drops to her arse.

It's the second time in short order that he's checked her out right in fucking front of me.

"Eyes up, Tiller," I snap as I throw a medicine ball in his direction.

He catches it with annoying ease and thuds it back against my chest. *Oof.* "Don't interrupt our final challenge."

Don't look at women who aren't your wife, I want to snarl back. But Emery can handle herself, and I know she's not interested.

As he hoists himself up again, she slides her attention to me for a second, a smirk pulling at the corner of her mouth.

I roll my eyes and pour myself into my final set of rows.

"Has anyone been in the lake yet? How's the water?" Kieran asks. "Refreshing enough to make Ty squeal?"

"Shut the fuck up," our teammate snapped. "I like a brisk dip."

"Liar."

"Don't need to go in the lake to enjoy it. Are we going boating this afternoon?" Max asks.

"No boat yet," I mutter.

"What do you mean, no boat?" he scoffs. "That sucks. You need me to make some calls for you?"

Jesus Christ, no.

But it's too late. He's texting someone he knows, and Emery is barking at people to get back to the workout, and suddenly we have an appointment to see a guy about a boat and maybe some jet skis this afternoon.

Fuck. Me.

I give up and drop to the mat to do some final stretching. I need to find some inner fucking peace, because the weekend has barely begun.

"Looking good," Emery says, appearing right above me.

I roll onto my back. "Thanks."

She holds out her hand and I reach for it, but instead of hauling me up and off the floor—something the little bundle of lean muscles has definitely proven herself capable of—she tumbles down onto my chest, as if I'd pulled her down.

I muffle a grunt of surprise. "What's up, pipsqueak?"

"Just establishing our relationship," she whispers in my ear. "Your jealous growling seemed to work, so I'm leaning into it."

I jerk my head around, looking for Max, but he's leading everyone out the door, heading up the path to the house now. "Did he do anything?"

"Nah." She rolls off me and pops up to her feet. This time when she offers me her hand, it really is to lift me up.

I grab a towel and wipe my face, buying a second to calm myself.

"Dawgs are a dime a dozen in this league," she says. "Honestly, he's not worse than your other teammates."

"But they aren't married."

She startles at the frustrated grind in my voice. That might be a bigger factor for me than it is for her. I'd rather not explain why I care. There is a part of me that is tempted to tell her the truth. Maybe I need another woman's perspective on how I've gotten myself into this mess—and how I can get out of it.

But it would feel like betraying Shannon, to tell anyone about my feelings for her. Even someone I trust as implicitly as Emery.

"Anyway, just... We don't need to be a PDA couple, you know?"

She laughs and throws her arms around me, hugging me fiercely. "Yeah, maybe it would be easier if we're 'taking things slow'. Nobody is going to believe that you want to drag me back to your room and rail me—"

"Stop," I groan.

That just makes her laugh harder.

I hug her back and kiss the top of her head. "How's that?"

"Brotherly." She pushes me away. "And sweaty. Go have a shower."

"You aren't going to suggest we share that, too?"

That makes her cackle. But then she stops and gives me a once over. Thinks about it longer than is necessary, straight-faced. "Should we, for research?"

The only thing giving her away is the mischievous twinkle in her eyes. But…it is believable.

I sigh and take her hand in mine. "Come on, you brat. It's going to be a long weekend if we overthink it."

CHAPTER 7
SHANNON

I'm climbing out of the pool when Russ and his new girlfriend stroll onto the terrace, hand in hand.

He's wearing the same Highlanders t-shirt he had on when we arrived, but now it's sweat-dampened, and he's turned his baseball hat around to wear it backwards, which makes his close-crop beard stand out more, in a distracting way.

She is very cute, as promised, wearing spandex short shorts and a revealing tank top, and she's beaming as he introduces us.

I'm sure it's just a matter of hours before he asks me to add her to the group chat, so as the senior WAG, I do my best Welcome Wagon impression. "So nice to meet you, Emery. I hear you're a hockey player, too?"

"Six years with the US national team," Russ says with pride. "But she's also building a personal chef business, too."

"Oh? Locally?"

"Um, no." She glances sideways at Russ. "I'm based in Minneapolis."

"Family," Russ adds.

Of course.

There's a funny pang in my chest at the thought of Russ falling for someone who is establishing a business in a whole other country. It makes me worry that he'll ask for a trade, which doesn't make any sense—he's just bought this place.

She starts chattering about her business, and how she might return to pro hockey at some point, but right now she's not sure about the new women's league. She didn't enter the inaugural draft, isn't sure if she wants to. She keeps talking even as I wrap myself in a towel, as Russ guides her to the door.

"You wanted to shower," he reminds her, and she blushes.

Great, now I have a mental picture of the two of them washing off their workout together. "I'll let you two go do that."

"Oh, no—" Emery cuts herself off.

They exchange a look so tender it makes me uncomfortable. Russ's eyes crinkle and the corner of his mouth quirks up.

"All right," she says, giving in. "Let's go. And then after we change, we're going to see a guy about a boat?"

"That's right." Russ rolls his big shoulders, pulling his sweat-damp t-shirt across his chest. "That's your husband's doing," he adds, his gaze finding and holding on my face.

"Oh no," I laugh. "How's that?"

"I said I wasn't in a rush to a buy a boat, maybe next year, and he immediately got on his phone and put feelers out there. Turns out, someone he knows up here has a boat and some jet skis he wouldn't mind unloading."

Emery leans in close to Russ, nestling under his arm like a possessive little kitten. *Mine*, her body language screams.

The ache in my chest intensifies, jealousy deepening. What would it be like to have that kind of touchy-feely relationship with my husband?

After they go inside, I head in as well, heading up to my own room. I can hear Max in the shower, so I knock to let him know that I'm here.

"Is that you, hun?" he calls out.

"Yep."

The shower turns off.

So much for my brief consideration of maybe joining him.

He opens the door, a towel slung low around his narrow hips.

I untie my bikini top, wanting him to see my tits, and I get the appreciative look. It's a little salve on that weird hurt in my chest.

"I should shower." I twirl the bikini top around on my finger, then hook my thumb under the strap on my bottoms. "You want to hop back in with me?"

"Can't. We're gonna go get Rusty a boat."

"He said that, but I think they're in the shower, too…"

He frowns. "Him and Emery? They told you that? That's fucking slutty, isn't it?"

I flush. Damn it. "It was just alluded to. Anyway, I'll shower real quick and then I think we're all going."

"Cool. I gotta call my agent back, anyway." He lingers a last look on my tits, which isn't quite as good as him coming into the shower with me and putting his hands and mouth on them, but it still feels nice, albeit in an unsatisfying way that leaves a subtle fever under my skin as I step into the shower.

I turn on the water, which is still hot from Max being in here. It comes out of the rain head above, a nice wide drenching that rinses me off, but doesn't do anything about the ache below the surface.

The shower has both a rain head and a detachable wand, which I eye, my pulse jacking up. Could I get myself off quickly with it?

There's only one way to tell.

My relationship to orgasms is funny. Sometimes I can't come at all. Sometimes it takes me a while. And sometimes, under the right circumstances—like being alone and my brain scratching at the right weird itch—I can very efficiently find a little dopamine hit.

The most important part is to not think about it too hard.

I grab the wand, brace my hand against the tile, and close my eyes. I think of sweat and bodies being pushed to the limit. I imagine low, private dirty talk. Filthy claims on every part of my body. A desperate, pleading protest rises inside me, *nooooo*, and that feels so good. Trapped in this shower. No way out. Warm bodies, strong arms. Muffled grunts and a hand over my mouth just in time as I choke out a body-wracking release, the shower head tumbling out of my fingers.

The dopamine rush makes me sag against the tiles, tingling through my extremities and making my brain feel a hell of a lot better.

I finish up efficiently, then brace myself for the afternoon ahead.

CHAPTER 8
RUSS

There's nothing quite like lying to undercut what should be a triumphant weekend of feeling like a king. This fake dating bullshit isn't for me, and we're only two hours into it.

It's not Emery's fault. She's amazing. And I know I should be grateful I have someone beside me this weekend who is firmly in my corner, who comes by being Team Russ naturally, but without the weight of actually trying to date.

I've never been one to date, even before I met Shannon. Discreet hook-ups? Sure, I like sex as much as the next person, although I can go longer without companionship than most of my teammates.

But relationships?

I don't do relationships. My parents' marriage imploded during my childhood, and then my father's second marriage was a toxic, indulgent mess. Two brilliant examples of what not to do with one's life.

Emery leads the way up the stairs. When we reach the top landing, Malik opens his bedroom door, and he gives her an appreciative once over that reminds me I'm not the only one who is shielded by her sharing my bed this weekend.

"That was a good workout," he says to her, as if I'm not standing right behind her.

I clear my throat, and he grins. Caught.

Emery takes my hand. "We'll see you downstairs after we clean up," she says sweetly.

I'm relieved to close my bedroom door and take a long, deep breath.

She crosses to her suitcase, open on one of the deep window seats. "I'll go first, if you don't mind?"

All business now.

"Be my guest." I flop onto the oversized armchair in front of the fireplace and close my eyes.

Immediately, I see Shannon climbing out of the pool, water sluicing off her long limbs, rivulets licking between her full breasts.

We met at the arena the day the Hamilton expansion team was announced fourteen months ago. There was a media blackout about who had been acquired, so we discovered who we were going to be playing with as each player arrived at the arena.

Max had already been tapped to be the team's captain, and he and Shannon were the first ones there.

We'd never met before, at least off the ice, and it wasn't like our lines were often pitted against each other on the ice, either. He came from New York, an unexpected star made available in the expansion draft by his hometown team. I was pulled off the third line in Los Angeles, where I'd been traded from Minnesota two years earlier.

What's the opposite of a star in hockey? I'm that guy. A journeyman. Someone who, when they list the relatively small number of players to have played a thousand games in the big show, is a surprise.

That's me.

My role on the new team was clearly spelled out in my first meeting with Dick Dorrian, the general manager—make every other team think twice about picking a fight with the new captain or either of the young stars-in-the-making, hometown hero Jenson Hale, and American import Hiro Watanabe.

On that afternoon, I strode into the arena focused on that plan.

None of us had come from the same team before, although a few of us had played together in juniors or minor league hockey.

I didn't expect to see Shannon and fall hard. She was the most beautiful woman I'd ever seen, without question, but there was something more than just a skin-deep attraction there. She had a quiet presence I found immediately calming, but beneath that I saw sparks of a wicked personality. She was simply captivating.

I've spent the last fourteen months wondering if what I fell into was love or lust or lunacy. Definitely lunacy, given what is riding on me not fucking what might be my last contract in the NHL.

In sixteen years of playing pro hockey, I've never made it to the Cup finals.

Because the universe has a funny sense of humour, sixteen is the exact number of wins it takes in the playoffs to go all the way. And for a hockey team to get there, they might need to play up to twenty-eight games in a row. An exhausting, brutal, destructive two-month-long journey that chews ups and rejects fifteen other teams in the process.

I've never made it to those final four wins.

I don't know what it's like to be that close to euphoria.

The last two teams I played on didn't have a chance of getting that close.

The Highlanders do.

And I've spent the last year so fucking close to losing my chance to be a part of that, all because I can't fucking contain myself when Shannon smiles at me.

She fucking smiles at everyone.

I am an idiot.

My life has never been this good.

Earlier this summer, I signed my first big endorsement deal. It came out of nowhere because I'm not really a household name anywhere outside of Scotland—and really only in hockey rinks there. Of course, there are only thirty ice rinks in the whole country, so that's not saying much.

That deal came about in part because of Max, ironically. He's also sponsored by the same energy drink company. We have the same agent—along with twenty other pro hockey players—and he recommended me for the international markets.

Because that's what a captain does, and for all his faults, he makes sure everyone knows how to get their bag.

The least I could do is stop thinking about fucking his wife.

Rivulets of water.

Fuck, that's a work in progress.

From my en suite, I hear the water cut out.

Sighing, I push myself up.

A minute later, Emery comes bouncing out of the bathroom, hair still wet, dressed in jeans and a plaid shirt just like the other girls had arrived in. *She's a quick study.*

"Hey, weird question," she asks, her thumb flying over her phone screen. "Have you heard the rumours about a new league forming?"

"A women's league?"

"No. Men's."

"Where? Here?"

She hands over the phone. "Watch for yourself."

It's a TikTok by an influencer who says they heard about it from a friend of a friend. A three-on-three league with no salary cap, called the Ice League.

I laugh. "Not a real thing. Don't believe everything you hear on the internet."

"This account has been right about some weird things before. I think they do have some insider information. And this isn't the first time I've heard whispers of this. You haven't heard anything?"

I stay off social media as much as is humanly possible, and I rely on my agent to pass on important news. Until he tells me this is a real possibility, I won't believe it. "As much as you and I love this game, hockey is fighting for fourth place in North American TV rights. There isn't enough money for the kind of thing she's talking about." I step around her. "I bet that rumour's going to take off like wildfire, though. A lot of dummies want to believe in fairytales."

For a hockey player, a league without a hard salary cap is a fantasy. The kind of romantic delusion that's right up there with running away into the sunset with your captain's hot wife.

I need to focus on what matters in reality. Getting my team as cohesive and hyped as possible before we head into training camp. I need to turn Hayden Calhoun from a reckless offensive-generating puppy on ice into a smart, mature two-way player. I need to mentor Malik Zondi to be the next me. And I have to find something, anything, *anyone* to redirect my lustful thoughts towards.

No more rivulets of water. No more black bikini fantasies.

CHAPTER 9
SHANNON

When I get out of the shower, Max is still on the phone.

I find clean clothes and put on underwear and a bra, then do my hair and make up next.

I'm almost finished when he steps into the bathroom and gives me a thumbs up for putting on a smoky eye with thick eyeliner.

"How was your call?"

"Good." He doesn't elaborate. "I like the black dress you hung up. Is that what you're going to wear?"

I put the finishing touches on my lip gloss, then press my lips together. "If you like it, then yes. That's what I'm wearing for dinner. This afternoon is jeans."

"Yeah, okay." He pauses. "The dress is great. Classier than what some of the other girls are wearing, probably."

I wince, knowing that's a dig at Harper, who is unbothered by fashion most of the time and primarily motivated by the function of her clothes, and Kiley, who is actually very fashionable, but also tall and plus-sized—which Max can't see past. Plus, it's a cottage weekend, for God's sake. Everyone should wear whatever they like.

But also, we try. All of us. We try to fit in, and be what they want, and we all do our best. I do it because Max demanded it in our marriage contract. Others do it...I guess for love. I wish I still did it for love. That's there, I think, but there's resentment piled on top of it.

Instead of reacting, I focus on giving myself a final critical gaze in the mirror.

Silence stretches between us. He wants me to agree with him, that we're better than his teammates and their wives and girlfriends. I'm not going to do that. Those women are my friends, and Max's need to constantly one-up everyone is exhausting.

When I don't reply, he comes closer, watching me in the mirror.

"Hun," he murmurs, pressing his front against my back. "What's wrong?"

"Don't say that our friends aren't classy."

"I didn't mean anything by it." He squeezes me tighter, holding extended eye contact in the mirror. It's unsettling. I hope he can't tell that I just quietly got myself off in the shower.

How would he know?

Twisting, I put my back to the mirror and wind my arms around his neck. Good wife, good wife, good wife.

Downstairs, someone hollers that it's time to go, and relief rolls through me. I pat his arm. "I'll get dressed really fast. Be right there."

He heads downstairs ahead of me and I pull on the dress, then check my hair in the mirror again.

I'm about to put on my shoes when I get a news alert on my phone from the Scoreboard app.

Like any good captain's wife, I follow sports news in surface ways. I never want to be caught off-guard or make Max look bad when we're at an event. But I don't usually click on headlines.

This one is different.

My heart in my throat, my fingers shaking, I stab the screen to read more beyond "Dumas to invest in new league?"

French billionaire Francois Michel Dumas, pictured here in Toronto this morning having brunch in Yorkville, is rumoured to be interested in funding a new pro hockey league. Spotted in both Toronto and New York this week-end, he's said to be meeting primarily with agents before officially announcing the rival league, anticipated to make a splash next season with no salary cap and a revenue model driven by streaming games online and designer merch collabs.

A trademark submission for the name Ice League has been submitted, an internet search confirms.

Known for savvy investments in other start-up sports ventures, Dumas's involvement suddenly vaults the Ice League from a novelty rumour to bona fide business-changer in North America's fourth-highest revenue professional sport.

He's been busy in the eight years since I last saw him, I think dimly. I remember him talking about hustling to get a piece of a racing team, and buying a rugby team.

It all seemed so indulgent, so wasteful with his money, but what did I know about business? Apparently nothing.

Because a French billionaire who once entertained the world's most rich and powerful on his yacht with me perched by his side is getting into pro sport in North America in the splashiest of ways.

These two worlds were never meant to collide. Not again, not after Max stole me away from "all that" and gave me respectability.

Back then, Max got a charge out of snatching me from the grasp of a much wealthier man.

Now?

Shock ripples through me as I wonder if Max knew this when he was talking to his agent.

If it informed the strange expression on his face as he looked at me in the mirror.

From the foyer, Max calls, "Shannon, get your butt down here!"

I shove my phone in a little purse and school my features.

CHAPTER 10
RUSS

It takes the rest of the afternoon to check out the boat and jet skis and arrange the necessary insurance. Emery, Mason, and Watanabe all decide they want to get their boating licenses, too.

By the time we're back at the cottage, with a plan to pick up the water crafts in the morning after a round of golf, it's well past dinnertime and everyone is champing at the bit for steaks.

The younger guys are also gagging to talk about the breaking Ice League news, but Kieran shuts that down pretty hard. On the off chance that this turns into hockey's LIVGolf vs the PGA , he doesn't want anyone to get caught out for having taken a stance one way or another.

"Let's wait and see what happens," he said as we all looked at our phones when the news broke. "And until then, it's the fucking off-season. The only hockey topics we should be thinking about are the ones we can control—our own strength and conditioning. Our own training. And a little rest and relaxation, too. Put those things away and let's go buy this man a boat."

So we did.

I have a fucking blessed life.

And once I got over the initial weirdness, it was fun to have Emery's hand in mine all day, too. Nice to not be the odd guy out. The vibe shift with my married friends has been good in an interesting way, too. I surprised them, I think, by having a woman with me this weekend.

Especially Kieran and Ty, who have both had suspicions about me and my feelings regarding Shannon.

The feelings are still there, of course. It's going to take more than a day of fake dating to un-train myself to devour how she looks in a bikini, confidently bounding out of my pool, holding out her hand and warmly welcoming another of my friends. It's going to take more than a summer to un-learn my visceral *get your hands off her* instinct when Max possessively tugs her close, his knuckles grazing the side of her breast or the curve of her arse just because he can.

But none of that feels as dangerously close to the surface as it all did at Kieran's wedding.

Emery is exactly the shield I needed. I thought I needed a rebound fling. It turns out I just needed a rebound fake.

"Thinking about your new boat?" my fake girlfriend asks, twirling around me in the kitchen. "You have a satisfied look on your face."

"Thinking about you, actually. Did you have fun today?"

"Yep. Makes me miss playing hockey, though." She scrunches up her face.

I tug her close, wrapping my arm around her shoulder and hauling her against me so I can kiss the top of her head. I'm a physical guy, and being single and celibate for an entire year has taken a toll I'm only just realizing now, belatedly. I don't want Emery like that, but having a legit reason to hold a warm woman close to me? I'm not above taking full advantage of the fake dating benefits.

"If you ever want an ear about getting back into it…"

"I know," she mumbles into my chest. "Maybe if I focus on getting more sponsors."

"That's the spirit. Lean into the Granger name."

She snorts.

"I'm serious, kiddo."

"You can't call me *kiddo* this weekend, *Rusty*," she gasps, poking me in the belly.

I chuckle and let her go just as Shannon comes in.

"Need any help?" she asks, a warm smile curling on her face.

Hot, visceral want tugs at my insides. "We're good," I manage to say. "You can relax outside—"

But at the same time, Emery nods. "Do you want to make this salad?"

"Of course." Shannon rolls up her shirt sleeves, revealing lean, tan forearms. "Put me to work. They're talking cars out there and my eyes are crossing."

"Fair warning, we're talking sponsorship deals in here," Emery says. "How are you with onions?"

"I like them better than cars." Shannon wiggles her fingers at the shallot Emery holds out. "I like sponsorship deals, too, by the way."

"Have you seen Russ's ads for BioPunk?" Emery asks.

I groan. "Don't."

"Of course I have," Shannon says. "Max is with them, too."

And his commercials are better. He's more of a natural in

front of the camera. I'm stiff and awkward, an oversized bear of a man—which has gone over better than expected back home in Scotland, where everyone on TikTok is taking the piss.

Good for BioPunk. Maybe even good for my name recognition outside of ice rinks.

Not good for my chances on getting another big sponsorship, probably, but that's fine. I only need the one. The BioPunk contract was a solid chunk of my down payment on this place.

Emery sets a red pepper in front of Shannon next. "And have you seen the TikToks?"

Shannon pauses, glancing sideways at me. "No."

"I need to get one of those *no phones allowed* signs for this kitchen," I say.

Emery winks. "I'll show you the best ones later. I have them saved in a collection."

"You're a brat," I growl at her.

"Am I a brat you want to make a gin and tonic for?" She bats her eyes innocently.

"Oooh, a G&T," Shannon sighs.

Damn it. "Aye," I grind. "I'll make you drinks."

"You do that and I'll set the table outside." Emery grabs the cutlery first, as I fill two glasses with ice. By the time she returns for the plates, I shove a cocktail at her, too.

She grabs it with her free hand and winks at me again. "Good boy."

Shannon's eyebrows pop up for a split second, as Emery somehow juggles all of that outside, but she doesn't miss a beat chopping peppers.

I clear my throat. "She didn't mean it like that."

Shannon looks up in surprise, her eyes flaring. "Like what?"

Shit. "Nothing."

I slide her drink onto the island next to where she's chopping and busy my hands with making my own drink. That doesn't stop me from noticing the smile that plays at the corners of her mouth.

"Okay," she says.

"That's not my— She's not—" I protest. But the explanation dies on my tongue. Because this weekend she is.

The smile grows. "I said okay. But if you keep protesting, I'll be forced to draw the conclusion that you are, in fact, a good boy."

I groan. "Really not."

"I don't know," Shannon muses innocently. She scrapes the perfectly diced pepper into a small bowl next to the bowl of minced shallot, then wipes her hands and takes a sip of her drink before ticking points off on her fingers. "You're a consummate host. You're the first person anyone on the team calls when they need a strong pair of arms. You make a mean gin and tonic." She pauses to lift her glass in a toast to me, which only makes all of this worse. "You've clearly caught yourself a good one with Emery, who probably has very high standards."

"The highest," I say dryly.

"And then there's the fact that you're blushing right now." Shannon's eyes are dancing, which is definitely more the cause of any manly flush I might be experiencing than teasing words from a girl who is like a sister to me. But I can't tell her that. She leans in and lowers her voice in a way that feels dangerous to my self-control. "It's okay, Russell. It can be our secret that you're a very good boy indeed."

Fuck.

My cock pulses to life, thickening as if on command.

As a lifelong dominant man, I've never responded to praise like this. Even knowing it's a friendly tease, though, my body doesn't care. If she wanted me on my knees, begging her for scraps, I would give her that in a heartbeat to hear her call me a good boy unironically.

She pats me on the arm, scalding my skin, and goes to move past, humming to herself in pleasure.

I twist, following her, and she turns around in surprise, backing up against the counter. I brace my hand on the cupboard to keep myself from leaning all the way in, and suddenly we're too close for friendly teasing. We're too close for the fact she's my teammate's wife.

I don't move.

Her cheeks turn pink, hot slashes that I feel in my belly. A warning I should heed, step back, give her space. Apologize, because I might not be a *good boy*, but I am a respectful man. But then, as the blood flow in my body redirects away from my cock, her eyes flash with something that looks a lot like arousal.

Outside, someone laughs loudly. There's a clatter of dishes, too.

Here, in the kitchen I bought because I'd convinced myself I needed to move on from this woman, she looks at me with a confused, desirous expression so raw it steals my breath. Her pupils dilate, her gaze turning liquid, and it's as if I'm suddenly seeing Shannon for the first time all over again.

Rough need closes like a fist around my brain stem, cutting off careful consideration and sensible thinking.

"If you need to ken a secret about me, Shan," I say

roughly, the Scottish side shoving to the fore. "Let it be that I'm definitely not a good boy."

Her breath hitches, her lips parting, and I know that I'll be stroking myself to that subtle, beautiful sound for the rest of my life.

In a single moment, she's imprinted on my plan to get out from under my desire for her in a way that guarantees I never will.

But she's still my captain's wife.

I drop my hand from the cabinet and step back.

Her gaze follows me, and hell if it's not magnetic. There's nothing I want more in this world than to step back into her orbit. The only thing that stops me from finding out if there's more where that shudder came from is the door opening behind me.

"Are you looking for this salad?" Shannon asks smoothly.

"Nah, just some ice," her husband says.

I gesture to the fridge without looking in his direction, then busy myself with tenderizing steaks until he's gone again.

There's a rattle of bowls as Shannon finishes the salad Emery started, then silence.

"Russ," she says softly.

I grab my tray of steaks. If I'm holding eight pounds of meat, I'm not likely to grab her. Or that's the theory. "We're good. Probably had too much sun today, but that's nothing some grilling won't fix."

I don't look at her as I head outside. If I do, I'll do something we'd both regret.

CHAPTER 11
SHANNON

I'm losing my mind.

What just happened?

What was that?

That was the old Shannon slipping through.

Horror jabs a finger in my chest.

No.

I drop my head to the counter and groan.

I've never, ever flirted with one of my husband's teammates before. Never. I don't even flirt with random people, not even to get a flight upgrade or a better seat at a restaurant, two situations that definitely justify a little flirting.

For most people.

Not for me, not anymore.

Because for Shannon Barker from Green Hills, Michigan, flirting has led to sex since she was fourteen years old. That's how old I was when I went to third base for the first time, gave someone an orgasm for the first time, and got really close myself.

Also the age when I learned that it's sometimes just

easier to finish myself off in the privacy of my own bed once everyone is asleep, a skill I still reach for to this day.

My mother—no dummy—got me on birth control and tried to control me in other ways, but I was a wild child. And when you're the prettiest girl north of Lansing, you don't take no for an answer. Not when your libido is in charge.

By the age of eighteen, I had my GED and a one-way bus ticket to New York City.

Honestly, it's a miracle I'm alive today.

So when I met Max, five years into my modelling career, it was a relief that he wanted to sweep me away from the glitz and glamour and chaos and danger.

And for eight years, I've lived up to the expectations of my new name. The only thing Shannon Tilman has in common with Shannon Barker is smooth skin and good posture.

And the occasional dirty thought I would never tell my husband about in a million years.

Maybe more than occasional, lately.

I need to be busier when we go home. Enough dilly-dallying on the podcast idea, for example. Kiley thinks we can launch it this fall, but I need to make a firm decision about the name and brand position we've been developing. *The View from the Wife Seat* is the currently leading contender for a title, but it's a bit of a mouthful, so Kiley is also trying to sell me on *WAGLife*.

In New York, the WAGs—ironically—didn't like the term. It was what outside observers called us, but internally, we were *spouses* and *better halves*. In Hamilton, everyone is a bit more irreverent, a bit silly.

Harper and Kiley will embrace the WAG label if there's fun to be had in it.

And they are rubbing off on me, although we did have a good debate about if it wasn't inclusive enough, given that not every hockey player in the NHL has a *wife* or a *girlfriend,* although the ones who quietly have partners and boyfriends don't want to be talked about on a podcast, either.

Kiley's very smart point is that WAG is the hook that brings people to pull up a chair and listen, and once I have their ear, I can explain how complicated it is to put your life on hold and love someone who has this insane career—and maybe give a bit of quiet insight into those who love from the shadows, too.

She's not wrong.

And lately, I have been wanting to find that outlet to talk about just how freaking complicated it is more and more.

"Babe, you okay?"

I jerk my body upright and see my podcast partner herself standing on the other side of the kitchen island looking at me in concern. Genuine, searching concern.

And if I were to crack open my chest and show my confused heart to anyone, it would be the girls before my distant husband.

No, I'm not okay.

I wish I *could* unload on her right now.

Max hasn't brought up the Ice League news yet. Nobody has, and it's driving me crazy. It's a ticking time bomb hanging over me, because I know Max has to be stewing about it. He *hates* Francois.

Plus, I just crossed a line with Russ, who has a new girlfriend. And also, why the fuck did *Russ* of all people flirt right back? When he has a new girlfriend?

Nothing makes sense.

But now is not the time to unload any of that.

"I'm great," I manage to say. "Just stretching my back. The car ride up here catching up to me, maybe."

"We'll have to go in the hot tub after dinner." Her gaze lingers on my face, searching.

"I'm fine," I insist.

Of all of my new friends, Kiley is the most likely to see through that lie. We've gotten closer over the summer as she's used her experience in theatre and live performance to help me develop my podcast ideas, and while she's not nosy about my marriage at all, I know she also doesn't have rose-coloured glasses when it comes to the WAG life. When she met Ty, she was recovering from being cheated on by her ex, and she was reluctant to take the leap to officially dating and all that this life involves.

She would be the first person to tell me that life is too short to stay in an unhappy marriage.

If only it were that simple.

And given how strongly she feels about infidelity—rightly so—I need to be extra careful this weekend. Whatever just happened with Russ cannot happen again. I can't give anyone the wrong impression. Not Russ, not Kiley, and definitely not my jealous husband.

Even if he's the only one who has broken our vows.

And Emery... I can't be disrespectful of Emery, either. Maybe most of all, because I remember what it was like to be twenty-four and idealistic, convinced that learning how to feed a team of hockey players heading back into training was the way to a man's heart.

"I was sent in to get the last of the salads," Kiley says. "There's apparently one in the fridge, too?"

I take a look, and sure enough, there is.

"Emery really is amazing," I murmur. Time to believe that as the actual truth it is, even if it makes me feel small.

"Isn't she, though?" Kiley says brightly. "I wonder if we'll see more of her once the season gets underway."

An uncomfortable pang zaps through me. I should want that for Russ. *I do want that for Russ.*

But there's something about their dynamic that set me on edge earlier. I don't see them as a couple in the long term. They aren't right for each other.

His words clang again in my head. *I'm definitely not a good boy.*

I've never before thought about the type of woman Russ might need, and I'm not a matchmaker in general. On paper, Emery Granger actually sounds perfect.

But does she know what to do with a man who growls under his breath that he's a bad boy?

I know that temptation well. Once upon a time, I thought I was smart enough and sexy enough to handle anything—and I almost drowned in the storm.

Max saved me from all of that.

When we get outside, I'm not surprised to see Max has parked himself next to Emery at the table, and he's pouring her a glass of white wine. He's drawn to pretty girls. I can't blame him for that—it's what saved me, once upon a time.

He glances up and gives me a quick smile. "Wine, hun?"

"I'm still working on a cocktail." I slide into the chair beside him, which puts me in the centre of the table. On my left is Hiro Watanabe, and on the other side of him is Ty, who is still standing behind his seat, chatting with Russ at the grill.

"Emery was just telling us about the program in Boston."

Max slings his arm over the back of my chair, drawing me into a conversation he loves—collegiate sports.

College in general. For Max, who has since gone on to incredible career highs, his college years were the best years of his life.

I've learned not to take that personally.

But those are conversations I struggle to relate to. Emery, it seems, doesn't have that problem.

"You liked it, I gather?" I ask her.

"Best years of my life," she gushes. "Did you go to Michigan like Max?"

Max answers for me. "Shannon didn't even graduate high school."

The terrace falls silent, fat sizzling on the grill the only sound for a moment.

I square my shoulders and lift my chin, flashing a brilliant smile at Emery. "I was intent on finding fame in New York. Ironically, I am from Michigan—the state, not the college. Got my GED and bought a one-way bus ticket when I was eighteen. Never looked back."

She nods along, more charitable than my husband. "New York is amazing. Was it scary being on your own at eighteen?"

"At first, yeah. I stayed in a hostel for a week, while I found a job and an apartment. And then it was sort of like living in a dorm."

"Except it was a fifth-floor walk-up and all of your roommates did cocaine," Max mutters.

"So more like your rookie year in the league, then," Russ interjects, drawing cackles of laughter from his teammates.

Max's ears turn red.

Across the table, one of the rookies gives me a shy look. "Was New York really a wild scene?"

More than this baby could ever know. "Yep."

"Sorry to interrupt, friends, but the steaks are getting close to being done," Russ says. "Grab your plate, come on up to the grill, and we'll pick the perfect one for you."

I smile at his casually bossy hosting style.

We form a line at the grill, the rookies jockeying for first dibs—after asking if the ladies wanted to go first, and we all let them cut ahead—then the couples lingering behind, chatting amongst ourselves.

Emery ends up just behind us.

"I want to know more about your time in New York before you met Max," she says.

"No you don't," my husband says.

Heat crawls up my neck.

Emery rolls her eyes. "Yes, I do. What did you do there?"

Again, Max answers for me. "Mostly modelling. She spent a fortune on private acting lessons that went nowhere."

Not nowhere. I learned how to act like I give a shit about college stories. How to hold on to a brilliant smile even as I turn brittle inside because I'll never actually be the pretty blonde coed he wants me to be, and not just because my blonde tresses are carefully created by salon artists. I don't even know if Max is aware just how boring brown my natural hair colour is.

From ahead of us in line, Kiley tilts her head sideways at me. "I didn't know you acted."

"Mostly voice over stuff," I say. "It was a long time ago."

"And there was your failed attempt at being a weather

girl," Max adds. There's laughter in his voice, but it feels pointed, and my smile drops.

I'm good, but I'm not perfect.

"New York was wonderful to us in many ways," I manage to get out.

Max shrugs. "Happy to move away, though, honestly. It's safer to keep a wife like this in the suburbs."

"Max, stop," I whisper under my breath.

"I'm just joking around."

What I want to say to my husband is, are you picking on me tonight because once upon a time, I let a billionaire fuck me in the ass? And now he's going to fuck your league somehow? Is that my fault?

But I can't.

So I swallow my protest and say a silent prayer of thanks when the line suddenly moves forward, and Kiley and Ty are picking their steaks, which Max finds way more interesting than tearing me apart.

That's fun for him, but not important. By the end of dinner, he'll forget he did it, and he wouldn't understand if I hung on to resentment.

When we get to the head of the line, Max goes first, and then heads back to the table.

"How are you doing, Shannon?" Russ asks, all casually warm and friendly. Different from how he was inside with me, but still nice. God, he's so, so nice.

I exhale and hold out my plate. "Ready for a medium-rare steak if you have one on the smaller side."

His eyes crinkle at the corners as he turns back to the grill. "Aye, I've got a strip loin with your name on it."

I'm surprised he knows my favourite cut. I'm touched. "Thank you, Russell."

From behind me, Emery squeaks.

I twist around to make sure she's okay, and she's jamming her two index fingers together. "What did you do?"

"Stubbed it."

"Your…finger?"

"Yep. I'm fine." She looks past me to Russ. "Nothing a little kiss won't fix, right, *Russell*?"

We both pivot back, and he's looking at Emery like she's the most adorable pain in his side ever, which is… interesting.

It's weird, mostly. But whatever floats their boat.

I murmur another thanks and get out of their way just as Emery smooshes her fingers against Russ's mouth, and he tells her to settle down.

As plates are loaded up with the salads Emery made, and we devour the perfectly grilled steaks, the conversation shifts to their afternoon workout, and their plans for tomorrow. Golf first thing, then collecting the boat and jet skis, and then in the afternoon, Russ has booked some ice time at the local arena. Both tomorrow and the next day, they'll skate together and bring the rookies into the fold, everyone sharing what they've learned from training with friends across the league over the off-season.

They drift to broader topics, too, like recently announced contracts, and the rookie camp that Jamie and Malik will be going to before training camp begins for everyone else.

But nobody brings up Ice League or Francois.

At one point in the conversation, my thoughts drift back ten years to Mediterranean summers that seemed so intensely glamorous for a small-town girl from Michigan. I thought I had the world in the palm of my hand, after a few rough years of missing out on more auditions than not, of struggling to make ends meet as a waitress and then a bartender.

When a roll of laughter snaps me back to the present, I realize I'm looking at Russ.

He's staring back, his brow pulled tight.

I flush and give him an apologetic smile before dropping my gaze.

"Has everyone had enough? I'm going to get these salads back in the fridge. They'll be even better tomorrow for lunch," Emery says brightly.

"I'll help." Harper stands.

"This is what we have rookies for," Russ says, waving them both back into their seats. "Mason! Zondi!"

The younger players jump to their feet and the whole table laughs.

"Thirty push-ups and then clear the table," Kieran says dryly.

Russ grins. "I'll be right back with dessert. Who wants crème brûlée, and who would prefer a coconut panna cotta?"

CHAPTER 12
RUSS

I know Emery is following me inside. I also know I can't stop her. It's a miracle she didn't drag me away before dinner.

"So…" she says as soon as the door closes behind her.

I open the fridge and ignore her.

"Russell," she chides after a minute.

I sigh. "It's not what you think."

"Really? Because, as we've very recently discussed, I was raised in the NHL and my brother is thrice-divorced."

"Thrice-married. Twice divorced, and let's hope that's where the stats end." I finish setting the ramekins I carefully filled yesterday on a tray, and grab the kitchen blow torch I'm sorely tempted to use on myself right now. "You invited yourself along for this miserable weekend, Buzz. So now we're in it. Whatever you think you've figured out, you're wrong. And if you keep poking that bruise, you're going to hurt an innocent woman. So leave it alone, do you hear me?"

"Oh." She rocks back on her heels. "Oooooh."

"Not oh. Not oooooh. Nothing." I yank open the drawers, looking for the damn dessert spoons.

"I put them over here earlier," Emery says, patting the island.

She parked herself next to them when she came in, knowing I'd eventually have to come and stand right in front of her, like a thirty-six-year-old schoolboy being called on the carpet for having an off-limits crush.

"This is more interesting than I thought," she says softly. "You're on the rebound from *Shannon?*"

"I'm not having this conversation with you," I grind out. Then I clatter the spoons onto the tray. "I love you like the sister I never had, but some things are not for you to find interesting. Understood?"

Her expression is undeterred as she looks up at me. "Are you okay, Rusty?"

I set my hands on her shoulders and lean in, holding her eye contact. "You saw the team this afternoon. We all want one thing, and one thing only—the Cup. That is the whole point of this weekend. That is what my entire focus will be when we report to training camp, and when the season begins. Anything else. *Everything else* is second to that, and anything that is in conflict with that goal is shoved into a box under the bed to consider when I retire."

Slowly, she nods, understanding setting in. "Which won't be that far away," she teases. "Because you're such an old man."

I laugh weakly. "Yep."

"I'll get the door for you." She grabs my hands off her shoulders and squeezes my fingers. "But for the record, I love you exactly like the big brothers I do have, and I would only want you all to be happy."

It's right on the tip of my tongue to tell her that I'm happy. Because of course I'm happy.

But the words don't come out.

CHAPTER 13
SHANNON

After dinner, Emery says she wants a bonfire. Russ has a big fire pit surrounded by Adirondack chairs—which Ani delights in correcting me are called Muskoka chairs in this part of Canada.

"I knew that," I groan.

Malik, who is from Vancouver, gives me a playful nudge. "I call them Adirondack chairs, too."

Max shoves his way between us, slinging his arms over both of our shoulders. "Hands off my wife, rookie."

"Of course, of course."

"Go sit over there." Max points across the circle, then scoops me up and sits down in one of the oversized wooden chairs ringing the pit, settling me sideways on his lap. "Hey, hun."

I lean into him, pressing my face into his neck for a second before Emery pulls my attention back to the group.

"This reminds me of summer camp," she says happily as she climbs onto Russ, poking him when he makes an audible oof. "In fact, I think…" She taps on her phone. "Yeah, my summer camp was like, twenty miles that way."

"Spoiled brat," Russ says fondly, shifting her to sit on the flat, broad arm of the chair, keeping his arm around her so she doesn't fall off.

"Did anyone else do summer camp up here?"

Everyone shakes their heads, no.

"I went to Boy Scout camp a few times," Kieran offers to a chorus of *of course you did*. "But it wasn't this bougie."

Russ grins good-naturedly. "Maybe that's why I bought this place, because I missed out on the coming-of-age camp experience."

Emery points over at us. "Did you ever go to camp, Max? You seem like a preppy camp boy."

"Hockey camp exclusively for me." He clears his throat. "But lots of my classmates came up here to go to summer camp, though."

They compare notes on which camps were more popular in their different decades of life, but from the same prep school circle, and I climb off of Max's lap, because Ani has pulled out Smores supplies.

I'm carefully toasting the marshmallow when suddenly I hear my husband say, "We should play spin the bottle."

I drop my marshmallow in the fire.

Fuck.

I twist around and give him a death glare. He did not just suggest that we kiss random people around the fire.

He grins at me, unrepentant. "Come on, hun. Just a fun game."

"Try to kiss my wife and die," Kieran growls.

Harper wraps her arms around him. "Yeah, sorry, we're a closed kissing loop of two over here."

There's a murmur of agreement amongst all the couples, and then Hiro shrugs. "I'll kiss you, Max."

Russ shrugs. "If need be, I would too, Tiller."

He says it dead serious, which makes everyone crack up.

But then Emery thumps his shoulder, and he grins at her. "You're not allowed to kiss Max," he says.

"You're not the boss of me. I'll kiss who I want."

He's laughing at her now. "And who around this circle do you want to kiss, Buzz?"

She wrinkles her nose.

He pats her hip. "That's what I thought."

She jumps up. "I need a marshmallow."

Kiley hands her the bag.

Behind Emery, Russ leans back in his chair. But his gaze doesn't follow her as she puts her marshmallow on a stick and proceeds to scorch it in the flames. His brow deeply furrowed, he stares across the fire pit at Max, and a skitter of unease chases up my back.

I don't want there to be tension between them.

I look up at Russ's girlfriend, waving her burnt sugary treat in the air in delight. I have to do something here to shift the energy.

Just then, Harper slaps her thigh. "Might need to get the bug spray out."

As good an excuse as any to leave the bonfire to the boys.

I jump to my feet and point at Emery. "You, come with us."

"Us?" Kiley asks, immediately standing with me. I love her for that.

Harper, Ani, and Becca promptly follow suit.

"Us," I confirm. Then I turn to Russ. "Do you have a wine cellar here in this palatial cottage?"

"Aye, there's the start of one, anyway. Through the kitchen pantry."

"Good. We're going to destroy it. Girls, let's go. Leave them to their kissing games or whatever they want to talk about. We have Emery Granger to get to know better."

The woman of honour claps her hands together and squeals, and Russ gives me a slow nod of approval. Finally, I feel like for the first time all day, I've done something actually right, because Russ looks happy with me.

Emery must read his expression differently, because she stops and gives him a reassuring pat on the cheek.

"It's okay, buttercup," she says sweetly. "I can handle the WAG gauntlet. My mom and sisters-in-law were all WAGs. I've trained for this."

"She makes us sound so menacing," I say in a stage whisper to Kiley.

"Not us," she whispers back. "Her brother's wives, though, might be monsters."

Emery tips her head back and laughs. "Definitely not the wives that were the problem. But that's a story for after we find the wine."

It doesn't take long to affirm that my decision to bring her deeper into our circle to ward off whatever that weird energy was with Russ was definitely the right call.

Emery Granger is a fucking delight. First, she finds us a bottle of white wine and expertly opens it, pouring us each a glass before saying, "What do you need to know about me?"

Straight and to the point.

I go first. "How long have you known Russell?"

Her gaze flicks to my face, curiosity and bald assessment equally present. Maybe this grilling with go both ways.

She thinks about for a second. "Almost seven years?"

Kiley and Harper exchange a look, clearly doing math on her age and Russ's age.

I clear my throat delicately. "And was it…a crush from the start, maybe?"

Emery snorts. "God, no."

We all laugh.

Then she blushes. "I mean, for a very long time, Russ was just…Rusty. On some levels, he's still that guy." She glances my way. "And old, no offence."

"None taken," I say dryly. "Although, to be clear, I'm not as old as he is."

Her pink cheeks turn scarlet. "I didn't mean that."

"It's fine." I wave my hand. "So, when did it change?"

"Very recently." She presses her lips together. "Very, very recently. And we're not, like…exclusive." She looks at me for a long second, as if she needs to make sure I don't judge her for that. "We live in totally different countries, you know? If the right person comes along and sweeps him off his feet, I'll be happy for them. I'm not a jealous human being."

I laugh lightly to cover up the wave of relief I feel that Russ isn't a hot second away from requesting a trade to be closer to his girlfriend. "Got it. That's cool."

She smiles brightly. "So we were friends first, and that feels like a better foundation for a relationship than anything else I tried in the past."

Kiley lifts her glass in the air. "Cheers to that."

Great. Even Russ's week-old relationship is healthier than mine. "Now that we're not getting interrupted," I say dryly. "Is there anything you want to know from us? Anything Highlanders specific?"

"All the hockey stuff is pretty familiar to me. Ummm…" She takes a long sip of wine. "Look, we don't need to…" She wiggles her fingers back and forth. "I know the score. You guys are genuinely lovely. But the sorority of WAGs only exists as long as the hockey player boyfriend or husband in question decrees it to be so, and Russ and I are still pretty new and pretty casual. You won't need to add me to a group chat, you know?"

I frown. "Russ won't string you along."

"I know." She beams. "No, I really, really do know that. But I have four older brothers who also play in the league. The oldest has been married three times. My sisters-in-law are not monsters," she clarifies to peels of laughter. "But I know how it is. *He* says when I'm added to the group texts, and *he* says when I'm taken off it, which isn't a game I want to play. So I'd rather you get to know me as Camden Granger's little sister, rather than Russ Armstrong's girl-friend. The former is forever, and the latter, while nice, is... who knows? But Rusty and I are also BFFs whether he likes it or not. So I might haunt you all, anyway."

"Ah," Harper says seriously. "So *you're* the monster."

Emery cracks up.

Ani grabs another bottle of wine. "Okay, so I have some questions about growing up in the NHL, in that case."

"On that topic, I am an open book," Emery says, leaning back against the wall. "What do you want to know?"

CHAPTER 14
RUSS

I'm asleep when Emery crawls into bed next to me, but since I usually sleep alone, I wake up at the slight pressure on the other side of the pillow barricade.

Then there's a giggle.

"Did you survive the gauntlet, Buzz?" I mumble.

"Oh no," she whispers.

"What?"

"I woke you up." I blink one eye open, squinting at the pillows. A wild riot of blonde waves peers back at me until Emery shoves her hair out of her face and grins. "Sorry."

"You don't sound sorry." I stretch. "What time is it?"

"Three."

"So, I'm on my own for golf at seven?"

"Definitely."

I reach over and pat her head. "Okay."

Then I close my eyes again.

"Your friends are hilarious." She sighs happily. "And they care so much about you being happy."

Huh? I sit up and rub my face. "What are you talking about?"

"Nothing." She rolls onto her back and smiles dreamily at the ceiling. "They're just really nice and I had fun."

Then she hiccups.

Her eyes flare and she presses her hands to her chest. "I am not a fish," she yells.

I jolt and curse in surprise.

She waves her hand at me. "It works."

"Aye, you aren't a fish. Success," I say.

"I cured my hiccups." Her hand stays pressed to her chest, and as the night's silence stretches around us, I'm surprised that she doesn't have another one.

"How...?"

"Dunno. I learned that on TikTok." Her eyelashes brush her cheeks. "Anyway, thanks for inviting me, Rusty."

I lay down again. "Any time, kiddo."

There's only a slight snore in reply.

I listen to the house settle. It might be my imagination, but I think I hear the click of another door closing at the far end of the hall.

I stay awake for far too long, listening for any other sound, with a vigilance that's both frustrating and unsettling. And even though none come, it's hard to fall back asleep.

CHAPTER 15
SHANNON

"That was too much wine," Emery whispers from her towel beside me on the dock.

"Shhh." My eyes are closed under my extra-dark sunglasses, and it's still too bright for this conversation. Or any conversation.

Especially with Emery. Because while we did have fun last night, and I am going to be more intentional in including her, I can't help but feel inadequate in my mental comparison. She's so young, but she's competed at the highest levels of sport, she got a degree, she's starting her own business. She can hold her own in any conversation, about anything.

When I was her age, I was a glorified hooker. And other than marrying well, nothing else has changed in my life. I have failed at everything I have ever tried—including, it feels like, my marriage.

It's a hot, still day on the lake, the kind of muggy humidity that encourages naps at the best of times, and this isn't even the best of times.

The guys haven't returned from golf and picking up the

boat yet. I really should take advantage of the gym being empty to crank out a run, but Emery attached herself to my side as soon as she woke up, and I don't like exercise to be a group activity.

A low drone in the distance catches my attention, a buzz along the water that gets louder as it gets closer.

"Is that them?" I ask, not lifting my head.

I'll let the eager youngster check.

"Looks like it, yep." She jumps up and waves.

Water slaps against wooden pillars, splashing as the engine is cut. Someone leaps from the boat to the dock.

"Let's tie it up. I need some lunch before we go out again." That's Max. "Hun, we're back."

I wave my hand in the air as Emery picks up her towel and announces that she's on it, lunch will be ready soon.

More footsteps. Laughter.

And then quiet again, and I let out a breath I didn't realize I'd been holding. Just me and the sun, at last.

Me, the sun, and my thoughts about last night, a kaleidoscope of intense feelings. Frustration, reckless confidence, unexpected curiosity, and underneath it all, a persistent longing for something different, something I can't even properly name, but something I know will cost me everything I currently have—all the safety and security I have carefully gathered the way a squirrel hoards nuts.

It's all too much to make sense of. None of it is what I thought this weekend would be. I desperately wish I could smash a pause button and just…think.

This moment to myself is as close as I'm going to get to that.

But then there's a creak, followed by heavy, slow footsteps approaching.

Not alone after all.

"Are you coming up to the house for lunch?"

I blink my eyes open as a shadow falls over me.

Russ is silhouetted against the sun, his broad shoulders and long legs stretching him endlessly in all directions, until he's all I can see. Blotting out the sun.

I look up at him through my sunglasses. "Your girlfriend drank me under the table last night. I need a bit more sun and lake time before I consider food."

"She has four older brothers," he says apologetically. "It wasn't a fair fight."

"I'm not complaining. She's lovely." I gingerly sit up, since we're apparently having a conversation.

He squats next to me, bringing himself closer to my level. "She said the same thing about you when she came to bed last night."

I try to picture them having whispered pillow talk at the other end of the hall. Max was passed out when I came to bed, and I'd been relieved, because it meant we didn't need to discuss Francois.

I change the subject. "How was golf?"

"Your husband won."

Now it's my turn to sound apologetic. "He does that a lot."

Russ laughs under his breath. "Aye."

I roll onto my knees, then he helps me rise to my feet. Standing this close, he's huge, and he makes me feel shorter than my five-feet-nine-inches. "I might have a swim, see how the water feels."

He raises his eyebrows raise. "By yourself?"

"It's not like it's deep here." I gesture at the lapping lake. "By swim, I mean immerse myself in the water and hold very still. And then climb out and lay very still on this towel again."

"Okay, now you're making me feel bad because my date gave you alcohol poisoning. I'll stay and play lifeguard, just in case."

"Oh God no, please don't feel bad." I sway my shoulder towards his. Not brushing against his skin, not that close, just being more inviting in my tone and body language. I don't want him to think I'm whiny. "Seriously, I started it. My only regrets are of my own actions. Emery was a delight."

"Still, as the homeowner, I'm going to insist on safety first." From behind his sunglasses, it looks like he winks, but I can't be sure.

Arguing seems futile and ungrateful, so I decide to just be quick in the water.

Instead of jumping off the dock where the water is deepest, I go down the ladder on the side. Large, smooth rocks greet my feet on the lake floor, stabilizing me. The immersion feels good, even as the briskness of the lake takes my breath away for a second. I force myself to start moving along the dock until I get to the end, where I can just touch with my tiptoes and he can see me from where he's sitting.

Since he insists on playing lifeguard, I might as well play by his rules.

"Haven't drowned yet," I say, infusing the words with bright cheer.

"I can see that. How's the water?"

"It's nice."

"I can tell from your teeth chattering how nice it is."

I laugh in surprise at the dry tease in his voice.

When nobody else is around, Russell Armstrong has an

unexpected edge to him. It's not bad. It's just…dangerous for me. Poor Russ is just caught on the periphery of my secret life crisis and he has no idea.

"It is both cold *and* nice," I insist.

"Sure." He's laughing now, too.

So I splash him.

"Hey now," he warns. And the slightly stern rebuke practically demands that I send a spray of lake water his way again.

He stands and puts his hands on his hips. "There's no splashing in the lake, young lady."

I laugh out loud. "Emery called me old last night, you know."

He groans.

"She called you old, first. Then apologized to me, and I made sure to explain that I'm not nearly as old as you are."

His mouth falls open. "All right. Okay. I see how it is. Hungover Shannon is quietly sassy, huh?"

"What? Me? Never." I tip my face up to the sun, grinning.

Which is a mistake, because I don't notice him peeling his shirt off. I only see the blur of movement as he launches himself into the air like a cannon ball.

The lake erupts, a shockingly cold wave splashing over me. I lose my footing and sink under the dark surface.

I grab at my sunglasses, making sure they stay on as I try to find my footing again, straightening up. Gasping.

And when I'm finally balancing on a rock again, Russ is right in front of me, grinning broadly. Water droplets slide over thick, freckled shoulders, and big hands slice through the water, treading with ease.

"Why'd you do that?" I gasp.

His smile widens even further. "I'm a big fan of natural consequences. Splashers get splashed back."

"I'm in a very delicate condition," I point out. "That was dangerous."

He laughs so loud it bounces across the lake surface. "You seem okay."

"Do I?"

He tilts his head to the side, his own water-dappled sunglasses obscuring what I'm sure is a mocking gaze, and then comes closer, his hand catching my elbow under the water. "Do you need a rescue?"

Yeah. From the feelings that his teasing fingertips are eliciting from my traitorous skin.

"I'm okay," I whisper.

"That's what I thought."

"My sunglasses got wet, though." I take them off, flicking the droplets everywhere. He takes them from me and swims back to the dock, setting them carefully on the boards. He puts his own next to them before diving under the water and swimming past me.

When he finally stands again, he's out where it's deep enough that it's just his head above water. "You never know what's going to happen on the lake."

"Good to know," I murmur back.

I should get out. I should go wrap myself in a towel, and then head up to the house.

Instead, I swim out a bit, tentatively testing my ability to tread water. Turns out, my hungover body doesn't mind that at all. The cool flow of lake around me feels…nice.

Russ watches me for a beat, then heads out to a buoy, his long, thick arms slicing through the water.

I wait for him to return, but instead he turns and swims toward the neighbour's wooden swim raft.

After glancing at the dock, I take off after him, cutting diagonally through the water, so I reach the ladder shortly after he does.

"Some lifeguard you are," I tease when I climb out of the lake.

"You told me you were fine." He shrugs, his big shoulders bunching and rolling.

It's a pretty wide platform, but he still takes up a lot of space on it. I'm not sure where to sit, so I take a page from his book and jump off, canonballing into the lake. Splashing him again.

Natural consequences for looking the way he does. For making me notice how huge he is, with that reddish brown hair dusting his chest. It narrows down the centre of his heavily muscled core, a fiery path of curls that disappears into the low slung waistband of his swim trunks.

I've never seen him without his shirt on, I realize dimly. He's jacked in a super solid kind of way. Totally different to Max, who's all lean, whipcord muscle.

I stay under the surface until my lungs burn, swimming all the way to the ladder in the quiet. When I burst back into the air and climb the rungs, he's moved over.

I flop down on the other half of the floating dock.

"How do you think it's going this weekend?" I ask. Changing the subject. Reminding myself of why we're here.

He looks out across the water. At first, I think he might not answer. Then he shoves a hand through his hair. "It's been good. Necessary. We aren't as cohesive a team as some others I've been on."

"How many has it been, seven?"

"This is my eighth team." He says it matter-of-factly, but there's something in his voice that grabs at me.

Like maybe he knows it's his final team. "That's a lot."

He nods. "Max has only had the two, right?"

"Yeah."

"Every team is different. Twice, I've done what Ty did last year, and join a team right at the trade deadline. Both times they were really gunning for the playoffs, and they were *tight* dressing rooms."

I hear that same tension in his words again. "How far did you get in those playoff runs?"

"Conference finals both times. Lost both times, but they were good runs. I want to do that again."

"Of course you do. And you will."

He frowns and swipes at his beard.

"Are you going to shave for the season?" The question bursts out of me.

He did last year, most of the time. The beard didn't come in until the playoffs. And even though they were only in it for one round, he kept it over the summer.

"Aye." He tugs on the short strands. "I'm going to be an ambassador for Hockey Fights Cancer and grow a moustache for Movember, so I'll have to shave at the start of that."

"Are you superstitious about it?"

"My beard? No. I've never found any correlation between superstitions and success on the ice." He pauses. "Well…"

"What?"

"It's nothing."

But his expression, staring hard across the late, his brows tight, says otherwise. "Tell me."

He chuckles. "No."

"Come on. I've been around hockey for a long time. I promise it won't shock me. It can't be weirder than needing to talk to your gear privately before the game. Or the year that two players both *needed* to put their jerseys on last."

His eyebrows jerk up. "I missed that one. How did they settle that?"

"Simultaneous dressing. On the count of three. And then one of them got traded at the trade deadline."

"It's nothing like that." He wipes his hand over his mouth. "I, uh, have just been thinking hard about how this my last chance at the Cup, and I got distracted last year. I'm not fooling myself about my role on the team or anything. I know I'm not the reason we lost, but I wasn't the reason we won, either."

"You want to make sure that you give it absolutely everything." I'm nodding along. This isn't a weird superstition at all. This is standard hockey player devotion. "That makes complete sense. That's normal, Russ. It's okay to put other priorities on hold. Is this about Emery?"

He jolts. "No. Not... No." His brows pull tight and he takes a deep breath. "It's not—"

I wait.

He's gone still, all of his muscles tense.

Slowly, he turns his head just enough to glance sideways at me.

I smile encouragingly. *It's okay.* I know all about soothing the frustrated beast inside a hockey player.

"I have to give up the idea of something, something I want very much." His gaze is careful, barely looking my way, but I feel his words in my chest. They're loaded with frustration. "And it's proving harder than I thought."

"But if you give it up, it will free your energy to focus on this upcoming season?"

Without hesitating, he nods. "Aye."

My heart squeezes for him. I try to think about what I know of this man. Not as much as I wish I did to give him the best guidance here. But at the end of the day, all hockey players are the same. Nothing else is as important as the ultimate prize. "You won't regret giving the team everything you have."

He doesn't look convinced.

I shift my hand over so I can bump my fingers against his. When I touch him, he takes a big, deep breath.

"I know it's a hard position to be in," I say. "Are you thinking about the *what ifs* of the road not taken, maybe?"

His shoulders relax, and he nods again.

"Well, I've done it, and I can tell you that once I made the decision, I only felt relief. So one way to test yourself is to make the hard break, and see how it feels."

He shifts to give me his full attention. "You've done what?"

"I've given up something I wanted—or what I thought I wanted—in order to get something else that I needed." I hesitate. I never talk about the choice to trade my Single Girl Life for Married Life. Some of the details feel too raw, still, after all these years. And it feels like betraying Max to tell anyone that I had to change myself to seal the deal on getting married.

"What did you give up?"

I shake my head. "Doesn't matter."

"I think it does."

I take a deep breath. "Actually, I think my whole life has

been a cycle of giving up one version of myself to discover a new one. And all that matters is that I've never regretted it."

Russ makes a thoughtful sound, then looks back out across the lake. "Was Tilman what you needed?"

All the air in my lungs punches out of me.

He snaps his gaze back to my face. "Sorry."

"No, it's okay." I whisper. "And yes. He was."

His finger nudges mine, in the same way I'd poked at him. "What was the previous version of yourself before him, then?"

"A party girl whose career never got off the ground. And that career had an expiration date, anyway." I say it as lightly as possible, but I can feel the rest of the truth barrelling in fast and furious behind those words. "But she also had an incredibly wild social life. It was an intensely *me* period, where I got to fly my freak flag as high as I wanted."

It's bittersweet now to admit that I gave up my entire identity for the safety and security of being Max's wife, when I'm on the cusp of what feels like another turning point where I'll give up that reward that I sacrificed so much for in the first place.

And I'm so focused on that feeling that I don't even realize I just told one of Max's teammates that I miss being freaky.

Damn it.

I tense.

"Hey, don't worry," Russ says. "That's just between us. It...helps, really."

I exhale in relief. "Thank you. And I'm glad to hear that. Because if you don't give it absolutely everything, I really think you'll always wonder what could have been. Just focus on what you need right now. Don't worry about what you wanted in the past."

He bends his long legs, wrapping his arms around his knees. I miss the warm press of his finger against mine. I try not to stare at his freckled shoulders or the light dusting of hair on his chest, now disappearing into the shadow of his thick thighs.

We're both silent for a good long stretch.

Then he looks at me again. "I should focus on what I need right now."

I nod, a weird lump in my throat. "Yeah."

His gaze is piercing. "You're happy, right?"

I don't know how to answer that. I dig deep and think about the last time that I was genuinely happy. "Moving from New York was scary. But I've found the best of friends here. I don't regret any of that." Then I think about the season to come, and I'm genuinely excited for them. "And now I get to cheer you on to victory this year."

I don't add that I think it's better to go down a path, no matter what, even if you find out later it wasn't the right one to get you where you want to go. That's the kind of bitter realization that doesn't taste any better if you're pre-warned.

Standing, I stretch my arms over my head. "Is it deep enough to dive in here?"

"Aye," he says, slowly rising, his gaze carefully tracking me.

Lifeguard, back on duty.

"Race you back to the dock," I say lightly before launching myself into the air.

Even with the headstart, he catches me halfway. I splash at him, but it's ineffective, and he reaches the shallow-enough-to-touch area first.

He's grinning when I join him. "Nice try. Oh, watch—"

A boat rips past.

Russ grabs my hand, hauling me past him, putting himself between me and the incoming big wave. I freeze, trying to grip the stone lake floor with my toes, and when the wave arrives, that doesn't help at all. He surfs the big roll of water, but I flail and get pulled under.

The next thing I know, he's lifting me back up to the surface, holding me against him, and all I can feel is his chest pressed against mine, his arms looped around my body. Plastered together, hearts pounding.

"You're all right," he says. A statement.

Lake water splashes all around us, cold and sharp.

I gasp and nod weakly.

"Shannon?"

I close my eyes and squeeze his shoulders. Smooth, tight skin. "Yes," I whisper.

He lets me go, and I let myself get caught by the next wave, grateful for the cold now on my overheated skin.

He sinks, too, until we're both submerged up to our necks.

I bob along for a few moments, until my breath settles down, then climb out and wrap myself in my towel. I curl up on one of the chairs on the deck, which gives me an accidental front row seat for Russ hauling himself out of the lake, decorated with water droplets that glitter like diamonds. He looks wild and rugged and golden.

"How about now? Are you hungry yet?"

I lift my gaze to his face and shake my head with a nervous jolt. "No. Still need more sun."

And some air.

He runs the towel over his head, making his damp hair

sticking out and up in funny ways. His gaze lingers on my face, his brows tight. And then he grins, the concerned expression evaporating. Or maybe I imagined it, projecting more into a conversation about hockey than rightfully deserves to be there. "All right. See you up there. Or back here after, if you're still recovering. But don't forget to put on sunscreen if you stay out, okay?"

I nod mutely.

At least I didn't ask him to put it on my back for me. I could hear myself saying that, too.

It's like all the normal social bounds I've taught myself over the last eight years are falling away at lightspeed this weekend.

Once he's gone, I focus on the hot, still air and the buzz of insects where the vegetation meets the edge of the lake. I close my eyes and I push away every single thought that threatens to intrude.

Freckles and big hands and thoughtful, careful watching.

He has a girlfriend.

It's a major red flag that I care more about that than the fact that I have a husband.

But even more unsettling is how unbothered I am when that same husband appears not five minutes later, holding a smoothie.

"Emery says that you're feeling a bit hungover. She wanted me to bring you this," he says.

I squint and take it from him. "Thanks."

"Where are your sunglasses?" He glances about, and spies them still sitting on the dock.

I wait for a guilty lurch when I realize they aren't alone. Russ's sunglasses are with them, very close together. Touching, as if they were put down at the same time. Max frowns.

Leaning over, he picks them both up and wordlessly hands mine over.

He doesn't ask who the other pair belongs to.

I don't volunteer the information.

"Maybe don't drink that much again tonight, hmm?"

"Yeah." I take another fortifying sip of smoothie. It's delicious. I need to ask Emery for the recipe.

"Shan—"

"Don't scold me, Max." I stand up. I know that's the main reason he agreed to bring the smoothie to me. I'm not being social enough. He's paranoid I'm going to reflect badly on him somehow. That, and he never passes up an opportunity to impress a pretty girl who isn't his wife. "We got a little carried away last night because we were bringing Emery into the fold. As Russ's new girlfriend, there was a lot to discuss. The bonding was worth the headache, and now that I've had a good swim, and this delicious smoothie, that's fading."

I refuse to be chided. I haven't done anything wrong.

Or at least, the mistakes I've made aren't the things my husband wants to chastise me for.

He looks like he wants to say something else, but thinks better of it. We walk up to the house together in silence. The kitchen is quiet now, people upstairs and in their various corners. The house sounds busy, though, and when I see the pile of hockey bags at the front door, I remember that the plan was to go into town for the afternoon.

The real reason Max doesn't want me to be hungover is that I'm expected to be a cheerleader today.

CHAPTER 16
RUSS

I lean my forehead against the tile in my shower, slowly stroking my cock—one of the more masochistic decisions I've made in a bittersweet weekend of self-inflicted pain.

Without spelling out the specifics, I asked Shannon if I should get over her for the good of the team, and she happily agreed. Zero hesitation. There wasn't an answer that would have made me happy, but having the woman I need to get over telling me that yes, I should definitely do that is more brutal than I imagined.

And still I'm hard.

Still I'm thinking about how it felt to have Shannon plastered against me in the water.

Focus on what you need right now.

At this exact moment, I need to know what her goosebumps taste like. What soft little sounds she might make if I chased her shivering reaction all the way down her torso.

I can still feel her in the circle of my arms, tensing muscle under soft flesh.

I can still see the lush bounce of her ass as she dives off the floating dock next door.

I want to chase her for hours.

I want to catch her and hike her up against my body, until her thighs wrap around my waist. I want to pull aside the tight little crotch of her swimsuit and stroke her pussy in the cold lake, and then stretch her out on the dock and feast between her legs until she's warm and wet and ready to take the long, hard length of me inside her.

I spill a fast and guilty release down the drain, my chest heaving as her laugh echoes through my mind.

So I'm not getting over her *today*.

But that was the right idea, that *is* the right idea.

I lather up with body wash immediately, a desperate and vain attempt to move on from *that* choice.

At least we have skating this afternoon. That will be a distraction.

Whether it is a good or bad one remains to be seen.

CHAPTER 17
SHANNON

I know a lot about my husband's teammates. And I watch all of Max's games, so I see them play frequently.

But until this afternoon, I don't think I've ever *studied* another hockey player the way I'm watching Russell right now.

It's impossible not to see him. He's the biggest man on the ice. The slowest, too, most of the time, until someone gets within a foot of him, and then suddenly he's in front of them, forechecking them so hard they go flying.

Over and over again.

The way he does it is a bit of magic, and even though they're all familiar with his play, he manages to surprise them often.

There's a lot more to what they're doing today. The skills coach, Thea, has cameras set up around the rink to record them, and right now they're taking a bit of a break between sessions by doing a little show and tell with favourite shots and moves. It's an intense session to watch.

It's all impressive. But my favourite part so far has been Russ being a beast on demand.

"They look great, don't they?" Becca Kincaid bounces next to me. "But I think they always do. I even thought they looked great in the playoffs."

When her fiancé had met the ire of fans and media alike head-on, taking the brunt of the blame for Hamilton's quick exit in the first round.

"Hayden really does look great," I reassure her. "He's a talented player, and he's just going to get better."

She glances around. We're alone right now in the stands of the community arena. Emery is skating with the guys, and Kiley, Harper, and Ani went in search of tea and coffee, because after a morning in the sun, the ice rink is extra cold for those of us not skating hard. I'm glad I grabbed Max's black Highlanders hoodie and a winter beanie.

Becca lowers her voice. "Can I ask you about your opinion on this Ice League that is launching?"

Tension coils between my shoulder blades. "What have you heard?"

"Just what's circulating online. Hayden says that Kieran told them to just ignore it."

"That's probably for a reason," I say carefully. Maybe that's why Max hasn't brought it up to me, too, although it's not like him to take advice from Kieran. "I try to keep out of the business side of things."

"Okay." She chews on her lower lip. "There's just so much speculation about it online."

"My best advice is to mute any accounts that get in your head. Staying offline is even better, but I could never."

Her eyes light up. "Really? Because same. I'm an Insta addict."

"I get it. Just curate what you see in the first place, that's the only way I've ever been able to manage it without going crazy with the what-ifs. And stay grounded in stuff like this." I gesture to the practice on the ice. "Look at how committed they are to this upcoming season as a team. Who cares about a rival league? Not the Hamilton Highlanders, that's for sure."

"Thank you." Becca's quiet for a minute, and in that moment Hayden skates hard for one of the cameras set up close to us. Then when he finishes his drill, he veers off and gives her a happy wave. She laughs and waves back. "I think he's going to want this camera set up for himself."

"Put it on the Christmas list," I say warmly.

"Put what on the Christmas list?" Ani asks, sliding into the seat beside me and handing over a takeout cup of tea.

"The camera set up."

"Oooh, yeah." Harper sits down next to Becca on the other side. "Good idea."

"What was Kieran's favourite present from you last year?" Becca asks her.

"Something personal in a TMI way."

Kiley does a double-take. "Really? You didn't tell me."

"Because it's TMI!"

"You need to tell us now."

Harper turns an R-rated shade of red. "Butt plugs," she mutters under her breath.

Ani leans toward, talking across us as she says in a stage whisper, "For you or for him?"

Becca squeak and covers her ears.

"No comment," Harper says, her gaze snapping to the ice. But when we protest, she smiles. "For him to use on me. Like I was the gift."

"Oh, that's good. That's very good." And as one, all of my friends start to think about how they can give themselves to their husbands this Christmas.

Me? I'm immediately processing the awkwardness of what Max would do if I gave him a sex toy and the promise he could use it on me. I had to learn how to get myself off with my fingers because he's so uncomfortable with the idea of a toy being "better" than him.

On the ice, Malik tries to hip check Russ and gets sprawled out on the ice for his efforts.

Russ shakes off the impact, then twirls his stick in the air before catching it and pointing it at the nearest camera.

Someone should turn *that* into a TikTok. He's so easy and natural when he doesn't think anyone other than his teammates will see the recording.

I'm glad Emery is on the ice with them, and not part of this conversation. There's a one hundred percent chance that her contribution would be a perky confirmation that Russ *loves* her sex toys and they use them every chance they get.

When we get back to the cottage, Foster puts the team through a hard workout and some recovery therapy in the garage while Thea reviews the video from the ice time and cues it up in Russ's viewing room.

As part of the good wife, good cheerleader role, I sit next to Max when she's ready for them to watch what she's cut for them.

I pat his thigh and bump his shoulder when it seems appropriate, although even after eight years of watching hockey, I'm never sure what is good or bad. When we break to have a pasta dinner Emery makes, he seems happy.

Seems being the operative word.

"Oh, before I forget," he says casually once we're all seated. "I found a pair of sunglasses on the dock at lunch. Who left a pair down there?"

Alarm prickles up my spine.

Russ doesn't react *at all*.

His careful silence pushes on my guilt reflex more effectively than anything else has so far. I think that deep down, I've always known I'm capable of deceiving my husband. Anyone, really. It's a skill I had to hone when I started spending time with incredibly wealthy men, because deception and denial are constants in their lives.

Max turns to me, sliding his arm over the back of my chair. "Shan? Was anyone swimming down there with you?"

"Wait, are they like, big? Oversized?" Emery interjects. She smiles brightly. "Might be mine."

"We were tanning together," I manage to say. "Before lunch."

"I must have left them down there. Thanks, Max."

"No problem," he mutters, looking like there is still definitely a problem.

Emery glances my way briefly, her smile firmly in place, her gaze soft and warm. Delayed guilt roils in my belly.

"This sauce is *incredible*," Ani says, changing the subject.

Emery laughs. "You want to know where I learned how to make it? TikTok."

Russ leans in. "Tell them about the hiccup cure."

"Oooh yes." She throws her head back, cackling. "Okay, so if you ever get the hiccups, just yell *I am not a fish* and throw your arms up in the air. They'll go away."

There's a chorus of disbelieving reactions around the table. She leans over, snuggling into Russ as she looks up at him softly. "Tell them how it worked last night."

He grins down at her.

Another visceral reaction slices through my chest, this one hotter and more deadly than the guilt.

"She crawled into bed, drunk as a skunk—"

"I wasn't drunk," she corrects. "Happily tipsy."

"Wakes me up—"

"Apologized *immediately*."

"And then scared the crap out of me with the fish thing."

"You skipped the part where I told you how nice your friends are," Emery says, triumphantly finishing their nauseatingly sweet little performance.

My thoughts right now aren't nice at all.

I stab my fork into my pasta, hating how delicious it is. Hating that Emery saved the conversation, diverted my husband's misplaced jealousy, and sparked this new wave of my own misplaced jealousy all at the same time.

I want to like her so, so much.

I *do* like her.

But in this moment, I hate her even more.

I hate how perfect she is for Russ. That my first assumption, that they weren't suited to each other, wasn't correct in the slightest.

And most of all, I hate that I read something into this afternoon that obviously didn't exist.

"What else have you learned from TikTok?" Kiley asks.

"What haven't I learned?" Emery taps her bottom lip with her index finger, thinking. "How to fold a bottom sheet easily, how to put a duvet cover on a king size duvet by yourself—a lot of them are bedding related—oh, and sleep related, too. Like hacks to fall asleep faster. There's this thing called *cognitive shuffling*—"

Max smirks. "TikTok dumbs everything down. I do cognitive shuffling but it's not that simple."

Emery frowns. "It's not dumbing something down to make it easily understood. That takes a lot of skill, actually. I learned about cognitive shuffling in sixty seconds, and it works the way it was described. Seems pretty simple to me."

"I'm sure." Except his tone sounds utterly dismissive.

God. Damn. It.

I stand up as quietly as I can, wanting to just remove myself from the table without causing a scene.

I long for my bedroom at home, my lovely dressing room, and my oversized bathtub.

"Everything okay?" Russ asks.

"Everything's great," I say, not making eye contact.

As I head into the kitchen, I leave Emery and Max arguing over the specifics of how to do something called cognitive shuffling. He insists there's a very detailed right way to do it, and she's gleefully insisting it's really just random word play with your eyes closed.

In the kitchen, I eat the last few bites of my dinner, then rinse the bowl and put it in the dishwasher.

Everyone else trails in a few minutes later. Russ's gaze finds me as soon as he steps inside. I turn and give Emery and Kiley my full attention. They're arguing about movies.

"We could watch *Cutting Edge*," Kiley says.

"Toe pick!" Harper says, twirling around in the circle. Kieran catches her, and she does a flourish with her arms to stick the landing.

"There's even hockey in that for the boys," Emery says sweetly.

Malik protests. "I like figure skating movies, too."

"Who doesn't?" Emery grabs the front of Russ's shirt and tugs. "What cocktail goes perfectly with a broken love triangle?"

The three words are a stab to my chest. And again his gaze finds mine, over her head. This time, I can't look away, and there's a loud rush of blood through my ears as his brows pull tight.

What are we doing?

He removes Emery's hands from his shirt and steps back.

Ani looks worried. "I'm not a big fan of love triangles."

That makes two of us. Anxiety twists inside me.

"Wait, have you never seen *Cutting Edge*?" Kiley shakes her head. "It's really not a real love triangle. She's not meant to be with her fiancé. It's Titanic rules. It's a *broken* love triangle, which is my favourite."

Emery nods vigorously. "Don't worry, she's not torn about the choice. And I wouldn't be either. D.B. Sweeney or…whoever the guy in the suit is? No contest."

I gasp, then clap my hand over my mouth.

Emery glances my way, her eyes twinkling. "Am I wrong?"

"Not wrong," I have to admit, my head spinning.

She grins. "He reigned supreme as the hottest hockey player on the small screen until Shoresy came into my life."

That reference to an irreverent Canadian hockey comedy shifts the entire conversation immediately.

"Shoresy!" Roan and Malik said at the same time. "Give your nuts a tug."

Even the main character's signature line is said in unison.

We've lost control of movie night.

"All right, show of hands. Who wants to watch *Shoresy*?" Russ asks.

Emery protests, turning on him, and he just covers her mouth with his fingers. I feel that touch on my body, in the cold lake water, and I go still.

Nobody notices as all the guys put their hands up.

"And *Cutting Edge*?" he asks, although we've already lost.

Still, the girls all put our hands up. My hand is shaking.

"Tomorrow," Russ says. "Maybe while we're skating?"

CHAPTER 18
RUSS

There is zero fucking chance I'm watching a rom com with Shannon, her husband, my fake girlfriend, and an audience of my teammates and their better halves.

Fuck. That. Noise.

It's bad enough that Emery is now on a mission to performatively prove to Max that I'm in love with her or something like that. I want to drag her aside and stage a break-up. Or at the very least, just tell her to cut it out.

It feels like this weekend is happening in slow motion around me, and I hate the feeling of not being in control.

So I'm taking control.

Emery growls and thumps me on the chest as I make the pronouncement that we're watching Shoresy. I spin her around and point her to the bar cart. "You're in charge of the cocktails tonight, kiddo."

She stomps to the fridge and grabs a bottle of beer. "Voila. Your Sudbury Special, sir. And I'm not skating with you guys tomorrow, because *Cutting Edge* takes priority."

I put a deliberate amount of chill on my response. "That's fine."

She doesn't pick up on the vibe, though, and when we all pile onto the couches in the viewing room again, she manages to arrange everyone in the blink of an eye so we're sitting next to Shannon and Max.

The massive couch still isn't big enough for the four of us.

I shift in my seat as the episode starts.

Immediately, the room starts laughing along as our favourite minor league hockey player chirps his way through reffing a junior game.

Shannon is as into it as anyone else. It's nice to watch her laugh. And it's hard to pretend not to watch her.

Emery pats my knee and leans against me. *Pretend with me instead*, she projects.

I don't want to, but I slide my arm over her shoulder, anyway—and my knuckles graze Shannon's shoulder on the other side.

She jolts, and then holds still, the soft muscle now firm against the back of my fingers. But she doesn't pull away.

I flex my hand, straightening out my fingers. Touching her from knuckles to fingertips. Warmth pours up my arm as she laughs with the next joke, shaking gently.

Grinning, I relax.

And when Shoresy talks about liking mature women, Shannon claps her hands and pushes her elbow into Emery, clearly delighted.

When he says he'll be so good to the woman he's pursuing, she turns pink and bites her lower lip.

Fucking adorable.

She deserves a man who will pull her close and repeat the line for her enjoyment.

What she gets, instead, is a pissed-off husband who starts whining about minor league players as if Shoresy is some real person who couldn't make it to the NHL, and not the figment of a clever writer's imagination.

Beside me, Emery shakes her head a little, then pushes herself off the couch. "Anyone want a beer?"

She counts hands, then disappears.

My arm, no longer having an Emery to rest on, is back on my end of the couch, and a sharp awareness of the space between me and Shannon prickles as the characters on the show argue about being less slutty in order to give their team everything they have for the rest of the season.

She glances sideways at me as Max turns and yells to our teammates, "Pay attention, titfuckers."

Shannon laughs and winces. Her preppy-assed husband doesn't sound right at all quoting Shoresy like that, and everyone in this room knows that.

But under the chorus of cheers and laughs, I can say, "It's not being slutty, by the way."

Shannon shifts closer. "What's not?"

"The thing I need to give up."

"You aren't struggling to give up the idea of *hammering ass* all season long?" she asks lightly, quoting the show in a mocking way.

I didn't say that, exactly. "Not with more than one person. Not with puck bunnies."

She lifts her shoulder in a don't care shrug. "Okay."

From the back of the room, Malik bounds forward and slides onto the couch on the other side of Max, pushing him into Shannon...and Shannon into me.

Emery returns, handing out beers, and just takes Malik's empty seat on the upper back right couch next to Roan.

The scene changes on screen, but I've stopped following. All I can feel is the press of Shannon's thigh against mine, from our hips all the way to where her knee is, just short of my own.

Her arms are crossed in front of her body, and her husband is right on the other side of us.

I can't move. I can't touch her any more than I am.

This is exactly what you need to give up, I try to tell myself.

But it's never going to happen.

As the hockey players on the screen have to grapple with the question of what they will do, and what they will give up, to be the best team in their league, I am forced to admit that I will not, cannot give up my one-sided affection for this off-limits woman.

CHAPTER 19
SHANNON

When Emery was between us, it felt safe to ignore the tingles racing along my skin because of his arm simply being stretched across the back of the couch, his fingers brushing against my shoulder.

But now that she's gone and I've been pushed right up against him, I can't deny that I'm painfully aware of his body.

And Russ... he's barely breathing.

I shouldn't be this aware of him. I shouldn't be aware of him at all, I know that, but I can't help it.

His thigh is rock solid against mine. Bigger, longer. He takes up a lot of space, all the time, but right here in this moment, he's so big beside me it would be comical if it didn't feel so dangerous.

I've never been with a man as big as Russ. The thing about billionaires is that they don't work out four hours a day.

Don't compare him to Max. Don't—

I close my eyes and exhale slowly, pushing all of that away.

"You okay?" Russ whispers.

No.

And then beside me on the other side, Max yawns.

And it's a lifeline.

"Tired," I murmur.

The episode is coming to an end, and as soon as the credits start, I tug at my husband's hand. "You want to go to bed?"

There's nothing Max likes better than going to bed early. He takes his sleep seriously, and he thinks it's more virtuous to wake up before dawn. Normally I don't join him, but tonight feels like a precarious moment, a turning point, for who I am as a person.

I am not going to flirt with my husband's teammate. I'm not going to press my thigh into his, desperate for some warmth and attention.

"Come on." I take Max's hand and tug him along with me.

He grins and waggles his eyebrows at his teammates.

I don't look back at Russ. I can't.

On the main level, I wind myself around Max and kiss his neck. He fills his hands with my ass and gives a good squeeze, pulling me into his body. I don't feel the hard thrust of an erection yet, but he's trying. When we get upstairs, he kisses me just outside our suite, pushing me against the wall and playing with my tits.

But as soon as we get to the bed, he yawns.

It feels like a slap across the face. As if I am boring.

He pushes me onto my back and climbs on top of me, only to yawn *again*.

I push him off me, accepting that this isn't going to happen.

"Maybe in the morning," he mutters.

But I know he's going to be up and out of bed before I even wake up in the morning. "Yeah, okay."

He sighs and heads to the bathroom to brush his teeth.

I change, then follow him.

He avoids my gaze in the mirror.

When we climb into bed, ready to actually sleep this time, I make another effort. I curl up beside him as he pulls the blankets up, and circle my finger on his t-shirt covered chest. "You could wake me up," I murmur. "You know, as early as you want. I'll go back to bed after. You can use me however—"

But he's already asleep.

Which is better than him chiding me and saying that's slutty, which is always a possibility—and he wouldn't mean it in a good way.

One of the continuous issues in our relationship, albeit in a one-sided way, is Max's discomfort with sex when he's not turned on. I know for a fact he is as horny as any other guy out there, and when the mood strikes him, he can be hot and filthy. But when his head is not in it, his head is really not in it. And there's no point in trying to push him. Nor do I want to be somebody who pushes him.

So I let it go.

I listen to his breath even out. I think about reading, but I don't want to turn on the lights. I think about finding something to read on my phone, but I actually don't want that background glare for long.

I find my earbud, make sure it's connected to my phone so I won't wake up Max, and open TikTok. I pretty easily find the video Emery was talking about with the sleep hack. I watch it three times, then put my phone aside and close my eyes.

I try it.

My heart is racing. It doesn't seem to work. I hate that Max might have been right, that it might not be this simple.

I try again, but I can't seem to make my thoughts random or soothing enough. I keep circling back to what we were talking about downstairs. I think of gruff Midwestern boys. I think of Canadian country boys like Shoresy. Hockey players who don't do it for fame or fortune, who don't do it for their legacy, but they do it because they love the game. They do it even if they'll never be famous. I think about that type of man turning that kind of passion in my direction, where I'm not an afterthought or a footnote in his hockey career, but I'm his entire life, equal to his love for the game that he adores.

I picture Shoresy jumping into the lake. Making me a drink.

I picture someone with golden red stubble on his jaw. Russ has a beard. He doesn't have stubble. It's not the same person. But if he shaved, it wouldn't take long for there to be a delicious scrape, a five o'clock shadow on his jaw that would feel so good running up the inside of my thigh.

My breath catches, hot fire inside me now. Terrible. I'm a terrible person.

That doesn't stop my back from arching off the bed, my shoulders and feet pressing down, my hips lifting against my fingers, that have found their way into my panties.

A crass, growly hockey player's mouth licking against my fingers. Jockeying for position because he all he wants to do is kiss me until I scream.

I got turned on watching the show, sitting on that couch. Being painfully aware of his body, the warmth of him, going out of my skin with need. This fantasy is my subconscious dealing with those feelings, that's all.

I need to come.

If I find a release, then this bombardment of thoughts will cease.

I give in. I don't think his name, but I feel the size of his shoulders between my thighs, his big fingers wrapping around my legs. Hear the burr of his accent and—

My clit spasms against my fingertips, and I'm tipped into an orgasm I didn't see coming.

I gasp a little shocked sob.

No.

For the first time in my life, I didn't want to come that quickly.

The fantasy fades, even as I try to hold on to the warm, dangerous feelings. I can't do that again, but wow, did it feel good.

I roll onto my side and push my fingers into my mouth, licking my own arousal off them. Pretending it's a Scottish tongue. Pretending I'm clinging to his broad shoulders as we kiss, as he tells me how good I taste.

Tears track down my cheeks as I silently sob. There's no clarity after this release. Only confusion and loneliness and a terrifying black hole where my vision for what's next should be.

CHAPTER 20
RUSS

I skip golf in the morning. I don't stick around for the girls to wake up, either. Instead, I do the rookie workout with Foster in the garage, followed by an ice bath and some red light therapy, hoping the latter works on jealousy as well as it does whatever else it claims.

Then I tag along with them to the rink in town, where Thea and Foster have an extra clinic planned for them this morning before we return in the afternoon with the rest of the guys.

Foster gives me a look when he sees me carrying in my bag.

"What?"

"You don't want to overdo it," he says calmly.

"Then I won't."

"You're not twenty anymore."

"Fully aware, bud. Thanks."

I take the warm up skate easy, then practice some angled shots off the boards at one end while Thea sets them up for some board battles. The mission this morning is to get them ready for the brute force of the NHL, and at first, they aren't sure that Thea Brown—who is a foot shorter than most of them—is the right person to teach them how to use their size, but she quickly wins them over with her keen observations and suggestions.

"All right, you're starting to get the idea of it. Mason, Zondi. Line up and let's do that again."

They take their mark ten feet from the boards, and on her whistle, they charge hard for the puck Foster shoots up along the boards.

Zondi's bigger and faster, but Mason hunches down, making himself smaller—and more compact. A coiled ball of muscles that can explode once he's got his skate between Malik's.

Just in time, Zondi figures it out, twisting and using his weight to power away with the puck.

"You almost had me," he says cheerfully, swinging back to high-five Mason.

I skate closer as Calhoun and Watanabe line up.

The most important part of this morning is not just Malik and Jamie learning from Thea and Foster, but also learning how to watch better hockey players the way the skills coach and trainer do—with professional objectiveness. Like scouts. Because there's a lot of pre-scouting done for us for games, but we need to do it, too. Watching tape. Remembering guys from game to game—which isn't easy, since we don't play the same team more than a few times a year, unless we get them in the playoffs.

Zondi doesn't disappoint. He makes the same comments I would, which is impressive for a twenty-one-year-old. Mason gets a little caught up in the battle, just cheering, but he's a younger prospect, and will get it in time.

Thea blows her whistle after Hiro wins the puck battle. "Now we're going to do it down by the net. Foster is going to be our goalie this morning. While he gets his pads and helmet on, let me run through the plan here. The name of this game is *get to the net*. That's the end goal. Get in the corner, win the puck, get it to a teammate, and then get to the net." She points to me. "Why is that, Armstrong?"

"Because goals are scored at the net."

"Correct. How many of us were the best shot on our minor teams?"

We all raise our hands.

"And in junior?"

They all keep their hands up. Mine comes down, because the Scottish whiz kid on ice was just average in the Toronto competitive leagues. I glance at Thea, silently asking if I can say something.

She smiles. "I bet Russ has some insight on this."

"Och aye. By the time I made junior, it was clear that while I had a lot of hockey skill, I wasn't going to out score other forwards. I even switched to D for a bit, which wasn't for me. I came back to being a forward with the right coaching, but always in a shut-down role. Nobody has ever expected me to score a lot of goals. But the only reason I ever do is because I know how to get to the blue paint."

Thea nods. "You're going to have this screamed at you by coaches across your NHL career. We're trying to help provide the context for that now, so it's easier to adjust your game accordingly."

Foster skates onto the ice, all geared up to have puck battles right in front of him.

Thea points me at the boards behind him. "Do a skate around, pretend to have a battle, and come to the point."

I glide behind the net, then bump into the boards where she's dumped the puck, duelling with an imaginary opponent before snapping the puck wide and clear. Breathing hard, I go straight to the edge of the blue paint, right in front, providing a screen for someone to make a shot on the net.

Thea does just that, trying to go five-hole.

Jenson blocks it easily, and I chip it right in.

"Perfect," Thea calls. She takes off her glove and counts out what she liked about my play. "Rusty wasn't interfering with the goalie at all, but he got into the perfect spot—and he's big enough, and tough enough, nobody will be able to move him from that spot. You are all going into training camp in a blessed position. The NHL always needs guys who can do what Rusty just did. Get to where someone like Jenson Hale or Hiro Watanabe can put the puck, and they will find you every fucking time. Now let's do that with some actual battling, mmkay?"

I get out of their way and skate to the far end of the ice, where I'm surprised to find Emery watching.

I skate to the door in the boards and head off. She meets me on the rubber mat, and follows me into the empty dressing room.

"When did you get here?" I reach back and yank the velcro that holds my jersey to my pants.

"A few minutes ago."

I glance up at the tight note in her voice. "Everything okay?"

She makes a face.

"Oh no. Buzz, what happened?"

"Shannon didn't want to watch *Cutting Edge* this morning." Her voice sounds really small.

I pause, waiting for the rest.

But apparently, that's it. Emery stares at me, like I'm supposed to interpret this in a significant way.

"So you drove twenty minutes to tell me this?"

"Russ!"

"What?"

"Last night, I think we freaked her out."

I unlace my skates roughly, then yank them off my feet. "There's no *we* here. I know you think you were doing something last night, but *you* didn't freak her out. I agree that *we* shouldn't do anymore of what *you* were doing, but—"

"Wait, are you…" She gasps and crosses her arms over her chest. "Russell Armstrong, are you mad at me for trying to help?"

"I'm not mad."

She rolls her eyes. "Okay. Anyway, what about you touching her while we were watching TV?"

I freeze, a skate guard in mid-air.

"Yeah, that wasn't real subtle." She sighs. "Okay, maybe it wasn't what I did. Maybe it was your—"

"We're both going to stop." My voice is hard and clipped. I try to soften that by looking at her. "She took her husband to bed, Buzz. That was as clear a reminder she could send me that I need to get over her. Not that I should have needed a reminder in the first place. I should never have involved you in any part of this. Think about how it must feel to her that you were insisting on watching a broken love triangle movie? What we have isn't a love triangle. It's a one-sided obsession from a man who should know better. It's fucking sad."

Emery glares at me for a long, silent beat before saying, "You're not sad."

"Stop."

"It's not one-side, either."

"*Stop.*"

It's less a word and more a roar.

I finish undressing in silence. Once I'm down to my shorts, I yank on a dry t-shirt and clean socks. I can shower at home.

"What did you tell them when you left?"

She shrugs and gestures in the corner, where her signature orange gear is set up. "I grabbed my hockey bag. I could skate."

"I'm heading back. I want a shower and a nap before we come back this afternoon. But they'll still be going for a bit if you want to."

"Yeah, okay. I'll skate with them." She doesn't meet my gaze.

I zip up my bag and shove my feet into slides before lifting it over my shoulder. I stop right beside her. "Thank you for caring about Shannon. I'm sure she's fine, but…it's sweet that the first thing you worried about was that she was upset."

Emery mimes her lips being zipped.

I nod. Right. I told her to stop, and I can't have it both ways.

I don't bother saying goodbye to the rookies on the ice. I'll see them soon enough.

My drive home is silent. Bracing myself, maybe, because despite minimizing the situation for Emery, I worry about what I might find at the cottage.

When I get there, though, I find Shannon and Kiley in the living room, deep in conversation about podcasting. I linger for a second, long enough for them to glance up at me.

"How's everything?" I ask.

Bright smiles from both of them accompany Shannon's reply. "Good. The lake's nice and brisk, if you're going in."

"Are you going swimming again?"

She shakes her head. "I've done enough of that, I think."

Right.

I head upstairs and lose myself in a steamy shower. This time, my cock doesn't want attention, which is good. He doesn't fucking deserve any.

CHAPTER 21
SHANNON

That afternoon, only the team goes to the rink.

Whatever the reason for that decision, I'm grateful, because I'm not up for playing cheerleader—even if means spending the afternoon with Emery, who couldn't leave fast enough this morning when I said I didn't want to watch *Cutting Edge*.

Now she looks wounded all over again. Spare me from the emotional seesaw of a twenty-four-year-old youngest sibling, I think. Except I know my cattiness is coming from a place of inappropriate jealousy.

So much for being kind, Shannon.

Fuck.

This morning, Ani had been with me in wanting to skip the movie and just hang out at the lake. And Kiley had been easily distracted with podcast talk.

I know how to sway a group decision so everyone sides with me. But I wielded that like a weapon, and that was wrong.

"Do you want to watch *Cutting Edge* this afternoon?" I ask her.

Her expression brightens. "You wouldn't mind?"

I'm planning to disassociate through the entire movie. But making Russ's girlfriend happy might be the only good thing that comes out of this weekend. "I don't mind."

While we make popcorn, I call a few beauty spas in the area. And by the time the movie is over, two aestheticians have arrived to give us all matching pedicures.

This is what I do best. I take care of others. I see what people need and I make that happen.

Ani can't stop raving about the movie. "You were right. It's not really a love triangle at all," she gushes to Kiley.

"I told you."

Across from us, Harper is sitting next to Emery and Becca, and they're talking about dinner tonight. And cooking in general.

"It's a shame you aren't in Hamilton," Becca says. "I'd love to take cooking lessons from you. Right now Hayden does most of the cooking when he's home, based on what he's learned from the team nutritionists, but it's pretty basic."

"More chicken and sweet potatoes than you know what to do with?" Harper asks, laughing.

"Yes!"

The newlywed puts her finger to her lips. "Let him just keep doing that. If he's going to be one of the clean-eating players like Kieran, that's a Him Problem, not a You Problem."

Kiley snorts. "Says the girl who eats ice cream for dinner."

"Second dinner, come on," Harper teases. "Sometimes it's the only thing I want at the end of a long shift."

"Do you have to hide it?" Emery asks.

"Nope. I don't know where his willpower comes from, but Kieran literally doesn't care that our freezer is stocked with six kinds of ice cream. There's a tub of sugar-free raspberry sorbet in there for him, too, and that's all he touches. And only if his macros allow it." Harper smiles fondly. "He did eat a fair amount of good cheese in Italy, though."

Becca giggles. "And Italy goes higher on the list for our honeymoon."

Emery leans in earnestly. "If you like those kinds of Mediterranean flavours, there are a lot of chicken dishes you can do that satisfy both your desire for something new and tasty, and Hayden's need for dinner to primarily be protein and complex carbs. You can email me his nutrition notes from the team and I'll make some easy dinner suggestions."

Unexpectedly, I'm taken back eight years, to when I first moved in with Max before our wedding.

It was the end of the season, and his team was on the cusp of not making the playoffs, although they did in the end. In hindsight, it was the worst possible time of the year to disrupt his routine, but I thought we were in love, and my lease was up.

To celebrate, I went grocery shopping and bought everything to make a nice meal. I was a working model at the time, so it wasn't like it was unhealthy at all. But Max had gone off on me, accusing me of trying to sabotage him.

It was our worst fight ever, and I almost moved out again. I almost called off the wedding, but he was full of remorse two days later when they won and two other teams lost, clinching his team's wild card spot in the playoffs.

Ever since, I've let him direct what we eat at home, and ninety percent of our meals are either prepared by a chef or delivered by a service, which a lot of other players do, too. So I convinced myself it was fine and normal.

Now I know it's not, but I still cling to hope. I would love to make my husband dinner—but I'm terrified he won't like it if I do. So I make him smoothies instead, because I know that makes him happy.

Hot, bitter tears well behind my eyelids and I lean my head back, pretending to be relaxing, until they pass.

"Hey, they're heading back," Kiley says, looking at her phone. "Ty just texted me. Apparently, there's a party tonight down the lake. Oh, it's the guy who sold Russ the boat. Shan, I think his son has that podcast I was telling you about."

I don't remember, because as soon as Russ came back, I lost track of our conversation.

Harper makes a little sound under her breath that catches Kiley's attention, and they wordlessly exchange some kind of lifelong best friend message.

"I don't care about going to the party," Kiley says out loud. "It won't be the best venue to network, anyway. We can go home tonight if you want."

"Wait, what?" Becca gives Harper puppy dog eyes. "Why?"

"Kieran pointed out that I'll need to run some errands tomorrow before going back to work. The day after is my first shift at the hospital after taking the summer off for the wedding," she says apologetically. "Sorry to break up the party early. But the guys weren't going to train tomorrow anyway, so..."

"And we drove up with them," Kiley adds. "No party for me."

"It's okay," I say under my breath. "I can't see Max wanting to go, either."

Right on cue, the front door opens and the guys start to stream in, disrupting what was probably our final moment of girlie peace together.

It doesn't feel like we did enough bonding.

Although Becca and Emery are again in deep discussion about food, so maybe they did, and I'm just the odd one out.

I turn back to Kiley and raise my voice to get over the din. "We'll get coffee soon and finish talking about ideas for the podcast."

Which is unfortunately the same moment my husband strides in.

Max looks back and forth between Kiley and me. "What podcast?"

CHAPTER 22
RUSS

We had such a good afternoon session on the ice with Thea and Foster. The rookies were happy to show off for the team leaders, and Max was in his element as their captain.

But the second we get back to the house, he hears something he doesn't like and Shannon disappears with him upstairs.

So much for a final team dinner together before Kieran, Harper, Kiley, and Ty hit the road.

Everyone pretends like they didn't see the start of an argument, and there's no yelling from upstairs, so I try to ignore the way I feel like clawing my way up there and demanding for Max to treat his wife better.

When Shannon emerges, her expression is perfect. A bright smile, full of warm goodbyes for the departing guests. "Max fell asleep," she says apologetically. "We'll see you back in Hamilton!"

The way she wears that mask is incredible.

She doesn't make eye contact with me, though.

It's the denial of her gaze that is the real tell, because ever since she's arrived, she's had no problem looking at me. Holding my attention. Sharing glances that even felt private, which I know is just me projecting my desire onto her, but it was something. Friendship, at the very least.

I watch her carefully as she curls up with Becca, Ani, and Emery on the couch. She doesn't really make eye contact with any of them.

And when it's time for the rest of us to head out to the party, it's almost like she lets out a sigh of relief.

"Go," Shannon urges when I hesitate to leave her essentially alone. "By the time you get back, Max will be up and ready for a late night bonfire."

Something tells me they might actually depart before we get back. But I can't force them to stay. I don't even know what they were fighting about.

I nix taking the boat, because it's dark and dangerous. Emery offers to be a designated driver by road, because she's happy to party on seltzer water, and Malik is happy to let her drive his SUV that sits seven, and then Becca and Hayden ride over with Ani and Jenson.

It's a short drive down the road that winds around the lake, walkable even, and when we pull in down the lane, there are easily twenty cars lining the drive. Music pulses from a terrace that promises to be just as big as mine.

"Let's go," Hiro says, leaping from the car.

There are a few other hockey players here, local Ontario boys home for the summer, and their extended crew. I lose names in a blur of introductions, but it doesn't matter, that's how many people are here.

Emery tugs me along, dancing her way to the middle of the terrace. "I could do this all night," she hollers next to my ear.

"Dance?"

"Yeah!" She beams at me.

I stick by her side for a while, then drift away to find a drink, but the line at the bar is long and nothing in the grab-it-yourself coolers looks good.

I wander back to Emery, who has found a group of girls to dance with now.

I love that she beats to her own drum. Little Miss I Can Do It Myself, she finds joy in everything. And one day she'll meet the right Mr. Sit Down and Let Me Help You, but whoever he is, he's going to have to like dancing a hell of a lot more than I do.

I glance around.

And suddenly, all I want is to go home. Maybe check on Shannon. But at the very least, I'd be happier climbing into bed and putting a movie on. I'm done with socializing. I'm done with the loud noise and the constant awareness of how everyone else is feeling at my own expense.

"Hey, I might…"

I don't think Emery hears me at first. Her eyes are closed and she's singing along to the music.

But then she blinks up at me and smiles softly. "Not your scene?"

"Not at all," I mutter. "I'm going to walk back."

"You sure? I can give you a ride."

"It's a nice night for a stroll. You're probably blocked in already, the way this place is filling up. Text me if you need anything or if the cops get called."

She snickers. "Never fear. And I'll get your teammates home safe and sound at the end of the night," she promises.

I don't bother to let anyone else know I'm leaving.

It's a quiet forty-five-minute walk back to my cottage, just my heels scuffing along the gravel side of the road and the occasional distant owl hoot.

Max's car is still in the driveway, but all the lights in my house are turned off, so I assume Shannon ended up turning in and they're asleep for the night.

Since I don't want to wake them, I head around the side, planning to grab a beer from the bar fridge next to the grill, but I pull up short when I hear splashing in the pool.

Shannon is doing laps. I don't want to startle her. Or at least that's what I tell myself when I stay in the shadows on the edge of the terrace.

It's dark enough that I shouldn't even know who's swimming. All I can see is a long, slim body slicing through the water. But I know it's her in the same way I know when she enters a room, even if my back is turned.

And right now, I can pretend for a second that she's my wife, and this is *our* cottage. That I've come back from an evening skate or running an errand, and I've found my woman taking a late-night swim.

If she were mine, I'd strip down and join her. Catch her in the water and wind her around my body, tangling us together until it's hard to tell where she ends and I begin. I'd taste her mouth and find out if her choice tonight was white wine, or gin, or apple cider for a change. I'd kiss her until she was breathless, and then—

"That you, Shannon?"

Max steps out onto the terrace. He's shirtless, wearing shorts and nothing else, his feet shoved into slides.

She swims to the side of the pool and hauls herself out of the water. "How was your nap?"

"Long, since you didn't wake me up."

"You said you were tired." She sounds resigned, and a bitterness starts to churn in my chest.

Max watches as she wraps herself in a towel. "Everyone else is at the party?"

If I were in his shoes, I'd be drying her off myself. Every last inch getting careful attention.

He doesn't appreciate his wife nearly enough.

"Yeah, they've been gone an hour and a half."

"You didn't want to go talk to the podcast kid?"

"Don't start again. I told you it's just an idea I'm working on."

"One you kept from me."

"Because you never support me in anything I do." Her voice raises at the end, sounding frustrated.

"It's not that I don't support you. It's that I think we need to work together and have shared goals. If you'd asked me, I'd have pointed out why a podcast isn't a good fit for you. I support you in good ideas, hun. That's just not one of them."

I ball my fists at my side, waiting for her reply. He's fucking playing her. Saying things that sound reasonable until you actually listen to the words themselves.

But silence is her only response.

"Hey, so…" He clears his throat. "We haven't had a chance to talk about this, but there's some exciting stuff happening with a new league."

Again, he waits for a reply. And even in the moonlight, I can tell she's not going to say anything. She's gone very, very still.

"My agent thinks I should consider a move at the end of

this season, if the timing works out. If I can jump to the Ice League, get announced as the first star player, it could be a real legacy statement."

What the fuck?

We share an agent, and I haven't heard fuck all about this—but this isn't a contract year for me, and I'm not really at the level to have any kind of legacy beyond being a legend to the two hundred people in my hometown back in Scotland.

"It's just…it would need to be the right deal. Something that would justify the reputational risk."

"Is anyone else going to the new league?" Shannon asks.

Max snorts. "Kieran won't let them even discuss it. He shut it down as soon as the news broke. Says he doesn't want anyone to get burned, but you know that guy just sucks the commissioner's cock."

You fucking idiot, I think. Kieran fucking tried to stop the chatter for this exact fucking reason. I can't believe what I'm hearing.

Blood roars in my ears and I miss the next exchange, but whatever they said, Shannon isn't happy. "I don't think—"

"Hear me out."

"It has nothing to do with me," she whispers. Not to keep quiet, because there's nobody else here. It sounds defensive and shocked at the same time, and raises my alarm.

"Well, it has something to do with you, doesn't it?" Max sounds…smarmy. "When was the last time that you talked to Dumas?"

The billionaire? Confused, I lean forward, trying not to miss anything.

"I haven't, Max. I don't. I wouldn't." She puts a heavy emphasis on the last word.

"Maybe you should." He closes the gap between them and tugs on the ends of her towel, pulling her against him. He lowers his head, hovering his mouth over hers. "Maybe you should go and visit him, for me."

"What are—:"

He cuts her off, kissing her roughly.

"Max, no." She twists her head away and he kisses her temple next. I stake a step forward, my fists drawing up. Ready. I miss what she says next, the words carrying in the wrong direction, away from me.

"Just a friendly dinner," he says. "A weekend in New York. Do some shopping—"

"I'm not going to New York." She ducks out of the towel, leaving it in his hands, and she paces away from him. Her long, bare limbs are visibly shaking, just like her voice. "I can't believe you would think—"

"It's nothing you haven't done before."

"Fuck you," she snarls.

My spine snaps straight up. Have I ever heard Shannon Tilman angry?

She turns on him. "I am not for you to trade away."

Max sighs. "I didn't mean it like that."

"Yes, you did. I'm not stupid."

"I don't think you're stupid."

"Yes, you do. You wouldn't ask me to do this if you hadn't already talked about it with someone. Who was it? Your agent? Or did you speak to Francois directly? What did you tell him? *Shannon would love to catch up with you. I'm sure I can arrange for her to come to New York.*"

When he doesn't reply, she laughs. "Damn it, I'm right,

aren't I? For fuck's sake, Max, it wouldn't even help you, don't you see that?"

"How do you know it wouldn't help?"

"Because I know him!" She throws her arms wide. "I know his world! I know my value in it, and I promise you, it's not what you think. Definitely less than when I was young and beautiful."

"You're still beautiful."

"Fuck off." She resumes pacing, then stops again. Furious. "Who the fuck are you to whore me out?"

"I'm your God damned husband," he roars. "Treat me with the respect I deserve. I'm fighting for our future."

"Our future is *set*, you selfish bastard."

"My next contract isn't going to be as good—"

"You have more money than—"

"I have nothing compared to him." Max's voice has taken on a sulky tone that I recognize from the end of the last season. He's not a good loser at the best of times.

But I can't make sense of what I'm hearing.

Max thinks the Ice League is a better bet for the next stage of his career? He *is* fucking stupid, if that's the case.

And the way he's treating Shannon is unacceptable. I'll stay in the shadows as long as she seems to be holding her own and getting some kind of cathartic release out of yelling at the dipshit, but the second he makes her cry, I'm intervening.

"Him, who?" Shannon gives Max a look I can't quite decipher in the moonlight. "Francois?"

"Do me a favour, *wife*, and stop being so fucking familiar about him if you won't spread your legs for him one last time."

She gasps.

I take a big step forward out of the shadows, but they don't notice me.

He hangs his head. "Fuck."

"I hate you," she whispers.

"Don't say that."

"I want a divorce."

He laughs. "Fuck. Definitely don't say that."

"We're broken beyond repair, Max."

"Come here." He drops the towel and moves to her.

I freeze, wondering if he'll spot me, but he's focused on her—and from the look on his face, he knows he's truly fucked up here.

He catches her hand and pulls her in against him.

"Max, don't..." She sighs, and I tense, ready to charge to her rescue, but then he's kissing her, and she brings their hands up, their fingers tangling.

She's not stopping him.

She's deepening their kiss, because of course she is. She's his wife, and this was just a fight.

Being married to Max Tilman probably means a stupid divorce-threatening fight once a month, followed by make-up sex.

Pain burns in my chest.

I need to walk away, *now*.

He pushes his hands into her hair, their kiss turning desperate. Then he picks her up, her legs going around his waist, and he carries her to one of my wide sun beds the girls got so much use out of this weekend.

That's my opportunity to leave.

I don't take it. I'm frozen to the spot, furious and unable to look away, as Max unties her bikini top, freeing his wife's breasts.

I can't see them, her back is still to me, but…

Fuck.

Fuck.

He fills his hands and groans, then he dips his head and gives her tits attention until her head falls back.

In the still of the night, I can hear her panting.

"I'm sorry, hun. You know I'm sorry, right?"

"Show me," she whispers up to the night sky. "Show me that you're sorry."

Her breathy plea is the jolt I need to leave them alone. I take a step back—right onto a twig that snaps louder than a gunshot.

Max jerks his head up, looking past Shannon's shoulder to make undeniable eye contact with me.

He wipes his mouth. "You looking at my wife, Armstrong?"

"Didn't mean to interrupt," I grind out.

"It's fine." He cups his hands possessively over her arse, keeping her straddled over his lap as he smirks at me. "You want to join us?"

CHAPTER 23
SHANNON

"What are you doing?" I whisper furiously.

But Max doesn't even hear me. He's still talking to Russ, his voice sharp and pointed. "I know you like looking at my wife."

"He doesn't," I protest, more out of self-preservation than an earnest defence of the truth. Because I think he does like looking at me, in the same way I like looking at him, but that's wrong. And my guilt for those exchanges is the only reason I'm sitting naked on my husband's lap right now, trying one last time to reconnect with him—he cannot invite Russ into this moment.

But I can't tell him that, so I have to lie.

And also remember that I'm topless and my bikini top is...somewhere. It's pretty dark on this terrace, but there is some moonlight. I can't just stand up and go inside without flashing our host. And if anyone else is back from the party, them too.

Oh my God, this is a disaster. My heart is pounding.

"He does," Max insists.

I cup my husband's face in my hands, making him focus on me. His expression is wild, still adrenaline laced from our fights. His rejection of my podcast idea. His stupid, arrogant demand that I try to get a favour out of an ex. And me foolishly admitting I want a divorce. *Fuck.* "He has Emery."

"He doesn't look at Emery the way he looks at you." Max's words slice like a scalpel.

Russ doesn't deny them, either. From behind me, he grunts. "You offering to share your wife?"

His words aren't precise like my husband's. He's all brawn, all heavy fists. Bruising.

Once upon a time, I liked bruises a lot.

"He's not." Desperate now, twisting on Max's lap, hating the way I'm getting turned on. "Please, Max, stop this."

"Shhh. It's okay if Russ sees how much I like your body. You're my wife."

It's a possessive claim that rings so, so hollow.

"Is that how it is now? You want to prove that she's yours?" Russ laughs, low and dangerous. "Go on then. Show me how you please your woman."

"You'd like that, wouldn't you?" Again, that scalpel precision, revealing something previously unseen. "You want to watch her get off?" Max pushes his hand between us, tugging my bikini bottoms aside to touch me—and he tenses when he finds me wet.

Fuck.

My husband is stupid in many ways—like how to influence a billionaire, for example, or how to keep a wife happy—but he's not stupid about this.

In the same way his sharp words have revealed something just under the surface between him and Russ and me, his rough touch finds evidence of something I'd rather keep hidden, too.

He shoves two fingers into me, making me gasp, then just as quickly he deprives me of more. His breath is ragged in my ear as he turns me around fully so my breasts are on display and my legs are spread, those bikini bottoms the only thing covering any part of my body now, and just barely. Then he lowers his voice, speaking to me now. "He didn't fuck anyone all last season, you know that. He's a monk."

"Not anymore," I breathe. And I mean Emery—Russ has a girlfriend, I keep reminding myself—but as his gaze finds and holds mine, I'm reminded of the other moments that didn't feel monklike this weekend.

The kitchen.

The lake.

The couch.

"I'm as hot-blooded as anyone else, given the right conditions," Russ says. Slowly, he steps onto the terrace and comes closer.

Max cups my breasts, his thumbs rolling over my nipples in a way that makes me squirm despite myself. And he keeps talking to Russ like they're having a regular conversation, just about…sex. Me. "You ever had a threesome?"

"A long time ago. Not usually my thing." Russ's gaze is scorching hot as he drags it across my face, taking his time before he makes eye contact with my husband. "You do this a lot?"

Do you whore out your wife? The unspoken question paints my bare skin, shame sliding into every nook and cranny.

"Never." Max smirks. "Not with Shannon, anyway."

My head whips around and I glare at him. As far as I

know, the answer is no, never. When we started dating, he was Mr. Strait-Laced. He hated what he learned about my sexual past, so I stopped sharing. It didn't matter. I chose him because he was different. I chose him for his stability and simplicity, because he thought I was pretty and wanted me all to himself.

I thought I would like that possessive vibe.

But Max didn't want *me*. He only wanted to keep anyone else from having me. We don't have a sex life that in any way would lead us to a threesome. He's lying to Russ to show off.

And now he looks at me, his gaze glittering in the moonlight. "Maybe it's time to tick a few more things off that list of experiences you've had that I haven't."

That's the worst reason in the world to do this. I shake my head. "Don't do this."

"Why not? You've done it before."

"Not like this." My voice cracks.

"But you like being watched, don't you?" He pushes his hand down the front of my bikini this time, and Russ's gaze follows.

Pinned down and helpless, I can't deny my physical reaction to this situation I would never have chosen for myself. But on the other hand, I like a lot of things that aren't good for me.

"Yes," I gasp, arching against his touch.

Russ's attention snaps to my face. I can't read his expression, because his back is to the moon, but I force myself not to duck my head, not to hide.

I am who I am. All this time I thought I was someone different, thought I'd shed that skin, but my husband has apparently never forgotten that my value is the good time I can offer someone else.

Tomorrow, I'm going to leave Max, and my world is going to implode.

Tonight, I'm going to make him give me what he never wanted to before—passion. Honest fucking passion. Even if it's confusing. Even if it hurts.

"Where is everyone else?" I ask Russ, my words strained because Max is playing with my clit, because his teammate is watching him as he does that, because... because...

"They're at the party. I walked back." He swipes his hand over his mouth. "We're alone. You can... I'll watch, if you want."

His words make my skin hot and tight.

"Turn around, hun." Max tugs at the strings on my bottoms.

I twist as it falls away.

I wonder how much Russ sees before my back is to him again, and heat licks up my spine.

Max arranges me, making me straddle him, and he has his dick out. A condom, too, which makes me wonder if his plan all along was to fuck me after making his grotesque request.

It's so hard to reconcile the sneering asshole who secretly judges everyone around him and the loving, horny man who is throbbing against my sex right now, eager to get inside me. Eager for his teammate to watch.

I wish I always had this Max, and not the other one.

"You feel good," I whisper, wanting to encourage him.

"Louder, Shan. Let Russ hear you."

Heat slaps my cheeks. That wasn't for his teammate, that was for him.

The asshole is always right there under the surface.

I widen my legs, sinking all the way onto him, and instead of repeating myself, I think of something Russ might like to hear instead. "We shouldn't be doing this outside. We might get caught."

Max growls and thrusts his hips up. "Russ will keep an eye out."

"I'll do my best," our audience says.

He sounds so close.

"Hard to tear your eyes away, huh?" Max squeezes my ass. "Maybe I should just share her."

My pussy clenches down in unanticipated alarm.

He takes that as an endorsement. "She likes the sound of that, man. I can feel it. Come here, touch her."

"You sure?" Russ is right there, right behind me.

And then there's a creak, his knee settling down on the lounger, and wild, reckless, foolish heat closes in behind me. He's not touching me yet, but he's close enough I can feel his big body. Every hand span that I ogled at the lake, every taut muscle that leaned over me in the kitchen. Right behind me, looming.

His breath washes over my bare shoulder, and then his hands ghost over my arms, my shoulders, barely touching me. I gasp when his fingertips are the first to make firm contact, pressing against my shoulder blades.

Tipping me forward, I realize. Leaning me into my husband, but also tilting my hips and popping my ass cheeks out.

Russ—Russell—is looking down my spine to my bare, spread ass.

"Fuck," he mutters. "You're so…"

His fingers trail down toward my , making me tremble.

He stops midway down my back, pausing for a beat before he drags his touch back up again, reversing the fiery course, and then he lightly wraps his fingers around my neck, giving me a hand necklace and tipping my head back.

His voice is rough, raspy. "Are you sure you want this?"

I reach back, tangling my fingers in Russ's surprisingly soft, curly hair. Connecting the three of us. One hand pulling Russ down towards me, the other bracing on Max's shoulder as he slowly drives up and into me.

Somehow it's a complete surprise, but it's also completely right that it is Russ who fills in the gap in this final goodbye of my marriage.

"We want this," I say softly, holding Russ's concerned but heated gaze.

Max doesn't argue. He's the one who invited him, after all.

Between my thighs, he keeps thrusting, moving in and out of me, but my awareness has shifted away from the steady pleasure there to the terrifyingly uncertain sensations skittering across my skin where Russ is touching me, making everything feel shimmery and surreal.

"You said you've done this before, man?" Max asks.

Russ grunts, his attention staying on my face as he answers. "Aye. There were two guys on my first team who were always, uh... They shared girls. Sometimes we just took turns and watched. Sometimes they invited me in like this. It's all hot."

I let out a weak, tremulous laugh.

It *is* all hot.

I had forgotten how good it feels to be sandwiched between bodies, to have my senses overwhelmed.

Russ brushes his lips over my bare shoulder to the nape

of my neck. "Not so big on sharing now," he murmurs, and it's so low I don't think Max hears it. "But I'll make an exception tonight."

"You ever double penetrated a girl?" Russ and I both tense, and Max laughs. "Come on, hun. You can take us both."

I moan despite myself at the mental image.

"You're such a slut, I love it."

Oh, how I wish that were true. He doesn't love it, though. He's going to regret this all in the morning.

Max shoves a condom at Russ, who drops it on the cushion beside me and resumes touching me. His hands cup my breasts the way Max did. His fingers are bigger, and my tits disappear into his fists.

I shudder at the new sensation, the ache of my nipples caught between his middle fingers and the way he bounces them. I'm new to him, too. Breasts he's never held before, a bit of unexpected fun.

I like the sounds he makes behind me, revealing what he likes.

"You're so soft," he murmurs. "You soft everywhere, Shan?"

"Yes," I breathe.

He ghosts one hand down my belly to my bare mound. He sucks in a surprised breath at the smooth flesh. I guess he really has been a monk recently if a Brazilian impresses him.

And then he groans as he slides his fingers between my lips and finds my clit.

He growls, his breathing going rough when I buck against his hand, caught between them now.

"Fuck, you feel good. And so fucking wet. You're soaking my hand."

"I'm telling you, man. She can take us both."

Russ keeps touching me, mostly my clit, but down to where Max is spearing into me, too.

And then he tips me forward again, his hand gone, but then back again from behind, and it's…not his cock, I realize. Just his fingers.

But he's doing it.

He's pushing into me from behind, adding to the sensation of fucking me.

Below me, Max is lost in his own fantasy. He thinks Russ has put on the condom and they're both fucking me now. "That's it. Take his cock, too."

I couldn't, though. Because even just Russ's fingers are too much. "Noooo…"

It's been a long time since I've been stretched like this, used like this, and it's a mind fuck how much I like it. But liking the idea of something and actually tolerating it are two different things.

Russ eases back and presses his face into my hair. "It's okay. You're okay."

I'm shaking.

"Take her ass, then."

I clench up.

"You got lube?" Russ's wet fingers trace over my tight rim.

Wouldn't it be something if my husband's magical pockets that had served up two condoms also had lube?

But we're out of luck.

Max groans. "You might not need it."

I gasp. "No."

Russ's other hand rubs up my spine. "It's okay, I

wouldn't. This is hot just like this. I could look at your arse bouncing all night."

"You want in her cunt alone? I'm almost done."

I close my eyes, hating how my pussy clenches down around my husband's cock at the casual way he'll offer me up.

"Nah, that's yours tonight." Russ catches my other arm, the one that's still touching Max, and he slides that hand off my husband's shoulder and brings it around behind my back. Moving as much of my touch as possible to his body instead. "I'll use her hand."

I shudder as he wraps my fingers around his cock like it's the most casual thing in the world, just forcing me to give him a handjob.

He's long and thick, overflowing my fingers, and when he thrusts through my grip, precum wets my hand.

I can't see him, I can only feel him, but my brain goes fuzzy, then refocuses, like an old-fashioned TV changing channels. I can visualize the length of him spearing into my body, demanding space.

Leaving streaks of precum everywhere he thrusts.

No condom. Nothing between us. Messy and raw.

"That's it," he breathes against my ear. "Squeeze me tighter."

Once I have the hang of what he's demanding, he wraps his arms around me, holding me up. His fingers find my clit again, and his lips brush my ear. "I want to feel you come."

I shake my head. That's not going to happen. It rarely does, but it's okay, because I just like sex. Being fucked is usually enough for me, and if I want a release, I can take care of that myself later.

Beneath me, Max is grunting, thrusting faster. His hands

grab my hips and slam me down, pulling me tight against his balls. I feel the start of his release into the condom, and then he's shoving me off and his hand is on his cock, peeling off the protection and stroking himself up onto his belly.

Russ catches me, his arms looping around my middle, and he presses his face in my neck as he moves me to the other side of the sun bed. I lose my grip on his cock, and I scrabble for it, trying to get him again, needing to finish him, make him feel good.

"It's your turn, my queen," he whispers against my spine, and in the shocked stillness that follows, he drags his mouth down the length of my back before he turns me over and lifts my legs over his shoulders.

I should stop him.

He shouldn't—

But then he's kneeling between my legs and his mouth is on my pussy, his tongue thick and sure, and I'm not going to stop him. I can't. I feel raw, nothing but nerve ends and swollen, aching flesh, and how does he know exactly where to lick to make it all feel better and hotter and so very, very *right?*

I murmur his name, sounding panicked, sounding *desperate.*

He reaches up my left side, the side of my body away from Max, and he grabs my hand, interlocking our fingers.

I squeeze down on his grip as he pushes my thighs further apart, as he licks deeper into me, filling me with his tongue and his breath and all the secret desire Max so casually revealed with his sharp words and dangerous offer.

His big arm shifts against the back of my thigh where he's holding me wide open, until his elbow is braced there instead and then his fingers join the overwhelming sensations at my pussy.

Oh, my *Lord*.

He plays with my clit like…

Like…

I whimper, crying out.

"That good? Like that?" His breath puffs against the wetness that tells him it's good, yes, very good.

I squeeze his other hand.

He squeezes back.

This is so wrong.

Maybe that's why it's hot.

Maybe I'm a terrible person, but I'm a terrible person who's about to come, and that makes it hard to remember to be Good.

He brings our tangled fingers to my belly, stroking me there for a minute before leaving my hand there.

When his body starts rocking, I realize with a jolt that he let go of me to stroke himself, resuming where I left off when he moved me onto my back.

He's groaning into my pussy now, lapping up my flowing arousal, and jerking off.

I can't hold off.

My knees pull up, my mouth falling open as I stare up at the stars and feel my orgasm race through me, like a wave rushing up the sand. Pure pleasure the likes I've never had before. And maybe that's true, because I have never come like this before, from someone else's mouth and hands and breath and tongue. Never, ever because of someone groaning into my cunt as they jerked themselves off.

It's not the kind of secret I should have with Russell Armstrong.

It's too dangerous to know how perfect this man is on his knees, between my thighs. I don't deserve him. I don't deserve this.

But as he chuckles with dark satisfaction, swallowing the last pulses of my release, I can't regret knowing how good I can feel under the night sky.

He pushes up, climbing on top of me, and I don't know if his plan is to jerk off on my belly or kiss me—oh, how I want his kiss—but I don't get to find out, because at the same moment, we hear tires on the gravel.

CHAPTER 24
RUSS

"Shit," Max mutters, hauling himself off the bed. "Shannon, come on."

I roll off her and lunge for the towel, tossing that her way as she scrambles to her feet, completely naked. She races into the dark house, following Max.

Chest heaving, cock aching, I search quickly for the two pieces of her bikini. I get my dick back in my shorts and her swimsuit shoved in my pocket just as the lights flick on inside.

"We're back!" Emery calls out, high on life.

Through the open door, and the pounding in my ears, I listen to her herd drunk hockey players into the kitchen, offering everyone electrolyte drinks and late night snacks.

I scrub my face, breathing in the scent of Shannon on my fingers. She's all over me. My beard and my hand, and I can't wash her off. Not yet.

I also can't sleep next to Emery like this.

Acting on instinct, I go down the path to the garage. Since Kieran and Ty have left, the suite above the gym is empty. Climbing the stairs, I let myself in. Without turning on the lights, I text Emery that I'm crashing on the couch here, and lock the door behind me.

Then I lean against it and close my eyes.

Fuck.

I can still feel Shannon's thigh twitch beneath my grip. Her fingers tightening in my hair, dragging me against her soft, hot pussy.

She got so fucking wet for me.

So responsive.

It took her a while to get there, but God damn it, what a glorious ride. I wish we'd had longer. I sink into the way her sounds made me feel. Sluggish, raw, primal.

I'm still hard.

Her sweet, musky scent surrounds me.

I can fucking feel her fingers desperately reaching for me as I lifted her off her husband and stole her for myself there at the end.

She liked stroking me. Liked the way I bossed her around, grabbing her wrist and putting it behind her back.

I thunk my head back against the door, groaning out loud as a whole-body shudder rocks through me as I viscerally re-live the way she tensed for me, a confusing mix of desperate need and uncertain worry. That shouldn't be fucking hot, but it is, because I soothed all of that for her.

Jesus, that's twisted.

The whole thing is fucking twisted.

I don't know what's going to go down in the morning, either. I'll have to follow her lead, but I'm guessing this was a one-time-only secret we'll never talk about again.

Fuck fuck fuck.

And her bikini is in my pocket.

I pull it out, my belly pulling tight at the memory seared in my mind of Max undoing these bottoms, the string falling away, revealing the bare curve of her hip and the shadow between her legs.

The pussy that she would eventually serve to me.

I pace away from the door, burning up now. Why didn't I fuck her?

You couldn't do that to her. Or to yourself.

Thanks, conscience.

But now I know what sounds she would make if I sank into her. I drop to my knees in front of the couch, the ache in my chest and the rampaging thoughts in my head still between her trembling thighs on the terrace. Burying my face in my hand that was inside her, I wrap my other hand around my cock and stroke just once before squeezing the base of my shaft.

I would take my time with her. Pin her down and wait until she softened for me, her legs falling open, her cunt blooming. My cock would fit right against her entrance. Hot, slick, tight. I'd want to thrust hard, sink all the way into her clutching body and claim her, but I wouldn't.

It would be even better to make her pant and beg for it. To wait until she's crazed with desire, and then give it to her inch by inch.

I rock my hand up my shaft, dragging my foreskin up around the thick flare of my tip. I stroked myself like this as I ate her out, but I didn't come close to a release. I wanted that to go on forever. Lost track of time and almost brought public humiliation on her.

It was the worst possible place for that. The wrong time.

But she tasted right. She tasted perfect.

I groan as my balls pull tight. Like a raging bull let loose in a pasture for breeding season, I'm going to come out of my skin with need. How the hell I restrained myself on that sun bed, I don't know, because right now, I see red. I want to mount her, rut her, feel that wet heat and bury myself in her tight squeeze.

Roaring, I climb on top of her and thrust, snapping my hips, driving my cock through my fist. Hot seed spills uselessly into my hand, making a mess of my fingers and my shorts and probably my fucking floor.

God damn it.

I roll sideways, onto my back, and I stare at the ceiling.

Training camp opens in two weeks.

And now I know what my captain's wife tastes like when she comes.

CHAPTER 25
SHANNON

Adrenaline carries us upstairs before anyone gets into the house.

"Well, that was…" Max shakes his head as I close the door quietly behind me and then lean against the door, covering myself with the towel and nothing else. "You used to do that a lot?"

"Not a lot." I take a deep breath and close my eyes. "Max—"

He closes the gap between us and takes my face in his hands. "It's fine. I forgive you."

Stunned, I blink my eyes open just in time to see him turn and head to the bathroom. He closes the door and then I hear the shower turn on.

Heart in my throat, I yank on clothes and crawl into bed, curling into a tight ball around one of Russ's soft pillows.

Downstairs, the young players have brought the party home. I strain to hear Russ's voice, to know that he hasn't been caught out, but there's nothing discernible.

And then fatigue rolls over me, and close my eyes, letting it pull me under.

I dream of rough, heavy bodies and being called names.

I wake up sweaty, my pyjamas twisted around my body, my legs fighting the sheet. Max is already out of bed, and I have the suite to myself.

It's still early.

My hands shake as I grab for my phone, as if my husband is going to send me a status update on our three-some from last night via text message.

Nothing.

And then, like someone downstairs can sense that I'm awake, there's a text message from Russ, of all people.

> **RUSS**
>
> Breakfast is on. Your husband is down here showing me game tape.

A perfectly normal message. So normal it's saying more than just the words on the screen.

I exhale wildly.

Oh.

Okay.

I mean, it's not. There's so, so much that's still not okay.

But right now, *this moment*, there's some fragile peace that has been negotiated between teammates, and that's all that matters.

I reply with a thumbs up.

And then I delete the perfectly normal message before I get out of bed and race into the shower.

———

With my face and hair done, and the rest of the house starting to wake up, I feel as prepared as I'm going to be to go downstairs and face the music.

I bump into Roan and Malik in the hallway. They look rumpled, but they're dressed for golf.

"Good morning," I say smoothly. Mask on.

They follow me into the kitchen. Russ is at the stove, his back to me, looking extra big and broad this morning in a faded t-shirt, stretched tight across his shoulders, and board shorts. Max is at the island, watching video on his phone. He doesn't look up.

And for a second, it feels like last night didn't happen.

But then Russ goes still, and turns. From across the kitchen, his gaze is sharp and searching. He doesn't look at me long, just a second, but that's all it takes for me to remember his hot gaze staring up from between my legs.

"Look at this," Max says, shoving his phone at Roan. I pivot and force my attention to their conversation. "He was never appreciated enough. Look at that slap shot."

"Who is this?"

Malik crowds in. "Craig Roslin. He still hasn't been signed, eh?"

"He will be. Someone will get hurt in training camp and he'll sign a one-year deal, come in as a trusted veteran." Max rounds the island and takes me in his arms. "How'd you sleep?"

"Not sure," I murmur as he hugs me. "Still waking up."

"Rusty, are you going to make my wife some breakfast?" He sounds so casual as he says it, but I hear the edge.

I hold my breath as I wait for Russ to say *aye, I already texted her about it*. But he just nods, his gaze polite but distant. "Breakfast for everyone, coming up."

I turn my attention fully to Max. My heart is hammering in my chest. "Have you been up for a while?"

"Yeah. I went for a run. Woke up Rusty, apparently." He squeezes me tighter, bringing his mouth to my ear. "He slept in the garage last night. He must be feeling guilty."

Shame slams into me as a bedroom door opens above us, and footsteps come running down the staircase.

"Good morning!" Emery says brightly. "Is everyone golfing?"

"I should pack." I pat Max on the chest and force myself to make eye contact with him. "We'll head out after your golf game?"

"Sounds like a plan." He twists as he hears Malik say something about the flex of the hockey stick in the videos they're still looking at.

Suddenly, it's just me and Emery standing together at this end of the island.

She gives me a friendly smile before sliding past. "What's for breakfast, Russell?"

He hesitates for a beat before answering. "Turkey sausage, fried mushrooms, and eggs to order."

"Need help?"

"Nah. Are you coming golfing with us this morning?"

She slides a glance back at me. "Might stay here and go for a final swim in the lake. How does that sound, Shannon?"

Like fair and just punishment.

"How many of us are golfing this morning?" Malik asks.

Max does a quick count. "We'll take two cars. I'll take Russ in mine, and you can drive everyone else."

I force myself not to react, not to tense up, but what the fuck?

Russ doesn't react, either. He just serves everyone breakfast, as if nothing happened last night at all.

His cleaning lady arrives as the guys are getting ready to head out the door, so I take that opportunity to escape upstairs and start packing.

Through the front window of our suite, I watch most of the guys pile into Malik's SUV, and then Max leads Russ to our car.

Max gets into the driver's seat with his usual restless speed. Russ moves slower, his shoulders rolling back and his face tipping up to the sky for a moment before he slides into my side, disappearing from view.

I pull out our suitcases, prepared to fold everything very, very carefully, just to delay the inevitable swim with the girls.

"Hey, Shannon?" Emery calls from downstairs.

I smooth my hands over the top of my folded clothes, take a deep breath, and lift my voice. "I'm upstairs."

Her footsteps fly in my direction, then she rounds the corner. "Can you take this back to Harper? She left it behind."

She holds out her hand, and a black bikini—my bikini, I'm pretty damn sure—swings from her fingers.

"Umm…" A dull roar starts in my ears. "Where—yes, I can—"

I snatch the two small pieces from her and fling them into my suitcase.

She smiles broadly. "Good. The cleaning lady found it in the suite above the garage when she was collecting the laundry, and I wasn't sure how Rusty would feel about being on bikini delivery duty."

Heat pools low in my belly. I can picture Russ returning

that to me in private. The tiny scraps of fabric dangling off *his* fingers in a very different way.

You left this on my terrace.

"He'd manage." The two words sound strangled. "But I can… Thanks."

She hitches her thumb over her shoulder. "I have to go find my own swimsuit now. See you down at the lake?"

"Yep."

She disappears and I turn, sitting on the edge of the bed, my fingers twisting together.

I can't exactly text Harper and say, hey if anyone asks, I gave you back a bikini that isn't yours. And I can't text Russ while he's a hostage passenger with my husband on the way to golf and be like, hey your girlfriend found my bikini but phew, she thinks it's Harper's, so go along.

Fuck.

Fuck.

The only thing to do is hope nobody ever brings it up again.

A swim. A lay out in the sun. Then a long, awkward car ride home where my husband won't have a room full of teammates to perform in front of. And on the other side of that?

I don't know what comes next. But I know it won't be anything like what my life has been up to this point for the last eight years. I blew that to smithereens last night, and the fallout will come as soon as we leave—or maybe it's already begun, with Russ hostage in Max's car.

CHAPTER 26
RUSS

As soon as I get in the car, Max peels out of my driveway, spraying gravel everywhere. Fucking idiot doesn't realize that's worse for his paint job than it is for my lane.

From the moment I woke up this morning, I knew I needed to smooth this over with Max. For Shannon's sake, and for our team's sake—and our own working relationship, which has never been close, but has always been professional.

So I wait until we're on an actual paved road, but then I refuse to wait another second.

"I owe you and your wife an apology for last night," I grind out.

He doesn't look across the car at me. "I need you to forget that happened."

I can't do that. "I didn't realize I was stumbling into the middle of an argument."

"It wasn't a real fight."

Sure as fuck sounded real to me. "I'm just—"

"Fuck off, Russ." He says it as easily as everything else

he's said this morning, from the too casual *good morning* when I found him running in the garage, to the way he sprawled in the kitchen, scrolling game video on his phone as I cooked, to the announcement that he'd be driving me to the golf course. "I'm telling you that was private. You probably misheard half of what we were saying, anyway."

I frown.

Other than wanting to make sure Shannon's okay, I don't really care about their fight. I mean, I know that married people do sometimes argue. I only used that as my entry into the conversation about what happened between the three of us. Max, though, seems fixated on me forgetting the *fight* more than the threesome.

Like the subject of the fight is what matters most to him.

They started arguing about the podcast Shannon's thinking of doing. Then they were talking about the Ice League, and Max was spinning some fantasy about it being a part of his legacy, spending the last few years of his career playing there instead of in the NHL. Bonkers dreamland bullshit.

"All right," I say slowly. "There was a lot of wind last night. I couldn't hear you, really."

His grip tightens on the steering wheel. "Good." He grimaces. "What has Marty said to you about Ice League?"

Fuck. Our agent. Of course, he doesn't want me to know about whatever angle he was trying to work—because Marty hasn't said shit-fuck-all to me about this opportunity, however real or not it may be.

Max and I might share an agent, but there's a code between players—we want to trust that our agent is doing the best they can for us, but also understanding that they might be able to do something different for another player.

There is also almost an entire league between Max and me, and we're at different points in our contract cycles. I have two more years left on my contract. He is in the final year of his, so he is actively looking for a new contract. And he is the type of player who could get one more big contract to get him to the end of his career.

He is a marquee player who would be very attractive to an investor for a new startup league, and also, being pursued in that way could, in turn, increase his value to an NHL owner.

I'm never going to be that kind of guy.

"Nothing," I can admit easily, because it's the truth. "I'm not the kind of player they'd be looking to snap up first."

"Yeah." He doesn't even bother to look sorry for that accurate jab.

"I'm not going to say anything to him, if that's what you're worried about."

"It's not just him. Just…forget the whole conversation."

"Done. And about the rest of it—"

"What about it?"

All right. I've tried. He doesn't want to talk about it. "It's buried."

"Good." He cranks up his music and we don't talk again until we get to the golf course.

We divide up into a couple groups, and Max puts himself in a group that isn't with me. Fine. Great, even. I don't want to spend a second more with him than I have to, and I have to spend a lot of seconds with him already.

I'm with Calhoun, Zondi, and Dodaj, and they're all buzzing after a good night out, and a good weekend with their teammates.

They're all so fucking young. So eager and full of hope for the season ahead.

I don't have a lot to say, so I keep my head down and focus on my swing. I have a couple of sweet birdies, and a beauty of an eagle on the eighth hole, so when we get back to the clubhouse, I'm the clear leader on our card—and when the others join us, it turns out I've beaten the whole crew today.

Max is *pissed*, and he takes it out on Mason and Hale. "This is what happens when you don't fucking understand the mission."

"To beat Armstrong on a course he's played five times in the last week?" Mason doesn't back down, which is both fucking brave and really fucking stupid for a rookie to snap back at his captain.

On the other hand, it's not like Mason's actually making the team as a 20-year-old D-man, and maybe by the time he does mature into the NHL, Max will be off in Ice League stardom.

Or he might be the punchline to a joke about Icarus flying too close to the sun.

I choke on an unexpected laugh, drawing confused looks from my teammates. "Nothing," I say, smothering my face in my hands. "Fucking nothing."

"Let's go. I don't want to get stuck in traffic heading home," Max growls.

"Glad we're driving back in separate vehicles," Haler mutters to me as we head back to the parking lot. "What's his malfunction?"

I shrug. "He doesn't like to lose."

Maybe that's why he's more pissed about me overhearing the fight about the Ice League more than the fact I made his wife come on my face. It doesn't even occur to him that he could lose Shannon. She told him she wanted a divorce, and he just kissed that out of her.

His career, though…

There is a certain confidence that carries men like Max deep into their career never having to grapple with what I have known since I was twelve years old: there is always someone to step into your skates, to take over your stall, who is a better, faster, smarter hockey player than you.

Even number one draft picks don't always turn into generational talent.

Maybe Max Tilman hasn't gotten over the fact that New York exposed him in the expansion draft, rejecting him as the generational talent he thought he was going to be for them.

I wasn't looking forward to being trapped in the car with him again for the drive back, but with this new thought in my head, I hop into the passenger seat.

Regardless of what personal issues we might have, understanding my captain better can only be good for the year ahead.

But where he wanted to talk about business—and how his is none of mine—on the drive to the golf course, on this return trip, he's moved on to stewing about what should have been his top priority: how fucking good I made his wife feel last night.

"We're going to head out as soon as I get back," he says.

"For sure."

"Last night won't happen again."

"I figured as much."

"Shannon can be emotional, and you got to benefit from that last night."

I frown, not liking where this is going. "We all got caught up in it a bit, but she didn't seem any more emotional than you did."

"That's your crush colouring how you saw it." He picked that word carefully. I bet he thought about it all morning, instead of focusing on his golf game. He spun around and around, trying to figure out what word would make me feel small and insignificant. To remind me that how I feel about Shannon is nothing of any importance.

Tell me something I don't fucking know, jackass. But I shove that thought deep, and shrug. "Sure. I don't harbour any illusions, Tiller. I know she's your wife, and she loves you. She only went along with it because you invited me in."

You did this to yourself and I won't let you reframe it any other way. Shove. Deep. Down.

He goes quiet. We slice down the narrow highway, thick trees on either side. Racing towards the inevitable.

"Lose the crush, Armstrong," he finally says. "She's not the angel you imagine her to be. She didn't think twice about helping you cheat on your girlfriend, did she?"

Fuck. Me. "Didn't cheat on anyone," I growl before I can stop myself.

He laughs. "We're all cheaters, buddy. Deep down, even Shannon's a slut. I've never encouraged it, because I knew it would get out of hand quickly, and I was right."

He called her that last night, too.

It's one thing in the heat of the moment. It's another to say it in the cold light of day.

My big, meaty hands ball into fists.

He notices. "Easy, big guy. It's fine."

"She was just trying to make you happy. It wasn't

anything to do with me. She thought you wanted to share her. If you regret that—"

"Don't give me marriage advice, buddy."

"Don't call me buddy if you won't take it," I snap back.

He slams on the brakes and wrenches the wheel, skidding his car onto the gravel shoulder. "Get the fuck out of my car."

"Gladly." I wrench the door open at the same time as I unbuckle. Then I see Malik's car behind us, pulling over, too.

"Fuck," I roar in frustration as I give our teammates my back for a second.

But Max, having thought about how to ambush me all morning, and probably having been a sociopath his entire miserable life, has it in hand.

Instead of pulling back onto the road and leaving me in the dust to explain, he does a U-turn and rolls down his window. "Left my wallet back at the golf course," he lies to our teammates, easy as can be. Captain Cool with a ready explanation. "Get Rusty back to his place, all right?"

He revs his engine and takes off back the way we came, leaving us in his dust.

I've just made everything so much worse. Fuck.

———

Shannon is in the kitchen with Emery, wearing a damp-looking bathing suit and wrapped in a towel as she eats a salad. They're laughing together, and they don't stop when we come in and start pulling out our own lunch options.

"Max had to go back to the course," I finally say, gruffly.

Shannon's expression is carefully unsurprised. "He

texted me," she says. "He's fine. We'll need to leave as soon as he gets back, though."

I want to ask what the fuck he said, but that's between them. I'm on the outside, just fucking everything up.

"Of course."

Emery glances at her watch, which gets text messages, too. "Excuse me for a second, I have to go call my mom. She's having a soufflé disaster."

She goes out on the terrace as Shannon excuses herself as well, heading upstairs. I try to ignore the racing footsteps. I try to stay downstairs. But it doesn't take long before I leave my teammates in the kitchen and follow her.

Knowing I probably don't have a lot of time before her husband returns, I knock on her door, and it swings open.

She's already packed, and she's standing at the window.

"Can I come in for a minute?"

She nods, not looking back at me.

I stay on this side of the room, but I close the door behind me. Then I take a deep breath. "Are you okay, Shan?"

She turns, looking surprised. "Yes."

"You sure?"

This time there's a beat of hesitation. Then she exhales and comes around the bed to stand closer to me. Not close enough to touch, but enough that I can see her chest rise and fall with each inhale and exhale. Steady. "Yes. I am," she says. "I'm sorry about last night."

I frown. "You don't have anything to be sorry for."

She swallows hard. Less steady.

I glance at the dark suitcase on the bed. His suitcase, that she packed for him. "Does he make you say sorry for things?"

"Don't say it like that."

I'll take that as a yes. Fuck.

Her gaze flicks nervously to my mouth, which has tightened into a line, and I can't help that. Then she looks back up to my eyes, and she slips on that mask that I've seen a dozen times before.

A bright, effortless smile. Clear eyes, all uncertainty wiped away.

"I know it's hard to understand," she says softly. "But I told you about my past. I know what I'm doing."

"If you ever need anything—"

For the second time in half a day, we're interrupted by the sound of tires out front. This time, it's her husband.

A visceral pain stabs through me at saying goodbye without a resolution, without being able to tell her everything I want to say.

She glances past me at the closed door. The message is clear. *Get out.* But her voice is soft and sweet, as it always is. "I'll see you soon, Russell."

I go to my own room. Emery has stripped the sheets off the bed, and the cleaning lady hasn't yet replaced them. I find them in the closet and make my own damn bed as I try not to listen to the sound of the Tilmans carrying their luggage down the stairs.

I wait until the last possible second before heading down to the front door to say goodbye.

Jenson and Ani are heading out, too, which makes the moment easier in some ways.

It's still fucking hard to see Shannon get in Max's car and drive away.

Then the young guys leave, and Hayden and Becca, and before long it's just Emery's rental car that needs to be packed up. Like a reverse of the start of the weekend.

She leans against her trunk and gives me her best sisterly inquisition look. "You okay, Rusty?"

I shrug. If I don't get the truth out of Shannon, I'm not about to give my own to Emery. "Of course. The countdown is on to the start of the season now. You should come see a game or two."

"I can't be your plus-one for the entire season."

"I know. I don't need that."

"You really don't." She pauses. "You should tell her how you feel."

"That's never going to happen."

"I think she needs to know there are other options."

I laugh without any humour at all. "She knows. She has her reasons and I respect them."

Once she drives away, I'm finally alone. I give my gorgeous new house the finger. "Really had different plans for you," I say out loud.

The house doesn't reply.

My phone vibrates. A text message from Foster asking if it's just me this afternoon.

Sure is. I'm all the fuck alone.

I've got a week here to myself before I'll head back to Hamilton, and I'm planning on doing nothing but skating and swimming and thinking about all of my life choices that have led me to this moment.

Two out of three of those choices are good for me. The last one can't be helped.

CHAPTER 27
SHANNON

The days that follow our return from the cottage are filled with silence.

Max throws himself into work, his favourite thing. He makes an appearance at rookie camp first, and then…I don't know what else. Captain things. He doesn't include me in any of it, a clear punishment for refusing to sleep with Francois, threatening divorce, and then…doing what we did with Russ.

And I refuse to be sorry.

I wasn't the one who invited his teammate to join us. It's not my fault that in the end, I enjoyed it more than he liked.

But I do miss how he used to lean on me as the Queen WAG.

So when I get an email from someone at the team foundation, asking me to step in as the chair of the Highlander Ball committee, I leap at the chance to do something, anything. The winter gala event raises money for the children's hospital and other local charities, and also celebrates the top community fundraisers, putting them in front of the big corporations who sponsor the team and the arena. I copy Max on my reply, accepting the job.

And then I call my favourite spa and book myself in for some self-care because I want to look my best for the first committee meeting I'll be joining.

The next day, we happen to leave the house at the same time. The silence is most profound as we politely jockey for access to the garage. He pulls out first, then I follow in my car. I catch up to him at the red light leaving our neighbourhood. He speeds away from me as soon as it turns green, and in the distance, I see him turn toward the highway. I head the other direction, into Ancaster Village.

The spa is at the end of the picturesque main street, across from a bakery and beside a sporting goods store that has a family law office above it—very small town vibes, even though we're technically on the edge of a pretty big city.

It reminds me of the town where I grew up, but with a lot more polish.

And when I was a kid, I couldn't afford a day at the spa.

Max's money makes my life easier in an infinite number of ways.

Inside, I hand over the credit card that he takes care of every month, to pay for the services that help keep me looking the way he likes. Smooth, soft, polished—every inch the perfect wife.

He joked on our first date about how I was too much for him, and I knew what he meant. When I protested that I was a small-town girl at heart, he asked me if I was the homecoming queen or the class valedictorian, as if those were genuinely the only two options he could imagine. When he found out I only had my GED, he almost didn't ask me out on another date. If he hadn't already followed me on social media, I think he wouldn't have. But then I posted another photo of myself on a yacht, and he was hooked right back in.

In the end, I think he saw mouldable potential in me. After all, I'd transformed myself from an edgy emo goth girl with a hick accent to a glittering, cosmopolitan black swan. Sure, I had edges he didn't like, but I, like a silly fool, was a little too honest with him in the early days about my eagerness to please. I would have agreed to anything to step inside the shield he represented against the outside world. It turned out, I only needed to transform myself into the girl next door—and sign a prenup that prevents me from accessing any of his hockey earnings if we ever break up.

"What are we doing today?" asks the receptionist. "Body wrap and polish, hot stone massage, the radiance facial, and the mani-pedi?"

The usual. I get waxed on an alternate schedule, like clockwork. Homecoming queens don't have body hair in Max's fantasy world. "That's right."

"Here's the usual form to fill out, Mrs. Tilman. You know the drill. Have a seat and someone will bring you your favourite lemon tea."

I do like the ritual of coming here. Sometimes I have the aestheticians come to my house, and I invite the other wives and girlfriends for a day of pampering, and that's nice in a different way.

But today I needed the setting for the pampering just as much as the pampering itself.

The lemon tea does wonders for my spirits. The polishing scrub and warm wrap help, too. The hollow feeling in my chest is smaller and fainter than it has been in a week when I get handed over to the massage therapist, who recognizes me. She's worked on me many times over the last year, and she immediately starts by asking about my trip to the cottage.

"How did that party in Muskoka go?"

I was here two weeks ago the morning after I sent Russ that text offering to help. He hadn't replied yet, and I'd just assumed...

Well, assuming is foolish.

Right after I left my massage, he'd texted me back and said he had it covered. In hindsight, I know now that was because of Emery.

I don't know what to make of his girlfriend. Or...his casual hook-up friend?

We've texted a few times since I've been home. She likes to send me TikToks about Russ, which from anyone else I would interpret as next-level subtle *he's mine* behaviour, but Emery doesn't give off that energy at all.

It's like she thinks we have him in common. Like we're some platonic polyamorous triad.

Sweet summer child.

I clear my throat. "It was really nice. I didn't end up having to do much. The guy who hosted had it all under control."

I can't imagine Max organizing a last-minute party for the team by himself. That's my job, and if he didn't have me...

He would have someone else. Literally, anyone else.

Nausea roils inside me, fierce and fast and unexpected.

By stripping me of his usual hockey-related wife tasks, Max has stripped me of everything that I am to him.

He doesn't have any interest in repairing our relationship because he knows I'll do it for the both of us.

She finishes with my back, then adjusts the warm blanket

to reveal my leg up to my hip, and cover the rest of me to keep the now loosened muscles along my spine nice and cozy. Then she pats my glute.

"There's a bit of new dimpling here." Poke. Prod. "Would you be interested in meeting with one of our technicians for a laser therapy consultation?"

I open my mouth to agree, yes, because the worst thing in the world is cellulite on my ass. Won't someone please think of the Insta stories?

She makes a tsking sound as she continues to examine me, and I can't blame her. The old Shannon would want to know about every imperfection. I would use the credit card that Max pays off every month to fix it, throw money at the problem of not being perfect.

But the last two weeks have taught me that I am so far from perfect it's not even worth trying. And that no matter how hard I try, I will never actually be perfect because my husband keeps moving the goal posts.

When everything else is stripped away, the only thing he values me for is my commodification as a sexy body.

By leaning into being as beautiful as I can be, I have reinforced that value to him, and I'm done with that.

I mumble some noncommittal answer, and we move on. We talk about other things that I barely hear over the panic surging inside me, the swell of emotion as I realize that this isn't what I want anymore.

I have spent eight years trying to be enough and never managing to get there. But in an urgent, chaotic, intense, moonlit hour, Russ showed me what I've been missing. Through the sounds that he made and the quiet, guttural utterances. The way that he reacted to my ass, even with the new bit of cellulite on it.

For the first time in years, I felt *wanted* in a raw, honest way.

Even as my husband was fucking me through that, it was only Russ that made me feel cherished. And when Max finished, without a thought in the world to my own pleasure, because he never cared about my pleasure, it was Russ who lifted me off, who moved me away. Who curled over me and whispered against my spine, "It's your turn, my queen."

It's your turn.

Three simple words I haven't been able to get out of my head ever since.

It's my turn.

And when I leave the spa mid-afternoon, the sign on the building next door calls to me. I don't have an appointment, but I've had a week to pick up the phone and make some calls.

I haven't.

There's no time like the present to rip off the bandaid and start putting myself first.

CHAPTER 28
RUSS

The last thing I expected to be doing two days before the start of training camp is signing energy drinks at a small independent sporting goods store in Ancaster, but the store owner contacted the team and Mabel in PR asked me to swing by and do a bit of fan service before we get into the pre-season.

Four cases of BioPunk later, my hand needs some physical therapy, but the fans who showed up seemed delighted—and the store owner is happy, which is great. It's not often that I get tagged for this kind of community outreach.

I'm thinking about grabbing a coffee and heading to the gym when I step outside and almost collide with Shannon, coming out of the door right beside the store entrance.

She gasps my name as I catch her by the upper arms, safely keeping her upright. I glance up at the sign above her head.

Buckley Family Law.

My attention jerks back to her face. I take in her red-rimmed eyes and nervously pinched mouth.

"Are you okay?" My grip tightens on her arms.

She exhales. "I'm fine. It's...." She screws up her face, her lovely eyes swimming in fresh, unshed tears. "Complicated."

"All right." I rub my hands lightly up to her shoulders, then release her.

"What are you doing here?" She gestures at the store behind me.

"Signing bottles of BioPunk."

She laughs in surprise. "Really?"

"Really."

"That's...unexpected. And funny."

"Aye." I grin, and her mouth turns up at the corners just a little bit. Shaky, but that's a smile. That's better. "Viral TikTok, apparently."

"Good for drink sales, good for the game."

"That's what Mabel said."

Now her eyes spark with something that looks more like joy. "I love Mabel."

"Hey, I was going to get a coffee across the street. Do you want to join me? I'll even show you the TikTok that went viral."

"Oh, I've already seen it. Emery sent it to me yesterday."

I chuckle under my breath. "Of course she did."

Shannon exhales and wipes the corner of her eye. "She's very much a friend collector, isn't she?"

"She is that."

She looks at me carefully. "Is she going to be visiting this fall?"

"Probably not." I don't really want to talk about Emery when Shannon still looks on the verge of crying. "Listen, I don't like the idea of you driving upset. If you don't want coffee, can I drop you at home? Or maybe call someone else to pick you up?"

"Oh God, please don't tell anyone." Alarm flashes across her face. "I can't—"

"Hey. All right." Without thinking, I draw her into my arms and give her a hug—and she tenses up.

I let her go immediately.

"Sorry," I mutter.

"No, it's…" She takes a deep breath and gestures across the street without looking that way. "Coffee would be good."

I manage to steer her across the street without touching her again, and inside the bakery, I order an iced black coffee.

"Same for me," she says.

The place is empty, which is good—nobody is going to hear our conversation—but also a bit awkward, because there's no white noise to provide cover.

"Do you want to sit outside?" the barista asks helpfully. "We have picnic tables in the garden."

The bakery is in a converted century-old house, and the garden out back is a little slice of overgrown heaven. And we have it to ourselves, but there's a breeze and some birds—it's not the awkward stillness of inside. Perfect.

"Have a seat," I say quietly but firmly.

She slides onto one side of a picnic table, and while I want to take up the rest of the same bench and wrap my arm around her, I resist that inappropriate urge and drop onto the other side instead.

She sips her coffee, and for a while, that's all that I need—just to see her and know that she's calming down, that she's not crying in her car. But as the colour in her face returns to normal, it's hard to keep silent.

"It's good to see you," I finally say.

She lets out a little frustrated laugh, but keeps her head ducked.

"Shannon."

She shakes her head.

"Look at me."

It takes her a second, but she slowly lifts her head.

"It *is* good to see you," I repeat firmly as I hold her cautious gaze. "And we don't have to talk about anything beyond that."

"This isn't too awkward for you?"

I blink in surprise. "No." I frown. "Not for me. And if it is for you, I—"

"It isn't." Her shoulders relax in visible relief.

"Has it been awkward…" I almost crush my coffee and carefully flatten my hand against the table. "At home?"

"Yeah."

"That's fucked, Shan. He—" I cut myself off when her expression pinches. I need to tread carefully. "We're grown ups."

"It's just sex, right? I've had a lot of sex." She doesn't look away as she says it, and it's not meant to be seductive at all—her face is all blotchy and red, after all. She's trying to be fearless, and it's working. Fearlessly bold, despite everything that's gone on. That's her natural instinct, and fuck me, but I love it.

More than anything, I want to lean in and ask her to tell me all about that sex. Even if it's been with her douchebag husband.

And while I don't agree that what happened between us is *just* sex, I'm glad that's all it felt like for her. She deserves any pleasure she can grab hold of.

"I'm pretty sure I confessed to some wild days, too," I say gruffly.

She sighs. "Ugh, that's enough of that. Distract me, please. Show me those TikToks of your countrymen ripping on your ads."

"I've got something even better." I swipe through my album of photos from my last trip home. "Did you know there's a statue built in my honour in my hometown?"

She gasps in delight. "No."

"Yes."

"Like…a permanent one?"

"Bronze, in fact. The real deal. I am the pride of Kinloss. And every time I join another NHL team, they add a new badge around the base."

"Oh my God." She claps her hands together in glee as I hand over my phone to show her photos of me standing in front of the bronze, idealized version of myself. The hockey journeyman and the hockey hero, side by side. "They're so proud of you."

"Aye, they are. It was a bit of a rude awakening to leave that enthusiasm behind when I was twelve and move to a land where, it turned out, everyone and their brother is better at hockey than I am."

Her gaze lifts from my phone to my face, immediately sobering up. "Twelve?"

I shrug. "It made sense at the time. I was being scouted a bit, but mostly by video. There are more amateur scouts in any city in Ontario than there are in all of the UK. My parents weren't together anymore, and they agreed my mum should bring me to Canada. She was the one with the dual citizenship, after all."

Shannon's brows pull tight. "Is she still here?"

I shake my head. "No. She moved back to Scotland as soon as I was eligible for the draft."

She reaches out and covers my hand with hers. "It sounds like there's some complicated history there."

I squeeze her fingers. "Aye. Maybe for another time, though. That's not the kind of distraction I wanted to offer."

"Any time. We can compare dysfunctional family tales."

"We have more in common than you might think," I say. "Your story about getting on the bus and heading for New York when you were eighteen. That was me and the draft. I went with another OHL teammate. He went in the first round. The next day, his whole family sat with me until the very end."

Her eyes are huge and filled with concern about an event that happened eighteen years ago and clearly worked out in my favour. "Were you drafted?"

"Halfway through the seventh round, aye."

She smiles, relieved for past me, and eases her hand out of my grip. I hadn't noticed I was still holding it. "I'm going to look for that video."

I laugh. "If you do, I'm going to have to look for your stints as a weather girl."

"You underestimate my ego, sir, if you don't think I'd like that. Once an aspiring actress, always an aspiring actress. I love an audience. Well..." She gestures at her face. "Usually."

"I'm not an audience, Shannon. I'm a friend."

"Those aren't the same thing?" She says it lightly, but her voice cracks.

Silence stretches between us. She drinks a good amount of her coffee.

I wait her out until she sighs. "Don't look at me like that."

"Like what?"

"Like you pity me."

"I swear to God, that's not what I'm thinking."

"What are you thinking then, with that unbearably soft look of understanding on your face?"

"That you're beautiful and brave."

She shakes her head a little, but that gets me another smile, so I'll take it.

But then she takes a deep breath, and my chest pulls tight even before she speaks. "I need to— I may have given you the wrong impression. With the tears and the fact that you saw me coming out of a law firm. And my..."

"It's okay."

"It's not, actually. Nothing is okay. I— I'm not leaving Max. I can't, apparently. Not yet."

Oh, fuck me. *That's* why she was crying? "Not...yet?"

She tells me, haltingly, about walking in without an appointment, just to find out what the process would be if she wanted to initiate a divorce—only to find out she can't, because she hasn't been a resident of Canada long enough. And either way, unless she wants to prove in a court of law that Max has been unfaithful, she needs to wait through a year of separation, which means living apart from him in a country where she isn't legally eligible to work.

"Aspiring actresses don't qualify for exceptional visas, it turns out," she jokes.

It makes me want to burn down the entire world. "What are your other options?"

"I don't have any."

"Of course you do." I reach for her, but she slides her hands away.

Right.

Fuck.

When I saw Shannon coming out of that family law office, I thought she was leaving him, and in that split second, the fantasy that I had tried so desperately hard to put on ice, so hard to get over, to rebound from—that fantasy roared back to life.

And now as she sits across from me, small and broken and trapped, I realize that what I had envisioned was coming from my point of view as a single, unencumbered man.

This life as the wife of a hockey player has trapped her, not only in misery, but literally trapped her in a foreign country with very few options. My simplistic fantasy will never be what Shannon wants.

We aren't in this together. I am, at best, a casual friend who she had a misguided threesome with.

I suck in a slow, careful breath. "Is moving back to the States not an option? You could work there? I—" I could help, I want to say. I settle on, "Your friends could help."

She blanches. "It's not that simple."

"Why not?"

She fiddles with her cup, nearly empty now. "You don't think that the press would immediately be on that? Here, a year-long quiet separation followed by a divorce once he's moved on—that's…that's civilized and—"

Civilized. The way she says the word sounds like a loaded bomb.

"You don't want to embarrass him," I say.

"No, of course not." She's earnest. He doesn't fucking deserve how kind she is being to him.

"Why not? He's clearly hurt you."

"It's—I told you, it is complicated. I am not—Russ, I don't know who you think I am, but I am not that girl. If I were to have a splashy divorce at the earliest opportunity in New York City, for example, sure that might embarrass Max, and he would hate that. But do you know what would happen next?"

Solemnly, I give her the respect she deserves and don't pretend that I've thought this through as much as she has. "What?"

"He would use everything that he knows about my past to destroy me. And any chance I would have of moving on from that, finding any kind of job that follows anywhere in my limited skill set, would be destroyed. I have already accepted that, on the other side of this divorce, when it happens, I will be a nobody, and I'm fine with that." Tears slip from her eyes.

I can't let her cry alone. I just can't. I reach across the table and gently swipe them off her face.

"I am fine with that," she repeats. "It's that whole audience thing, you know? Double-sided. Two weeks ago, I had plans to start a podcast, and now—" She stops and stares at me, her eyes painfully bright. "And now the thought of everyone in the world having access to this *wound* that is my marriage makes me want to shrivel up into a tiny ball and never be perceived ever again by anyone."

CHAPTER 29
SHANNON

I've said too much. Way, way too much.

But as Russ holds my face and wipes my tears away, I can't stop myself. I've kept all of this inside for so long, and now that it's spilling out, it's like an avalanche of confessions.

"I—I can't, I *can't* make this antagonistic. It would spiral out of control so fast. I need to wait, and I need Max to…" Oh God, I feel faint. "You can't tell him."

"I won't."

"You can't…" I try to focus on his face. On the light dusting of freckles across his nose. His thick brown eyelashes, golden at the tips. His close-cropped beard. There are so many parts of Russ I've never let myself notice before, and they're all so close now, leaning in across the picnic table.

"I. Won't."

"You're a protector," I whisper, dropping my gaze. "I see that. You can't try to protect me here. I don't need that."

For a moment, he holds my face, and I think he might tell

me to look at him again. But then he releases me, letting me hang my head. He gets up, the picnic table creaking, and he comes around to sit beside me, shoulder to shoulder, but he's facing the other way, out to the back of the garden.

Close enough to lean on him if I want to, but no longer demanding eye contact.

Finally he asks, "You okay, Shan?"

I swallow around the lump in my throat. "Yeah."

"Are you safe, I mean?"

My gaze jerks up, looking sideways to meet his laser-sharp attention.

"Has he ever—"

"No." I cut him off because I don't want to have to defend Max any more than the bare minimum. I'm furious with my husband right now, but he's not going to hurt me. Not with his hands. Not even with his words.

My husband hurts me with his silence, and his absence. That's enough.

Russ nods.

I drain the last of my coffee, just a sip, and it's not enough. My throat still feels dry. "It's for the best that I try to make my marriage work for a while longer. I hope that, as my friend, you can support it."

His throat works.

I look away. I need to hold myself back from begging. Please, Russ, please support me and support us in this.

The more desperate I get, the faster he'll agree. But I can't push him like that if he doesn't understand why this is important to me.

I twist away from him. "I need some water. I'll be right back."

He stops me, his hand on my arm first, and then his arm

wrapping around my waist, pulling me back against him. "I'll get it for you," he whispers into my hair. "And I'll keep your secrets, too. I promise you that." Then he releases me and stands up. "Stay here and enjoy the garden."

He grabs my empty cup, leaving his own half-finished coffee in his spot, and gives me another soft smile before heading inside. I watch him stride toward the back door of the bakery, his long legs eating up the lawn, the sun glinting off his reddish-brown hair that looks golden in the late autumn afternoon light. In another universe, I'd have been a small-town girl from Michigan who went to a hockey game and bumped into this lovely Scottish mountain of a man. I'd have flirted so hard, felt so lucky to have his attention.

I'm lost in that fantasy when I hear my name. Not in a light Scottish accent, but my husband's voice.

"What the hell are you doing here?"

I jerk my head up, expecting Max to have confronted Russ, but we're alone. Max is holding his hands out, palms up, and I belatedly process his words differently. He's not angry, just confused, because I'm not one to sit in a garden, and per our shared calendar, he would have expected me home an hour ago—not that he would care about that.

"Ummm…" I glance at the bakery. "I'm just— How did you find me?"

He laughs and taps my phone. "I always know where to find you. You've got your location turned on. I was wondering what you wanted for dinner."

A chill rolls up my spine as I scramble to my feet and grab the offending device. "Oh. Okay. Well, I was just coming home."

"Do you want the rest of your coffee?"

To my horror, Max reaches across the table and grabs

Russ's cup. I'm staring at it when the back door of the bakery slams shut.

In slow motion, we both turn in that direction, because it's the kind of sound that makes you go *what the fuck*, but there's nothing—nobody—there.

I snatch the coffee from Max and jerk my head toward the street. "Let's go."

"What's your rush?" He glances around. "This is a cute place."

That's when I notice that he's dressed up, and he got a haircut today.

When I'm the only woman in his life, Max Tilman is all about hockey. He showers obsessively and smells like body wash. He wears athletic clothes and eats meals prepped for him by a sports chef.

But once in a while, he starts dressing with more care. He wears cologne, something I only experienced when we were dating.

It's a pattern I've come to realize that, on some level, means he's trying to impress somebody. It never lasts that long. A few months at most, and then I get my husband back.

Ironically, the easy looseness that happens because he's filled with confidence in his pursuit of another woman often has a knock-on effect of him being nicer to me. Guilt, maybe, although it would never stop him from having little affairs.

This is a cute place.

Max has sought me out and is now…flirting with me… because he's just come from another woman.

I'm sure of it. I recognize all the pieces, little flags that I used to process in a bizarre form of coping denial. Yes, it pricked at me as wrong, but I focused on the good parts of our marriage and consciously ignored the bad parts.

I can't ignore anything anymore.

I look at the bakery, where I'm sure Russ is lurking right now. Hiding because I begged him to give me space to salvage this marriage for a little while longer.

Because I couldn't bear to throw my husband's life into upheaval, or bear the consequences of that coming back on me.

What a joke, and I am the punchline.

"I'm tired," I manage to say coolly. "I want to go home and take a long bath."

"Maybe I'll wash your back."

It's an empty promise.

We take our separate vehicles home, and he gets a phone call from his agent as we walk inside. I go upstairs on my own to run my bath. As it fills, I look at my red-rimmed eyes in the mirror. Did Max even notice that I was visibly upset?

I don't let myself think about Russ wiping away my tears. I don't let myself think about today at all. I just wait for the tub to fill, then I slip into the steaming water and feel hollow inside.

CHAPTER 30
RUSS

I get to the arena an hour early on the first day of training camp.

The coaching and training staff are already there, setting up for the player meeting. Handouts neatly set on chair seats, water, fruit, and protein bars set up on a side table. Whiteboards at the ready behind a familiar podium.

I snag a mandarin orange and head to the dressing room. The carpet is freshly steam cleaned, and the uniforms hanging in our stalls have never been worn before. This year's practice jersey is a particularly nice design, so I snap a few photos of the gear before anyone else comes in.

This room won't look this neat or clean—or smell this good—again over the next eight or ten months.

Please, God, let it be ten months this year.

I take a moment in front of Max's stall, too. I look at his number. The C on his jersey.

And I tell myself, it's not the man inside the uniform I need to play with. It's the jersey itself.

In the hallway, there's a clatter of noise.

I peel the mandarin in a single, perfect spiral, then head down the short hallway to the locker room where we leave our street clothes, our personal belongings, and change into our preferred base layers before practices and games. I toss the peel in the garbage and turn right, pushing out a side door into the main corridor that will take me back to the meeting room.

By the time I slide into my seat in the middle of the room, I'm ready enough. I've compartmentalized the fact that everything that I thought that I knew about loyalty—to my captain, to my team—is now in question.

I've been around the league a long time. It's not like this is the first time I've been aware of a teammate's marriage falling apart, but it's the first time I've been personally invested in the outcome.

And I can't shake the feeling that there's so much more on the surface that none of us have ever seen.

Over the last week, I've started a dozen text messages to Shannon. I deleted each of them before hitting send.

The way he tracked her down at the bakery, I can't be sure he isn't looking at her texts, too.

And it's that dark thought that is on my mind as our general manager welcomes all the players in the room, both those of us on the team, and the prospects and professional try out (PTO) candidates attending camp as well.

After the GM speaks, it's over to the coach, and then Max is invited to stand.

"Welcome back, captain," our coach says, handing over the podium.

Tilman looks like an NHL superstar. He's got the flowing hair, the easy smile that promises he has a good dentist on speed dial, and the restless energy that betrays his preference to be on the ice right now. Plus, he looks like a stud in the team-branded polo shirt, and he knows it.

"Boys," he starts. "You all look good. You all look hungry. That's good. Because last year we had a taste of success, didn't we? I want a four course meal of it this year. That's my promise to each and everyone of you. I'm going to demand you serve your absolute best, or you'll have to answer to me in the locker room. But first things first—you gotta make the team. You gotta impress Coach. So tomorrow and the next day and the day after that..." He pauses for effect, and lets his gaze roam the room. It feels like he connects with every player in the room except for me. "I'll see you on the ice, brothers. Because I'm going to gunning for the top spot on the roster."

I don't look across the room to where Ty Connor and Kieran Marsh are sitting. Ty and Max are both straight centres, and Kieran can play wing, but he typically prefers to be a centre. When Max is healthy, the lines look very different from when he's not.

Tension like that doesn't affect me. At training camp, I'm more likely to be replaced by a six-foot-seven nineteen-year-old who feels immortal and wants a chance at the bottom of an NHL roster.

None of the prospects or PTOs this year really fit that description, so I'll keep my head down, do what I need to do, and in two weeks, the regular season will be upon us and I can start counting the games until Shannon is free of her marriage.

"Thanks for that, Max," our GM says, stepping back up to the mic. "Now we'll get into the program for the morning. Open your handouts to the second page, please."

I follow along.

At some point, I feel Max's gaze on the side of my face. Slowly, impassively, I glance his way and nod with a respectful energy I definitely do not actually feel.

As if I'm saying, I know you've claimed your wife back from me. You've won whatever horn-locking game that was.

I thought it would feel more dangerous to hold the secret that Shannon wants to leave her husband. I thought that would be hard to know she's going to be single soon and to keep from him, my teammate. But it's actually incredibly easy to partition off that knowledge because keeping that straight in my head is how I can keep her safe.

"There are two schedules to follow today. Each of you have a ten-minute slot with media, and another time to report to the trainers for initial physical assessments. Tomorrow, we hit the ice." Coach raps his knuckles on the podium. "Remember what my expectations are for you all this year. I have a high standard for competition and work ethic. If you have a chip on your shoulder, you won't make it here. That's a promise. All right? Let's go."

The second day of training camp is a bag skate to show the trainers our aerobic ability. That's never my favourite. I'm never the fastest, but I'm not the slowest, which feels like a miracle. And at the end of the skate, I get a clap on my shoulder from the coach, then I get to sink into a cold plunge before getting taped up by the trainers.

The third day is where everything goes off the rails.

"Harder, faster, harder, faster. Do you understand?"

"Yes, coach," we all say as one.

"Let's run that again. Armstrong, hang back with me a minute."

Everyone else loops back to the end of the ice where the assistant coaches are. I heave myself up from my kneeling position and skate over to where our head coach is looking at his clipboard at the boards.

"Sir?"

He flicks a gaze at me. "You're slow."

My legs feel as fresh as they're going to all fucking season. I'm not slower than they should expect me to be. "Yes, sir. I'll be faster."

"Tomorrow, you're going to be skating with the B group."

What the fuck? I haven't stood out, maybe, but I'm a quality depth skater with size and weight on my side. There's no fucking way I'm not starting on the third or fourth line on opening night, so why wouldn't I train with the A group?

From across the ice, I see Tilman shift his focus our way from the drill they're setting up to do.

Ah.

So apparently my quiet deference over the last two days wasn't enough.

"B group," I repeat. "You got a plan for me there?"

Coach's eyebrows raise. "The same plan I have for you in every practice, bud."

All right.

He jerks his head. "Get over there. Join your team."

I queue up. One of the trainers skates over and runs over the drill, getting me up to speed as I watch Jenson take the pass on his forehand, switch the puck around to flick it behind him, then drop back and pick it up again before getting around the D-man in his way.

Clever puck work is never my first or even fifth go-to move. I want to smash my way into that defence man and ditch the puck to a faster teammate, but that's not the moment I'm being asked to step up to.

It feels good to snatch the puck and drop it back. I don't slow down and pivot fast enough, though, and the assistant coach running the play has snagged it away from me.

"Next time," she says cheerfully. "Get back in line."

"Not fast enough, big guy," Tilman drawls as he skates past.

My shoulders come up, but I don't reply. I just get in the queue again.

Then there's a thump against my back as he rocks up behind me. "Did ya hear me, Rusty?"

"Sure did."

"You can't be slow this year." He sounds so fucking cocky.

Shannon's desperate plea echoes through my veins. I can't make this antagonistic. It would spiral out of control so fast.

She's right that I can't interfere. Their marriage is so much more complicated than I understand and until she untangles from it, all I can be is her quietly steady friend.

Which means swallowing my frustration and shrugging. "Yep. Need to be faster."

"Think you can do that? Think you can step up and be something you've never managed before?"

"We still talking about hockey?" I jerk around as Ty Connor shoves his way, casually, between us and grins at Max.

"Hockey's the focus, don't worry." I say it to both of them, but also to myself.

And hockey requires that I put up with a shitty training camp. With being relegated to group B tomorrow. With keeping my head down and not taking the bait.

Even if I'm ready to murder someone.

Even if I want to dismantle the legal and immigration system that has Shannon trapped in a relationship in which she's clearly not happy.

It's not time.

Not yet.

CHAPTER 31
SHANNON

"Shannon, thanks for joining us. Max looks good out there."

I smile and nod in agreement as one of the other committee members for the Highlanders Ball makes small talk. Very deliberately, our next meeting coincided with the end of the first week of training camp—the team foundation knows how to make people feel special, giving them insider access to the rink, and the players.

The event looks like it's in good shape. We're slightly behind our target for sponsored table ticket sales, but I've volunteered to make some phone calls and send some emails this week. We'll hit our fundraising goal, I guarantee it.

We're in a suite not that far from the press box, so this end of the arena feels pretty bustling. I can feel curious journalists glancing in our direction.

Smile. Laugh. Nod again. Look engaged.

Don't let on that I haven't seen my husband in almost a week.

After Max came to find me at the bakery, the Prince Charming routine faded faster than it ever had before. Now

I'm just getting the silent treatment and he's not even sleeping at home half the time.

I'm numb to it all.

I've shaken nearly everyone's hand and circled the room when my phone vibrates.

KILEY

Are you at practice today? In a suite filled with people?

I make my way to the front of the suite and scan the stands. From the opposite end of the arena, a few small figures wave from the upper deck.

I've been putting off talking to Kiley about the podcast. Dreading this, in fact, but now that she's here, and I'm finished with the committee…it's time to rip off the bandage.

KILEY

Come join us if you can get away

SHANNON

What section are you in?

I excuse myself as soon as she replies. The arena feels massive when it's empty. The concrete stairwells echo and the curved mezzanine that wraps all the way around the building seems to go on forever. It does eventually deliver me to their section number, though, and I find Kiley in the stands with not just Harper, but also her twin brother, Grant, who is one of the team's doctors.

"Hello, friend," Kiley says happily. "I haven't seen you since the cottage."

She pats the seat next to hers, and I sink into it. "I know. I've been busy. I'm working on the Highlanders Ball. That's what you spied—the committee getting a little reward of watching practice."

"It's a good one. Did you see the fight?"

A frisson of fear races up my spine. "Who fought?"

"Two young dumb bucks." Kiley shakes her head and glances over at Harper. "Mason and Zondi?"

Between them, Grant gets a message on his phone and clears his throat. "Speaking of, I'm needed downstairs. Excuse me."

He hops over the seats, gives his sister a shoulder squeeze goodbye, and disappears.

I take a deep breath, glad it wasn't Russ and Max.

Focusing on the ice, I try to spot either of them. Max is readily found, but Russ doesn't seem to be skating today.

I bite my lip, wanting to ask Harper and Kiley if they know where he is—but dreading them picking up on my curiosity as meaning something more than just an idle question.

Then there's a whistle on the ice, and everyone huddles up around the coach for a quick chat.

I shake my head, clearing it of thoughts of hockey players. That isn't as important as my friends who are right beside me. "So, what's new with you guys?"

Harper's expression brightens right up. "Did you hear Kiley's news?"

Kiley grins. "We've bought an apartment. Well, Ty's bought a condo, and I'm gonna live there rent free."

"Hey, congratulations!" I know that Kiley currently lives in a small run-down World War II era apartment building in a cute, walkable neighbourhood not far from the arena. Harper lived in the same building before she moved in with Kieran last season, and when Harper moved out, Ty moved in to her place—subletting it so he could be closer to Kiley.

But the two of them living upstairs/downstairs from each other wasn't really long-term NHL-calibre accommodations, so now that he's convinced her to be relationship official, a move is definitely in order.

"Thanks. And we get possession pretty much immediately because it's vacant already. It's got a very different vibe from my place, and everything I own is hand-me-down anyway, so I'm treating it like a blank slate and finding all new stuff. Well, new to us. Ty loves art deco and mid-century modern, so I'm getting up to speed on retro furniture pretty quickly."

"It sounds lovely." I pause a beat, then glance at Harper, testing the next thing I feel I need to say. "I don't want to be a downer. I promise I'm not trying to be. But you know you need to save all of your income as yours, right? Don't split anything. Let him pay the bills, especially as life gets more expensive."

"Oh, I know, and he is. He's great about that."

"Good, good. Of course he is."

Harper nods along. "I had the same talk with her, don't worry."

Heart pounding a mile a minute, I smile through the discomfort.

Down on the ice, everyone skates off, Max last.

I remember when he started paying my bills. It felt so romantic, not having to worry about rent or anything else. And then my lease came to an end, and of course it made sense to move in with him. His Upper East Side apartment in a building with a doorman was better than my shitty walk-up. No brainer.

But then I was in his way during play-offs. We fought. I learned not to throw surprises in his path. Then came the pressure to work less, as if me being more dependent on him would be easier. Followed by a romantic proposal. A legal meeting that went by in a blur. *"It's all pretty standard."* A wedding that same summer. More pressure to give up work.

A move to another country was just the last in a long line of small maneuvers to make me wholly dependent on him.

A credit card he pays off every month can't be used surreptitiously for divorce lawyers. It can't cover my rent for the next twelve months while I wait out a separation period.

And our marriage contract foresaw me being the one who would leave him, and it punishes me appropriately.

Another group of skaters arrives, and with a jolt, I realize I recognize the biggest, tallest person on the ice.

"Why is Russ skating with a bunch of AHLers?" I sound alarmed, because I am alarmed.

Kiley glanced at Harper, who shrugged.

Neither has been around long enough to understand the nuances of training camp groups.

I frown.

To distract myself, I circle back to Kiley's moving plans, because a weird idea occurs to me. "Are you planning to sublet your apartment?"

She shakes her head. "Luckily, we don't need to do that. We'll get possession of the condo two weeks before my lease is up, which is basically perfect."

Damn it. "Well, that's good!"

Kiley tips her head to the side. "Why? Do you know someone who needs an apartment?"

I shake my head, "No," I lie. "I was just, you know, curious."

Which is a silly response. I should have said it was for someone I met through volunteering.

Or you could tell her the truth.

I could. I probably should.

But I can only peel off so many layers of my skin in one day, and there's something else I need to talk to her about, too.

And when Harper gets a phone call from her mom and excuses herself to go up to the mezzanine, I realize there's no time like the present.

"Listen, I need to hit pause on the podcast idea."

Kiley's face falls. "Oh no. Can I ask why? Is there anything I can do to lighten the workload?"

I shake my head. I practiced this. But my voice still catches. "I think there's a reason I spent so long developing the idea. I don't think I'm the right person to host it."

"I think you're perfect."

I laugh weakly. "Definitely not. But I love your vote of confidence, thank you."

"Let me know if you ever change your mind. I remain excited about producing a show for you."

"Thank you. You're the best."

She glances at her watch, where a text message has just shown up. And she smiles with a secret pleasure that makes my chest hurt, it's so beautiful.

"Is Ty finished now?"

"It's fine, I can keep talking about this," she says hastily.

I shake my head. "Go. Find your man. Make him buy you lunch."

"I'll see you tomorrow night? Did you see that Jenson booked a suite for us?"

I noticed the group texts about the WAGs sitting in a

suite instead of family seats closer to the ice. I hadn't replied yet because... Well, I hadn't replied for silly reasons. I'm going to cling to this girl group as long as I can. "Yep. I'll see you back here for the game."

When she leaves, I lean forward, bracing my elbows on my knees, and I watch Russ skate circles around the less skilled players. He steals their pucks and gets in their way. He fucks up their shit in every possible way, until he's called over by the coach, presumably to give the rest of them a chance to do anything without a mountain ruining it for them.

He spends the rest of practice chatting with the coach, looking as casual as can be. I walk down to the edge of the upper bowl and sit there, as if being fifteen feet closer will make a difference.

Or maybe I want him to see me, because when he looks up, I wave.

Even from this distance, I can see the surprise on his face. He waves back.

I pull out my phone, knowing he won't see the message until he's changing back into his street clothes.

SHANNON

Good practice today. What's up with the AHL group assignment, though?

I'm about to go into a Pilates class when his response finally arrives.

RUSS

Who knows. Just gotta roll with the punches. It was nice to see you in the stands.

I have to put my phone away after that, but when I finish the class and check again, there's another message.

Wild, electric heat rolls through me. He shouldn't. And I shouldn't encourage him. But my phone has a password on it that Max doesn't know. It's one of the first questions the divorce attorney asked me, and thankfully, despite all the other ways our lives are entangled, our phones have always been ours alone.

Except for my location tracking, which I've now turned off—probably one of the reasons Max stopped speaking to me again.

The first pre-season game of the year is my first chance to catch up with the WAGs who don't live in Hamilton year round. Magnus Gustafsson's Swedish girlfriend, for example, whose English is broken but enthusiastic.

Some of them, like Andrew Mitchell's girlfriend, Lauren Point, don't even live in Hamilton during the year. The lawyer met the west coast D-man back home in Vancouver two summers ago, and given that the team is away half the time during the season, and a decent number of those games are up and down the west coast, she's stayed with her firm there.

"Until he puts a ring on it," she jokes to Kiley.

Kiley glances my way, clearly remembering my warning. "That's smart," she says. "Save your money, too. Make him pay for the flights."

Lauren winks in agreement. "My sister is a lawyer, too—family law—and her mantra is, *don't do anything you wouldn't advise a client to do.* So you bet, I'm putting the onus of financial responsibility on the higher earning partner." She pauses for effect. "With appreciation shown on my knees, of course."

Kiley hoots and claps her hands. "That's it. That's the right answer."

I grin and go take my seat as the game starts. Because it's a home game, they're playing their top lines, even though this is mostly a chance for the coaches to see some of the players who are on the line to get cut out of training camp. And because it's an away game for Montreal, the other team sent their B-squad.

It doesn't look that way off the first face-off, though.

Hamilton is *rough*, and it hurts to watch.

We're in a suite today, which comes with food. The temptation to slide out of my seat and go peruse the buffet is high, but I stay parked on my butt until the buzzer goes at the end of the first period.

Then I hightail it to the back of the suite.

Lauren is already tucking into the salsa. She gives me a sympathetic look at the state of the game.

"Maybe the second period will be better." I reach past her and grab a plate, and then load up on veggies and dip. And cheese. Tonight calls for cheese.

I was really hoping the tension at home wouldn't be reflected on the ice, but Max isn't playing well at all. And Russ has barely had any ice time, too. Right now, I imagine the two of them circling each other in the dressing room like cage fighters, blaming the other for their bad first period showing.

When the truth is probably that it's my fault. Not for anything I've done, maybe, but for what I haven't done.

I clear my throat. "Lauren, can I ask you a legal hypothetical? Well, it's not really hypothetical, but I don't know all the details. It's for a friend."

"Umm…" She shrugs. "I mean, with the caveat that this is not legal advice because you haven't hired me…yes."

"I get that." I take a deep breath. "I know this woman who is in a difficult position because she's here in Canada and her marriage has broken down, but she can't move back to the States, for financial reasons. No job prospects, no family or friend supports there. And she can't afford to wait out a year-long separation here in Canada, either."

"She's American?"

"Yeah."

"Does her spouse have financial resources?"

"Yes."

"Is there a prenup?"

"Yeah."

"Is the spouse opposing the divorce?"

That gives me pause. "I think so. I'm not sure."

She takes a deep breath. "Well, as an American, the easiest divorce would be found by going to Guam, which only has a residency requirement of something like a week, last I checked. But it takes money to get done that quickly and if it's not agreed upon by all parties, then it can be challenged in court. I wouldn't want to be on the receiving end of that lawsuit. Otherwise, any competent attorney should be able to advise on the states that have the shortest residency requirements, or refer to an American lawyer."

I don't think that was mentioned in my first appointment, but I wonder how many cross-border divorces the small town family law firm I randomly walked into has ever handled.

When I don't reply, Lauren pulls out a business card. "You can pass this on to your friend. I'm actually an immigration attorney, but as part of that, I do refer to family lawyers on both sides of the border. Another option is appealing to the American consulate for assistance, and we can help with that, too."

I'm stunned. "Thank you. I'll pass that on. That's…I wasn't expecting to have so many options…to tell her about."

The suite door opens and a little blond tyke comes barrelling in.

"Charlie!"

I crouch down and get in front of Becca and Hayden's son. "Hey, mister."

He giggles and dodges around me, but I dart my arm out, catching him around the middle.

"Noooo," he howls, kicking his feet.

His mother swoops in and scoops him up.

"Thanks," she says breathlessly. "Look, Charlie. There's

food up here, like I promised." Then she looks at me. "We sat down by the glass, but then he got hungry."

"You came to the right place." I offer Charlie a carrot.

He looks at it suspiciously. I swipe it in the thick Greek yogurt dip, and he takes it from me more readily. "Thank you."

"You're welcome. There are meatballs and garlic bread, too."

He gets a big grin on his face at that.

I leave them to it and go back to my seat, thinking about what Lauren said.

The second period starts with Kieran at centre instead of Max, and two prospects on either side of him. Then Russ comes out after the first line change, and some kid on Montreal's team picks a fight with him, which makes no sense because Russ is twice his size and Montreal is leading two to nothing.

Russ grabs a fist full of jersey and holds the kid at arm's length, letting him pinwheel fists of fury for twenty seconds before Russ takes him down to the ice with a single swinging left hook. As he stares down at the other player, he shakes his head, then skates back to the Hamilton bench, not looking at the refs.

It doesn't work—both players get a penalty called on them—but the fans think it's funny to watch on the Jumbotron as Russ pretends not to be aware he's going to have to go to the box.

Then he grins and nods, and heads to the sin bin for two minutes.

Since both teams have someone in their respective boxes, the teams play four-on-four, a prime opportunity for Hamilton to score as the better skilled team.

We do, Hayden Calhoun posting the first goal for Hamilton tonight, bringing us to within one.

Becca and Charlie cheer like mad, and we all cheer with them.

But when the final buzzer goes after the third period, that's the only goal we've scored.

I'm dreading Max coming home tonight.

And Lauren's card is burning a hole in my pocket.

CHAPTER 32
RUSS

"All right, that wasn't what we wanted it to be," Coach barks as he strides into the dressing room. He doesn't wait for the door to shut behind him, so guaranteed, that's the lead quote in the sports press tomorrow. "But this is what the pre-season is for, working out the kinks. And tonight, there were a fuck ton of kinks. Tiller, I don't know who you think was going to pass to you while you hid behind their D-core, but that's not a system we've ever practiced. Gusty, Mitchie…if we're not checking, we're not winning. Right? Throw your bodies around more." He glances at his notes. "Hooner, good goal. But you were still a minus one for the night. You can do better, too."

Calhoun hangs his head. "Yes, sir."

"If you played less than fifteen minutes tonight, the trainers are going to put you on the bikes. Everyone else, grab some food. Tilman, Calhoun, Hale, and Zondi—press room. And we have a practice in the morning. If you're not early, you're late. That's it."

Nobody says anything until he's gone, then the volume

rises quickly. I've already stripped down to my base layers, so I get up to head to the training room.

Max gets in my way, frowning. "Where the fuck do you think you're going?"

"Bike," I growl. "I only played fourteen minutes tonight. No thanks to you."

"What the fuck does that mean?"

"Nothing." I go to step around him, and he shoves his arm out, putting his palm in the centre of my chest.

The room goes quiet.

"Hey," someone says behind me. Kieran, I think.

"Get your hand off me," I say tightly.

"Your ice time is your own fault," Max snarls. "Don't put that shit on me."

"You saying you didn't tell the coach I was too slow to practice with the A-squad?"

He laughs. "Do I live rent free in your head, Rusty?"

I'm not laughing. I'm wondering if he watched any part of the game tonight when he wasn't actively on the ice. Because I might be a gentle giant, but I am still a giant. I don't care if someone postures. I don't care about chirping or smack talk. But the second someone drops their gloves and comes at me, it's on.

And Tilman's hand in the middle of my chest is the dressing room equivalent of flinging his gloves across the ice behind the ref's back.

I grab his wrist and remove his hand from my body, squeezing tighter than I need to. "Projecting much, Tiller?"

"What the fuck does that mean?"

"Okay," Gustafsson says as he and Marsh get between us, and Hale starts barking orders to everyone else. "Move along, nothing to see here. Shouldn't you be on a bike? Calhoun, press room, now."

The room mostly clears out, until it's just the veteran core, and Jenson because he's an alternate captain.

"I didn't start it," I point out.

Marsh rolls his eye at me. "Can you fucking finish it? Politely?"

He means I should apologize to Tilman for a perceived slight.

Except Max and I both know this isn't about his usual diva feelings. There's nothing *perceived* about the beef between us.

"Politely, I'll just ask our captain to keep it professional in here." I shrug. That's as good as they're going to get from me.

Everyone waits.

Max doesn't say shit.

So I shrug Gusty off of me and stalk out of the room.

While I'm on the bike, I can see on the closed-circuit TVs that Tilman goes into the press room next. He looks pissed off, and manages to make the press think that's aimed at himself.

I know better.

"I'll be right back," I tell the trainers.

Quickly, I head to the locker room, adjacent to our dressing room, where our street clothes live—and where we usually lock up our phones.

I grab mine and head back before I get in trouble. This late after a game, nobody cares if we've got our phones on us. Other teams have different rules, but the Highlanders are pretty flexible as long as we're doing what we should be.

Hopping back on the bike, I fire off a warning message to Shannon.

RUSS

Got into it a bit with your husband tonight.

Sorry.

SHANNON

What does that mean?

RUSS

He got in my way. Said some shit about my game. Put his hand on my chest.

SHANNON

Please tell me you didn't smash him like that poor Montreal kid

I grin. She watched me play.

RUSS

I did not. But that Montreal "kid" deserved it, and he also started it.

SHANNON

Not the point

RUSS

I just wanted to give you a heads up that he's mad at me

SHANNON

he's just…mad in general

RUSS

Will you be okay?

SHANNON

I don't expect him to come home tonight

I frown.

RUSS

Why not?

SHANNON

Don't worry about it

I'm going to sleep now, try not to get into any more fights

My frown deepens.

I finish up my workout, then roll well and get some work done on my glutes before I head to the shower.

Most of the team is gone, so the last person I expect to see again is Max. He's just finished showering, and he's only wearing a towel, so I don't think he's going to pick another fight with me—not before he gets dressed.

Still, I try to give him a wide berth.

Hostility rolls off him in waves, and he doesn't carry on to the locker room.

I sigh. "Given the circumstances, I get that I'm not your favourite person. But this…" I make a little buzzing insect noise at him. "Attention seeking bullshit needs to stop."

"Fuck you."

"Fuck you, Tiller." Suddenly, I'm so fucking tired. "Be as mad as you want. I don't care. But stop making it my problem. You made your choices and now you have to live with the consequences."

"You don't know what you're talking about."

"Fucking quit it with the victim mentality, Max!" I'm breathing hard. And I'm shouting. Any minute, someone is going to come to find out what the commotion is. I lower my voice. "Bottom line: you put another hand on me, and I will smash you. Understood?"

"Is that a threat?"

"It's a fucking promise, asshole." I give up on the shower and go straight to my locker. I'm not changing, either. I just need to get out of here.

He watches as I grab my keys and wallet. I'll get my suit tomorrow. "You shouldn't have watched us that night."

I cannot believe how badly he misunderstands where that night went wrong. But that's not my problem. I shrug. "You shouldn't have fucked your wife on my terrace. Have a good night, Captain."

CHAPTER 33
SHANNON

The only bright light out of the week is that after that miserable loss to Montreal, Andrew Mitchell proposed to Lauren Point.

The next day, we take her out for brunch.

"Now it's my turn to ask you for advice," she says to me after we order. "We're going to have two weddings, a traditional Coast Salish ceremony for our families, and then the following weekend a reception in Vancouver for everyone. I want a few different dresses, and Ani's given me the names of one designer, but she thought you might have some other suggestions as well."

I pull out my phone, trying to think. "You want Indigenous designers?"

"Yes."

"So the first place I would look is in the Instagram follows of the other designers you've already heard of. Fashion is just like any other industry. People follow their friends and their competitors alike, just to keep tabs on each other."

"I tried that this morning, but I didn't get very far. I'm not very social media literate."

I smile. "You're a bit busy doing more important things."

"Right now, nothing feels more important than my wedding dresses." She blushes. "Is that horrible?"

"You're talking to the queen of vain. Of course it's not horrible. Those are photos you will be looking at for the rest of your life. You want the weddings to be perfect." I text her a few links. "These are all Indigenous dress designer followed by my friend, Olivia Nash. She's a Pacific Northwest girl, from Seattle, and I love her sense of style. She's in New York now—that's how we met—but her heart is definitely on the west coast. I'll ask her directly for some recommendations, too."

"This is incredible, thank you." She hands her phone across the table to Ani. "Check this out."

The dress conversation spills into wedding photo talk.

All of it feels surreal to me. At some point in my near future, I'll be boxing up my wedding memories and putting it all behind me. I think about my wedding dress hanging in the spare room closet, not far from where Max is sleeping right now—when he even bothers to come home.

As I expected, last night he slept somewhere else. With someone else, probably.

Maybe I'll burn my wedding photos.

After brunch, I drive Kiley to her brother's apartment so she can pick up her dog, Puck, who she shares with her twin, Grant.

"Do you want to come for a walk with us?" she asks. "We're going to a park first so Puck can do her business, then we're going to check out the new condo and take some measurements."

I have nothing else to do today, so I agree.

We talk about her conflicted feelings about leaving behind the clerical work she was doing at the hospital for the more precarious nature of regional theatre work. As we leave the park, she stops to take a picture of a restaurant so she can text it to Ty, then she explains it's for a recommendation list they're building together on the Lusty app, a travel and lifestyle app for "people with wanderlust" where they first met. Apparently they take their foodie lists very seriously, and it's deeply entertaining to hear how in-depth their debates get.

By the time we've reached her new building, I'm in a much better mood than I've been in all week. More than any of my other friends, Kiley can reliably be counted on to not make every conversation about the WAG life.

Ironic, then, that we were once considering a podcast together with that exact title.

At the front door, she types in a code, saying it out loud for me. "Remember that for when you come over."

I laugh. "Will do."

It's a gorgeous new building, with a great lobby and fast elevators that whisk us up to the top floor. They've bought one of two penthouses on this floor, and the apartment is flooded with light.

"Wow, these windows," I say, taking it all in.

"I know, right?" She closes the door and unclips Puck's lead. "Go on, girl. Get your sniff on."

"What are you measuring?"

"Everything."

I play with Puck while Kiley does what she needs to do. Then the energetic pup curls up in a beam of sunshine for a little nap, and we step outside onto the wraparound terrace.

"This is a beautiful place," I tell her, meaning it with every fibre in my being. "I'm so happy you get to move here soon."

Kiley being Kiley, she takes the compliment, but her gaze searches my face with an astuteness that makes me feel very vulnerable.

I turn and glance out over the city. We can't see the arena from here, that's on the other side of the building.

"At brunch, Lauren mentioned that you'd asked her for some advice," Kiley says softly.

I'm prepared to lie here. I have a complete, easy explanation. The same thing I said to Lauren—it was for someone I know, someone in a bad spot.

But my friends are going to learn the truth soon enough, and I'd rather they hear it from me. "I'm leaving Max."

"Oh." She leans against the railing next to me. "How are you feeling?"

"Numb."

"What do you need?"

"A time machine." My voice cracks. Not completely numb.

She pulls me into her arms and I sob on her shoulder. She rubs my back and doesn't say anything else, which is exactly what I need her to do.

"I can't talk about it yet," I finally whisper, wiping my eyes.

"Okay."

"I haven't told anyone else." Except Russ, but that's... different.

"I won't say anything."

"I don't know when the separation will happen. It's complicated because I'm here on a spousal visa."

"Oh, shit."

"Yeah." I swallow hard.

"Whatever you need, we'll make sure you get it. We're friends no matter what, Shan."

I lift my head and look her in the eye. "That's not how it works with the team. It's okay."

"Fuck the team. That's how it works with *me*."

I hug her back. "Thank you."

"I can do different voices. Do you want me to call Lauren and get a referral to another lawyer? She'll never know it's me."

I let out a watery laugh. "No, it's okay. I think I'll call her myself."

"Good. Remember what Emery said about how they control the WAG groups. That's not how it's going to be for us. You leave our group chat, babe, we're just dragging you into a new one."

I burst into tears all over again. I don't deserve these friends. But I love them so, so much.

"Call Lauren," she whispers. "It'll be confidential. That's her job."

I nod. I will.

Puck pats at the glass door. Kiley cringes. "We're going to have to come up with a better system for that to avoid the paw marks."

Inside, I try to grasp for something I can help with. "Do you need any decorating assistance?"

Kiley shakes her head, smiling gently at me. "We have it covered. The only thing I want you to do is come and visit once we move in."

A little frown tugs between my eyebrows despite myself. My mask is slipping and I hate it.

After she reconnects Puck's lead, she holds the door open for me.

The elevator whisks us back down to the lobby in seconds, and Puck is excited to lead us off. I'm leaning over, telling the dog to be patient, so I don't notice Russ standing at the elevator doors right away.

"Kiley," he says. I jerk upright. His gaze sweeps over me. "Shannon."

"Russ," I manage.

Great. Now everyone has been named.

Kiley tugs Puck around Russ's legs. "We were just here to measure upstairs."

"You live here," I breathe.

He nods, turning slowly as I reluctantly follow my friend. Watching me, even as he steps backward into the elevator car.

"Russ lives here," I say to Kiley once we're outside.

"Yeah." She gives me a curious look. "You didn't know that?"

I have helped a lot of the team find accommodations and furnishings. Russ, though, never asked for my assistance. Where he lived has never come up. "No."

"It's how Ty heard about the condo even before it was listed."

"Ah."

Kiley and Puck walk me back to my car. I ask her if she wants me to drive her to her apartment on the other side of downtown, but she says Ty is going to pick her up shortly, now that they're finished practice.

She gives me another hug before I leave. "Hey," she whispers. "You don't have to *do* anything to be worthy of our friendship, you know that, right?"

"I—" I don't know what she means.

"Decorating help, being resourceful. Always having whatever someone needs, or knowing how to get it." She shrugs. "That's all amazing. But that's not why I like you."

I stare at her. "Right."

But as I drive away, I actually can't figure out why else anyone *would* like me, unless they wanted to sleep with me.

That unsettling thought drives me to make two phone calls that afternoon. The first one is to a therapist. The second is to Lauren Point.

CHAPTER 34
RUSS

"You got a minute to talk?"

I look down at the ice, where the A-squad is currently practicing. "If you don't mind listening to me huffing and puffing, sure. I'm running stairs at the arena, waiting to practice with the B-squad. Again."

"I talked to Dorrian about that. They appreciate your leadership role on the team."

I snort. "Okay."

"It's just a balance thing during training camp." Marty sounds too smooth. Like Shannon's calm mask.

Lies, all lies.

"Whatever. I'm guessing that's not why you called me."

"No. It's about the Ice League. You've heard the rumours."

"Mostly try to ignore them, but aye."

"They want to announce the first wave of players soon."

I stop at the top of the concrete steps and turn around. I'm at the very top of the upper bowl. "So it's really happening."

"There are pros and cons on getting in on it."

"Where are the teams going to be located?"

He hesitates. "Quebec City. Vancouver. New York. Chicago. Vegas. And Los Angeles."

I whistle. "Nothing in the Golden Horseshoe?"

"No."

So it would mean moving. "Not interested."

"You should hear about the bonuses being offered before you say that."

I don't need to. "I'd rather not know what I'm missing out on, Marty."

"All right. Don't say I didn't try to make this happen for you."

I watch Max pick up speed on the ice. I fucking hate how fast he is—except when we're playing against another team, and he's using that for the greater good. "I'm not a UFA anyway this year."

"They're negotiating with the NHL. They'd be willing to buy out contracts."

And then it sinks in. There won't be any teams within 800 km of Toronto…and in exchange, the league will put pressure on teams releasing veteran players like me. People who can always find a job in the NHL, because we're good and reliable, but we're also replaceable by the next generation of players like Malik Zondi.

Here I was blaming Max for being demoted to the B-squad, when all along it might have been a just-in-case call by our General Manager.

Fuck.

Me.

"Have they locked up the stars for each team?"

Another hesitation. "Not gonna talk about other players yet, Rusty."

I'll take that as a no. "I'm still out. Thanks for thinking of me. Sorry you won't get that cut. But I'm staying put. Can you put a phone call in to Dorrian and make that clear?"

I walk back down the stairs and turn to run up them again, my thoughts churning. Every high-value free agent is a possible candidate for this launch. All of them would be pressing their agents to get the most amount of money possible. Basketball or baseball star level of contracts. It would have to be, to get them to leave the NHL.

It's not a given at all that Max will win that lottery.

But if he does, he and his wife will move far, far away from here. From me.

———

That afternoon, the training camp roster is cut substantially. Among others, Jamie Mason gets sent down to our new AHL affiliate in Niagara Falls—and I return to the A-squad for practice.

When I wake up the next morning, the team group chat is hopping.

JENSON

Don't forget it's school photo day today

KIERAN

Please don't piss Mabel off and forget your time slot

MALIK

I'm already at the arena having breakfast

MAX

Also don't forget that the press has more
access today than usual

JENSON

Best behaviour for school photo day!

TY

Stop trying to make fetch happen, Haler

HAYDEN

Don't use twenty-five-year old movie
references, boomer

TY

it's not a… well, fuck you

I chuckle as I do a search for when Mean Girls was released. Then I drop a thumbs up response on every message except for Max's, and head out the door.

Even though I know that the day I ran into her, Shannon was just visiting Ty's empty penthouse upstairs—which remains empty for now—I still expect her to be on the elevator every time I call it.

In the same way she imprinted on my cottage, a single exchange of nothing more than names has seared her into my awareness here in my own fucking apartment, too.

Maybe it would be for the best if Tilman left for the new league.

Maybe I should call up the French billionaire and offer to blow him myself to make that happen.

The arena is attached to a mall that is attached to a convention centre, and the team photos are happening in both spaces, so there's a parade of players going back and forth through the mall. Fans have turned out, and the team is managing that well, with posters and players signing for the public at posted times.

Despite Haler's cute comparison to school photo day, there's nothing quick about it. And it's not just a single head-shot, either.

They have a long list of still and video images they need for promotion throughout the season. Every time we score a goal, get a star of the game, pass a significant milestone, or anything along those same lines, a photo of us in this year's uniform needs to be added to a graphic. The league also wants some photos.

It's endless.

Some people get goofy with it, which is fun and fine. I tend to treat it as a straightforward task that is best accomplished as quickly as possible.

When I arrive at the arena, I head to the players' lounge and find a few people have joined Zondi for breakfast, including Ty, who has brought Puck with him to work today.

"She likes to go on the ice," he says with a grin.

I grab a banana. "That makes two of us."

As I eat, I double check where I am on the schedule.

Signing in the mall first. Then back to the arena for the on the ice pictures and video. Then back to the convention centre for the green screen and isolated black backdrop stuff.

They could do it all at the arena, but by having us parade back and forth through the mall, it makes the day more interactive for fans. There's no arguing that our PR team knows what they're doing, so I just go where I'm told.

Fingers crossed, I'll be finished by noon. Then I can get a workout in, and get home in time for a nap.

We're only playing five pre-season games this year. Tomorrow is our third, and our final home game before the season opener. The last two games will be short day trips to Detroit and Buffalo, and almost certainly they'll rest those of us who are going to be on the team coming opening day.

So tensions have eased, more or less, and the vibes are pretty good considering the shitty start we've had to the year.

I have a busier line than I expect at the signing table. A lot of BioPunk bottles. A few jerseys.

By the time I get to the convention centre for my last set of photos, I'm running on autopilot.

Sixteen years in, all of this start of the season stuff is pretty routine.

So I don't hear the start of a whispered conversation about a Big Problem that has developed, but the second I hear Shannon's name, I'm dialled in to the rest of it.

Apparently, Mabel is distressed that nobody knows where Max is and he's forgotten about an extra photo shoot —this one for the team foundation. Shannon's already there. The kids are already there, she says, and that's enough for me.

I am willing to run the risk of sticking my neck out only to have to hide in the shadows again if Max shows up at the last second to belatedly play the role of responsible captain and adoring husband.

But there's a solid chance that he is done for the day and won't be coming back, either because it wasn't on his team schedule, or because he's ghosting Shannon in this moment the same way he's been ghosting her since we got home from the cottage. And I can't leave her hanging.

"Hey," I say to the intern, who needs to work on his whisper volume. "Tell Mabel a player is on his way."

"I think they need Mr. Tilman," he says with a note of worry.

"Sure. But I'm going up there, anyway. Bump me down the list here. I'll be back in an hour."

———

The team foundation photos are happening one level up, in another conference room. At the top of the escalators, I nod at Aaron Green from the Observer, one of a dozen reporters I've seen around today. He's working on his laptop in a quiet corner just outside the room where Shannon is.

Taking a deep breath, I pull the door open and step inside.

My gaze goes immediately to her. She's standing with the photographer and Mabel from PR.

Blonde waves spill out of a high, loose ponytail. It's artfully casual, and entirely off-limits. I want to mess it up. I want to bury my fingers in her strands and tighten my hand into a fist. Push her down to her knees and make her suck my cock.

She'll have to take off the tight-fitting, sexy version of her husband's jersey first, though. It makes my chest burn to see her wrapped in it, and the asshole isn't even here to appreciate her.

From the expression on Shannon's face, she isn't happy to see me as the substitute, so I beeline to Mabel and say, "Seems like there was a mix up. I'm not exactly a pretty face, but I can fill in."

"You're perfect," she says, lying through her teeth, because we all know the photo shoot was for the captain and his wife. "Shannon, we might not..."

The wife in question immediately nods, understanding intuitively that she can't be in the photo shoot with a man who isn't her husband.

How about the man who makes her come during sex? Because that's sure as fuck not her husband.

While Mabel murmurs with the photographer about rearranging the kids who will be in the promo material for our winter Highlanders Ball, Shannon pretends not to look at me.

Fine. I can be painfully aware of her from across the room.

I cross to the pile of toys on the black cloth photo backdrop and introduce myself to the hired child models who are dressed up like they're going to a fancy ball.

"Hey, kids," I say, squatting down to their level. "I'm going to be in these photos with you today. I'm a hockey player."

"They told us," one of the boys says. "You're married to the pretty lady."

"Ah, actually not. There was a change of plans. Her husband couldn't make it."

"You're the replacement," a girl says.

I wish.

I gesture at her sparkly ballgown. "How do I get a fancy outfit like this?"

She giggles. "It's kind of itchy."

"Even better. I love itchy clothes. Especially ones that are too tight and make it hard to breathe," I say straight-faced.

More giggles.

The girl tugs at my jersey. "I like this."

I spin on my heel, an idea forming. "Do you like the version that the pretty lady is wearing?"

"Uh huh."

"Then you should go and ask her for it. It would be funny if you wore her jersey over your sparkly dress, don't you think?"

Her eyes sparkle in agreement and she takes off running, stopping right beside Shannon and tugging on her hem.

Shannon looks nervously in my direction. "Maybe we can get her one—"

"The others are all too big," I say, cutting her off. "Yours is just right to puddle on the floor at her feet."

I rise, excusing myself from the circle of kids, and cross to her.

Her cheeks turn red even before I lower my voice. "If you need another jersey to wear instead, you can have mine."

She stares at me.

I'm not sure she's going to do it, but then she yanks the custom jersey off, over her head.

She's breathing hard as she hands it to me. Glaring, too. She's so fucking beautiful, and I'd done holding myself back from making sure she knows that she's wanted.

I let myself look my fill at her before I step back and put Shannon's custom WAG jersey on the little girl. "There you go, princess. Fits you perfectly. You can keep that one."

God bless Mabel for always having a rack of spare jerseys, ready for any occasion—although the way her gaze is darting back and forth between Shannon and me, I imagine she wasn't anticipating her enforcer draping his number on the captain's wife at this photo shoot.

"Don't want you to get cold," I say as I turn back to Shannon. The thinnest of excuses.

The look of raw but willing vulnerability that she gives

me right before I slide my jersey over her head is fucking everything.

It's a confession. It's a plea.

She lets me slide her arms through the oversized sleeves. My gaze drops to where my number is, the same part of her arm where I pressed my fingers when we were watching Shoresy.

I want to claim her with so much more than just my jersey.

"We're ready to start," the photographer says.

"This won't take long," I say just for her ears. "Wait for me."

Shannon's gaze pleads with me to just go and do the thing I came here to do—cover for the team, maybe. More accurately, protect her from embarrassment. But more honestly, as soon as I heard her name, I knew I wanted to see her.

And now I want more than that.

I want everything, damn the consequences. Damn the embarrassment.

But the second I turn around and let them put me in the photo with the children, Shannon flees for the door. The last thing I see as she sprints for the hallway is my number on her back.

I know it's a matter of seconds before she takes off that jersey on the other side of the door.

But I also know that her purse is still sitting on a table against the far wall. She hasn't left the building. And the second we're done here, I'm going hunting for her.

CHAPTER 35
SHANNON

Outside, I pause in the quiet, carpeted corridor, grateful that it's basically empty. There's a guy on a laptop at the end of the hall, and I give him a polite wave before ducking across the hall into an unused room.

I'm not needed for anything to do with this team anymore, and it breaks my heart.

The only person who wants me is the one person I can't give myself to. My heart cracks open and my hands shake as I pull off Russ's jersey.

It's heavy as I turn it over in my hands and trace the letters of his last name across the back.

Armstrong.

I should feel guilty for liking it so much. Instead, I feel a softer, achier kind of guilt for taking the jersey off.

I need to get this back to Mabel, somehow, without making eye contact with her or ever explaining why Russ put it on me in the first place.

Maybe I should text her that it's in this room, and just… never see her ever again.

I pat my back pocket for my phone, but it's not there. It's in my purse, and…

Fuck, I left my purse in the other room.

So the eye contact is going to have to happen, because Mabel will find it when they finish up.

I pace across the room to the far wall, anxiety rising.

I don't know how people punch walls. Punching this wall looks terrifying. I try shoving at it and that does nothing, so I lean against it and just groan.

When the door behind me opens, I nearly jump out of my skin.

Russ raises his hands. "It's just me."

That soft, achy guilt pulses like a glowworm in my chest. Of course he came to find me. Sometimes I think that no matter how far I run away in this world, Russ Armstrong will always find a way to walk through a door and make eye contact with me. No matter how long I live, I will always have this desperate *what if* pounding through my head.

In another lifetime, he could have been my soulmate.

In this one, he's a mistake I need to stop making—for both of our sakes.

He looks taller than usual. I look down and he's wearing his skates still, guards on.

"Where are your shoes?"

"I left them across the hall with your purse. I told Mabel I'd come and find you."

"And you did." I laugh weakly. "That was fast."

He winces. "You were easy to find. You waved at a reporter I know on your way in here."

The anxiety explodes in my brain, like an oncoming car turning on their high beams. "A reporter?"

"It's okay." He comes closer. "Aaron's a good guy, and

you wearing my jersey isn't sports news. There are some weirdos on Twitter who might find it interesting, and I really liked it, but it's your personal business."

I throw the offending jersey at him. "Not funny."

"I'm not laughing."

He closes the gap between us. The uniform he's wearing today is pristine. It still smells *new*. It is a neon sign that he's off-limits. If cooking Max a nice dinner when we first moved in together put his playoff chances in peril, me having an affair with his teammate would definitely fuck up the entire season.

But as Russ stands in front of me like a shining, over-sized, brand-new man, I can't pretend I'm unaffected by him.

Still, I have to try to resist.

"Russ, we can't…" I trail off as he lifts his hand.

His fingers hover just above my bare shoulder, his attention locked on the thin strap of my tank top. "Can't do what?"

"Anything."

"But we already have." His hand lowers, those fingers making contact with my shoulder.

I shudder at the deep, profound ache that spirals through me from that warm press. I miss being wanted.

I miss being desired. That's all that this is. I'm vulnerable to his attention because I haven't been a good enough wife and—

He drags his fingers up my neck and tips my chin up. My lips part, traitorous lips, but my eyes go wide at the same time, and he clearly reads my panic. "I'm not going to kiss another man's wife, don't worry."

I gasp and jerk away from him, because that's what I want more than anything else.

I want him to kiss me.

I can't unfeel all the emotions he unlocked inside me, I'm not that strong.

Russ catches me and spins me around, pressing me against the wall. Crowding against me. His breath is warm against my temple, and I want to melt into him. "There was nothing wrong with what we did. It felt good because it was good. You're incredible, a goddess, and feeling you come on my tongue is one of the highlights of my entire fucking life."

His hand traces up my spine. I shiver at the memory of his mouth moving along that same path. When he called me his queen.

"But you won't kiss me," I say bitterly.

"Not today. Not while you wear his ring."

I choke on a sob.

Russ exhales and stills his touch, his hand curling around the nape of my neck. His other fingers wrapping around my hip. He presses his face into my hair from behind. "It's okay, Shan."

"Fuck you. Nothing is okay."

He doesn't respond to that. He just holds me tight, pressing me against the wall, until the fight leaves my body and I sag.

Then he turns me around and pulls me into his chest, hugging me even tighter than he pressed me against the wall.

"Why did you..." The words clog in my throat. I hope he can read my mind with the rest of the unspoken question. *Why did you get physical like that?*

After a long pause, he grates out, "You looked like you needed it."

I have to fight against this, because I hate what it would mean if he's right. "You don't know what I need."

"Maybe I don't. But neither does your husband."

"God damn you." But my voice cracks.

"Where is he, Shan? Why isn't he wrapping you in his number and holding you tight?"

I can't tell him. So I just shake my head, and he pulls me into his chest again. I lose myself in the embrace of a man who isn't my husband, and I cry. The weakness I feel right now is exacerbated by the strength that radiates through this man.

But as the fight leaches out of me, it's replaced with a new calm. An uncommon steadiness that I barely recognize.

I take a deep breath.

Russ rubs my back. "That's it," he murmurs. "Take another deep breath, just like that."

"Don't coach me," I mutter. But I do it anyway.

And it does feel better, but I don't love it. I can't let Russ take care of me. I can't want.

He eases back and looks down at me. "You're a mess, aren't you?"

Somehow that works better for me.

I exhale and nod. "Yeah."

"That's okay. It's okay to be a mess." His gaze searches my face, his eyes seeing too much. "Max is still staying somewhere else?"

"Not every night." I swallow hard. "It's not like he's moved out. He's...there's someone else. And...it's not the first time."

His expression betrays a flash of thunder before he tightens it up. "Shannon."

"I know. I *know*. But…it's complicated. The history between us, my past. I never expected him to be faithful, I think. Deep down. But this is the first time that I…"

Russ grips my shoulders. "It is *not* your fault. Don't say that."

"You don't understand."

"Help me understand."

"I feel like I've betrayed my wedding vows. That's different. I let myself down."

"He invited me to join in that night. That wasn't you."

"I'm not talking about the threesome. I mean the rest of it. At some point this summer, I lost my loyalty to my husband." I lick my lips. "I wanted them to mean something. My wedding vows. If they couldn't mean fidelity from him, they could at least mean loyalty from me. And in exchange for my loyalty, I got something in return. Safety and security."

To my own ears, it sounds like the worst kind of denial. I can't imagine how it sounds to Russ.

"Don't judge me," I say.

"I'm not," he says, and his voice is warmer than I deserve.

"Before you, I was faithful to him. Fully."

"We didn't do anything. You haven't betrayed him."

"If only that meant something."

"What does that mean?"

"Nothing."

"God damn it." He growls in sudden frustration. "Don't … what is the point of sharing half of anything with me? Be messy. I can handle it."

"Maybe I can't!"

"Then let me handle it for you." He ducks his head, grabbing my gaze again. "If I can't be your lover right now, at least let me be your friend."

I have enough friends, I want to snap. And not nearly enough lovers.

But that's not really the truth, either.

And if there's something I have learned from my friends this summer, it's that there is more strength than I ever realized in being truly, fully honest. For them, it's with their husbands. For me…I need to start with myself. And then the man I wish I could take as a lover is a good next step.

"You want to know what it means? It means if you would cross that line with me, I would be your lover. I would cheat on him, because he cheats on me all the time. You are the only reason I have stayed faithful to him this time. You are more noble and respectful of this marriage than either of the two people inside it."

I shudder as his hands glide up my sides, and over my shoulders. He cups my face, holding my gaze, as he brushes his thumb over my parted lips.

His gentle touch against my mouth is more intimate than any kiss could ever be.

I suck in an aching gasp.

Pain lances his expression, but his voice is light. "Then it's a good thing I've already made it clear that married women aren't my type."

"And if I weren't married?"

He looks at my mouth, and fire licks up my spine. "Then this would be a very different conversation."

I square my shoulders. "I've put things in motion with another lawyer. I'm not a pushover."

"I don't think you are. I think your life is more complicated than anyone could ever imagine, and I wish it didn't scare you so much to let me in a little."

"As a friend."

"Yes. As a friend." But he says it in a way that promises he wants more than that.

I reach out and take back the jersey he hooked over his arm. "Then, as a friend, I'm keeping this."

"You are?" His gaze flares.

Good.

I need him to know that I want more than just friendship, too.

"I need something nice and warm to sleep in this winter. Since I'll be lonely and separated and—"

He crushes me against the wall again, this time with me facing him, his arms bracing on either side of me. "Fucking do it. Wear my number every night. And know that once you're free, I'm going to claim you for myself."

CHAPTER 36
RUSS

I shouldn't have said that. But I can't regret it. If Shannon has moved on from her marriage, then she's fair game to be wooed. And once she's single, there won't be anything holding me back from finally making her mine.

CHAPTER 37
SHANNON

Bringing Russ's jersey home feels like both the worst thing I have ever done, and the best kind of wild rebellion against the gaslighting and bullshit of my marriage.

But it's not like I expect Max to be home that afternoon. So when I pull into the garage, and his car is there, I know I can't very well carry the jersey upstairs without making everything worse.

And the fact that I have it is special. I want to keep that my little secret.

I roll it into a tight ball and put it in my workout bag, grateful that I went to early morning Pilates today before going to the convention centre.

Inside, I hear Max in the kitchen.

Lauren's warning that I should maintain a normal relationship as much as possible while she investigates my options for divorce rings in my ears.

"Hi," I say calmly.

He looks up from a prepared salad from the fridge. "Hey."

I get myself a salad, too, and he hands me the vinaigrette I like. It's a familiar routine, but hollowed out, like we're just going through the motions of being married.

The first bite tastes like cardboard, and it doesn't go down easy.

I can't do this. Sorry, Lauren.

"There was a photo shoot for the Highlanders Ball."

"I couldn't do it. I told someone."

"Okay. It worked out."

"Yeah, I heard Russ showed up." He takes a big, wolfish bite of salad.

"He did."

"Must have been cozy."

"I wasn't in the photo."

"We couldn't have that. People might get the idea that he's stealing my wife."

I don't rise to the bait.

"Maybe we need to do some of that couple's counselling Haler's doing to make his wife happy."

I don't like the way Max says that.

And I really don't want to go to therapy with him.

I don't trust you enough to do that, I want to say. Instead I just shake my head.

"No." He shoves his bowl away. "No, my wife doesn't want to fix our marriage."

"What do you think therapy would that accomplish?"

He doesn't have an answer for that.

"I wanted to repair whatever is broken between us for a long time."

"You," he snaps. "You are what is broken between us."

I gasp. "Excuse me? I'm not the one fucking someone else

right now. You want to try counselling? That will be the first thing I bring up, you *asshole*."

"You still have a higher number than I ever will," he sneers.

Like a fucking child.

"I tried for a long time," I whisper, shaking with fury now.

But I'm done trying.

"So what's your plan?" He crosses his arms over his chest. "You think you get to stay here in the house I pay for?"

This is exactly what Lauren warned me about. "Who *are* you? Do you think you can threaten me?"

"I'm your husband, and you don't fucking act like you know that."

His arrogance is incredible. But now that the truth is spilling out, I refuse to back down. "I know exactly who you are. You are a coward. You are weak and you need me, and you're mad that I'm removing myself from being in service to you. My husband? Try *master*. That's what you wanted to be to me. No fucking thank you. I wanted to be your partner."

He goes very still. "Is that what you think?"

I try to soften my voice, because I'm probably never going to have another chance to say any of this. "I am grateful to you for the life that we have shared. But as I told you that night, I want out of our marriage. I cannot be with you anymore. And you're trying to villainize me for that, when I've never done anything but try to help you. Even as our relationship has imploded, I've saved you. I haven't heard anything more about Francois' Ice League! I saved you from something embarrassing, because that's what a good wife does. And that will forever be our secret. I keep all of your secrets even though I don't love you anymore."

He stares at me, his eyes getting hard and cold. Deep down, Max is a liar and he does not live in honesty. It's probably asking too much for him to listen to my truth.

"I assume you know how to take yourself off of the WAG group chat." His words are intentionally sharp, and slice deep with precision.

"Max. I want to do this in a civil way and—"

"The most civil for me would be you removing yourself from my life as soon as fucking possible. You have outlasted your usefulness. And since you don't want to go to counselling, let me take this opportunity to remind you of the contractual limits of our prenup. Also, it's my understanding that we need to be separated for a year here in Canada before you can apply for divorce. So I suggest, *wife*, that you start looking for a job. It might be a challenge, given that the only experience you have is on your back, but—"

I've taken a swing at his face before I realize it. My palm connects with his cheek at the same moment his hand comes up and grips my wrist.

He doesn't move.

His gaze glitters. "But there is another option. If you would be willing to reconsider helping with Dumas."

"You can't be serious."

"I'm very serious."

"I thought—"

"You thought wrong. Ice League is going to happen, and I want to be a part of it."

"There's a third option," I say desperately. I yank my wrist out of his grasp. "Guam. With the right amount of money, a divorce can be granted there in seven days."

"You've looked into it, then?"

Fuck.

That glittering gaze turns dangerous. "No, Shannon. I don't want a quick divorce from you without getting something in return."

I can't breathe.

"Meet with Francois. Help close the deal on me headlining the league." Max shrugs. "And then you can have your quickie Guam divorce that will free you to be with your stupid Scottish crush."

"You can't believe for a second that I would just want out because you're a horrible husband, can you?"

"No."

Desperation claws at my insides. "How do I know you'll honour this agreement?"

"If you have enough influence with Dumas to have him extend an offer to my agent, you'll be able to persuade him to rescind it if I don't keep up my end of the bargain."

I hate how he says influence and persuade. He makes them sound X-rated.

But the worst part is that I know he's right. That is exactly the power I hold here in this moment.

I lick my lips. "I'm not moving out of this house until the divorce is finalized. And if you change the locks while I'm in New York, all bets are off."

"I'll book you a room at the Ritz."

My stomach turns at the thought of Max acting like my pimp in this transaction. "I'll book my own accommodation."

Francois always preferred The Lyle Hotel on the Upper East Side, anyway. More discreet, more luxurious. Better soundproofing.

For a moment, I consider saying that. Using my own scalpel to try to wound Max the way he wounds me. But you can't hurt someone like Max. You can only try to hold on, survive, and get out by whatever means necessary.

Which means I also can't beg him not to tell anyone about this.

Fingers shaking, I take out my phone. I can feel him smirking as he watches me book a flight for tonight. And a hotel for three nights, at least to start.

Maybe I'll get lucky and Francois won't even be in New York this week, and I'll have a final shopping trip on Max's dime.

But deep down, I know I'll stay in the city until the billionaire can see me. I'll fly anywhere in the world to have an audience with the man who holds the key to free me from this marriage.

———

It's late by the time I get to the hotel. I haven't been back to New York since we moved.

Max wouldn't have been comfortable with me visiting without him, and then our summer was just really busy. I meant to come back, but it just didn't happen.

And now, as I take a town car into the city, I feel like I've come home.

At the same time, I'm not exactly eager to move back. For one thing, I don't think I'm going to be able to afford the rent. And there are already way too many reminders of my marriage here.

But if I dig deeper than those years, New York is also where I discovered myself.

And then, unfortunately, lost myself for a period of time.

So coming back is a reminder of those coming-of-age experiences that I had, and I have a lot of nostalgia for that time in my life now that I'm safely past it. Plus, the shopping is unparalleled.

Maybe I stayed away for a whole year because I worried that I would miss it. And while it is good to be back, I realize that I didn't miss it, and I won't miss it when I leave again, because I know it'll always be here for me to return to whenever I need another reminder of how far I've come.

It's your turn now, my queen.

But on the other side of this trip, I'm hoping that I will have some time to make somewhere else my new home.

Lauren warned me that when the divorce is finalized, I will have to leave Canada pretty quickly to "exit" off my spousal visa. And then I'll be able to come and go like any other American visitor, but that's all I will be. I won't be able to live forever in Hamilton as a hockey player's ex-wife.

I try not to think about what that means for a fledgling relationship with Russ.

But he travels enough that it shouldn't matter where I live. Lauren lives on the other side of the country from Andrew, for example.

I ignore the wave of grief that rolls through me at the thought of being forced away from my new home just as I was putting down roots.

One thing at a time, Shannon. First, you need out of your marriage.

Even though it's been years, the hotel's detailed guest notes means they act like they remember me and I get upgraded to a suite when I check in.

"Right this way, Ms. Barker."

I smile at the use of my maiden name, which I used to make the reservation because it's what I had the account for this hotel chain under. *That* sounds good.

The concierge shows me to my room personally, and asks me if I need anything.

"Not tonight," I say, already thinking about a shower and bed. A decade ago, I'd be just getting started for a night of being seen at clubs.

There's only one person who needs to see me this trip. And I've put off contacting him long enough.

Since my phone number has changed, I go with an email from my rarely used old account to his private address because I'm hoping he still checks that constantly.

From: Shannon Barker
To: Francois Dumas
Subject: I'm in NYC for a few days and I'd love to catch up

Francois,

It's been a long time. But I've been watching your Ice League news with great interest. Do you have time for a drink? I'm in the city for at least three days. And if you're somewhere else in the world, just let me know where. Your girl is overdue for a vacation.

Shannon

P.S. If texting is easier, this is my current number: 742-555-0081 and I'm on WhatsApp with that

CHAPTER 38
RUSS

To keep myself from texting Shannon, I meet up with Gustafsson, Zondi, and Watanabe for dinner at a steakhouse across the bay in Burlington.

Zondi is our most promising rookie this year, and we need him to feel hyped for the rest of training camp.

Selfishly, I could use some hyping up, too. I need to get my head back in the game.

On the drive, I have my phone read me the scouting report for the game we're playing day after tomorrow, so I'm prepared for practice in the morning.

Detroit is expected to send a prospect heavy squad because they haven't cut as many players as other teams at this point in the pre-season, which should make us the better team, but sometimes the chaotic oversized puppy energy of prospects thinking they might make the big show can surprise us.

A text notification drops as I'm getting off the freeway. A message from Max to the whole team.

MAX

What's up, fuckers? Anyone going out
tonight?

Fuck me.

MARSH

not me, sorry bud

JENSON

I'm chilling in my backyard if anyone wants
to come over for a beer

Despite my growling chant of *No, no no noooo*, the next response is from Zondi.

MALIK

A few of us are at this steakhouse in
Burlington

He drops a pin.

I pull up to a red light and consider pulling a U-turn and heading home again. Making some kind of excuse.

But there are cars on either side of me, so I have to advance when the light turns green. I'm two blocks away now.

MAX

Sounds good. How long will you be there?

Might join you in an hour or two

MALIK

Yeah, probably two hours at least.

The good news is that Tiller never shows up early to

anything, so if he says one to two hours, he means two. I have to chuckle at Zondi already clocking that.

No dessert for me, no real hardship, and I should be able to be out of there before he arrives.

I pull into the parking lot at the same time as Watanabe.

"This might turn into a party," he says with a laugh as he checks his messages.

"Sounds like." As we head inside, I schedule a text to myself to send in seventy-five minutes, a trick one of last year's prospects taught me. No hockey player is ever going to ask twice if you get a text from a supposed booty call.

It's handy if you find yourself stuck with a chatty team-mate and you just really want to have a nap.

And also, apparently, if you can't stomach the thought of socializing with your team captain.

Great way to start the season, Armstrong.

So much for the hype. Here's hoping the steak is good so I can salvage something from the evening.

It's not really a lie that I'll have a date, though. It might be a date with my right hand and the promise of Shannon wearing my jersey this winter, but it's the best date I'll have had all year.

CHAPTER 39
SHANNON

The reply from Francois arrives at five in the morning, and when my phone vibrates, I sit straight up in bed, heart pounding.

The email is short and to the point.

From: Francois Dumas
To: Shannon Barker
Subject: RE: I'm in NYC for a few days and I'd love to catch up

My beautiful Shannon, of course I have time for you. Would you like to come to a dinner with me tomorrow at the New Museum? Or were you thinking something more private?

F

I'm taken back a decade to when I met Francois for the first time. I was twenty-one. He was in his late forties, and sounded like a prince. He wasn't in New York very often the first year we knew each other, but the year after that, his time in the city increased and he bought an apartment.

I've never seen the inside of it, though. We always met here. A decade ago, I didn't wonder why that was. He's not married, or if he is, it's not public knowledge. I don't think he has any children.

But it may have simply been to prevent attachments—either on his part or mine.

Francois is a deeply emotional lover. It would be easy to think he loves you.

At five in the morning, though, I know he's a workaholic who can go eight years without talking to a girl, and then slot her in with ease.

Something more private.

My stomach turns.

I hit reply and fire off a quick acceptance of dinner the following night. I need the probably false hope that what I've come here to do can be accomplished outside of this hotel suite. At the very least, I need a day to prepare myself. I need a new outfit.

I need an Olivia Nash dress.

And maybe some Livy Nash advice.

———

"Shannon!"

"Livy!"

She's waiting for me at a cafe just down the block from her East Village boutique.

"I can't believe you're awake," I say, squishing my designer friend in a tight hug.

She laughs and returns the embrace. "Do they hug harder in Canada? This is a good one."

I exhale happily and let her go. "The friends I've made there do, anyway. But it's so good to see you."

"At seven in the morning, too." She waves her hand at me. "What's up with this? Why are *we* up?"

"It's a long story for another time," I say. "Have you ordered coffee?"

"Yep. I took a guess and if you don't like what I've asked for, I'll drink both of them."

"I'm sure it'll be perfect."

It's a hazelnut oat milk latte, and it *is* perfect. I savour the first couple of sips, then put it down. "How about you? You didn't say why you were up when I texted you."

Her cheeks turn pink. "It's kind of dorky."

"I'm sure it's not."

"My dad has been tapped to be the next ambassador to France."

"Wow." I blink hard. "Wow!"

"I know. It's sort of extra. And there's a friendship dinner tomorrow with the UN Ambassador and some business leaders that I'm going to with my parents. So I've been watching French TV in all my spare time to get caught up on the latest world events from their perspective."

Of all the dinners in Manhattan tomorrow, what are the fucking chances?

"At the New Museum?" I ask faintly.

She laughs, surprised. "How did you know?"

"I, um, have also been invited. As a plus one of an old friend. That's why I need a new dress. I didn't bring anything appropriate."

Livy claps her hands. "I can totally help with that."

"I'm thinking of finding a salon this afternoon to take me back to a brunette, too."

She flicks a curious glance over my hair. "Interesting. Were the lowlights a test?"

"Subconsciously, maybe. It's a new thought. Do you think it's a mistake?"

"I don't think it's ever a mistake to go back to our natural colouring. With, of course, some salon improvements."

I give her a wry smile. "Of course."

I'm grateful she doesn't ask for any more details, and then the waitress comes around to take our breakfast orders, which gives me a chance to think about how I'm going to navigate the dinner with Francois and Livy both knowing me.

Livy reminds me a lot of Becca Kincaid in her youthful exuberance. She's an earnest, eager young designer who dressed me for a charity fashion show three years ago, while she was a student at the Fashion Institute of Technology. We've kept in touch since, but our friendship is ninety percent clothing oriented. Based on the fact that she immediately started a boutique with a friend after graduating was a clue that she came from money, but I didn't know she had family who became ambassadors.

I smile at her over my latte. "And how is the French news familiarization exercise going?"

"I have enough to work with. Most people just want a small prompt, and then they will fill the conversation with their own opinions if you let them." She winks. "I'm very good at letting them."

"A girl after my own heart." I take a deep breath. "Speaking of opinions and letting people talk, do you know Francois Michel Dumas?"

If she says that he's her godfather, I'm calling quits on this whole thing and heading back to Canada to live out a year-long separation in purgatory.

But she shakes her head. "I know the name, thanks to the news. Sports?"

"Among other things. That's who I came to see. I asked for a meeting and he offered dinner, which turns out to be... your dinner."

"Is this about hockey?"

It's about so many things. Sex, jealousy, money, power. Fame. Legacies. "Yeah. It's about hockey."

"Cool." She flicks her gaze up to my hair, then down my body through the cafe table. "I have a pink and white and rose gold gown that would look stunning on you."

I breathe a sigh of relief. "Amazing. I can't wait to try it on."

CHAPTER 40
RUSS

If I were a paranoid man, I would think that Max has clocked that I ducked out of dinner last night just before he arrived. From the moment we arrived at the rink for practice, he's been extra tense.

Malik seems aware of it, too, so maybe it's actually about something he did or said after I left.

Or it might just be that Zondi sees through his bullshit because the entire short period he's been on the team, Max has been on a sharp downward spiral emotionally. Where the rookies and young players from last year have carried over goodwill towards the captain for his star power and leadership, Malik only has the last five weeks to go on and it hasn't been great.

It doesn't help that I can't even meet Max's gaze for a second.

I thought I could keep a lid on my disdain for our captain, but now that I know he's cheating on Shannon again, that he's never been a faithful husband to her, it's all I can do to keep my mouth shut when he strides in acting like he's King Shit.

We have our team meeting first and go over the plan for the game tomorrow. One of the coaches takes us through video that shows pretty much what I've already read in the scouting report.

"What's the plan for tomorrow?"

"Always be checking," we say in unison.

"That's right. Disrupt, disrupt, disrupt. We're going to practice that today. If you're not on the penalty kill team, go get dressed and hit the ice. PK guys, hang back because we have some more notes for you."

I head for the dressing room because that doesn't apply to me.

After quickly changing into this season's practice gear, I hit the ice. Our jerseys lean hard into the bagpipe-playing wild boar aesthetic that I get no shortage of grief over from Scottish fans online.

Since I'm the first guy on the ice, I get to dump the bucket of pucks set out by our equipment guys, and I notice the practice pucks also have the bagpipe front and centre.

I wave over the PR intern. "Can you ask Mabel if I can say shite on the team's TikTok account?"

He blanches.

I laugh. "Just ask her. Say, 'I'm repeating this word for word because he told me to'."

He laughs nervously. "Okay."

By the time everyone else is on the ice, I've taken a ton of shots on net and I'm the good kind of warm, all loose and limber.

When we circle up around the coach, I stay on the other side of the group from Max—far enough away I can't really hear him if he mutters anything, but unfortunately, that also puts me in his line of sight.

Avoid, ignore.

I can feel him staring at me, and it starts to be a bit of a game.

Ignore, avoid, disrupt.

Then we get set up to run some checking drills.

The point of these in practice is to better anticipate how really good players will avoid getting checked. It's not to give your teammate a jarring bone crunch the day before a game.

We set up in two groups at either end of the rink. At the whistle, two guys take off, as if one is on a breakaway and the other is the only person who can stop him.

Zondi manages to clip Marsh pretty good, enough that he loses the puck. Kieran gives Malik a high-five for the effort, and they switch ends. Hooner isn't as lucky up against Connor, but Ty has some words of advice for Hayden just before they, too, switch ends.

Two by two, we run the drill. Tilman takes on Gustafsson just before I take on Watanabe.

"Well, that's not a fucking fair size match," Hiro says goodnaturedly to me as I help him up off the ice after simply putting my body in front of his at the last second.

"You still managed to snap the puck back at the last second, which is all you can do if someone wants to brick wall you."

"True." He claps my arm as we switch.

The groups weren't even numbers, so the last rush is two-on-one, and then we line up again.

This time, the lines get rejigged a bit. The two on one rush is done right at the top, and by the time it's down to the last pair, it's me at one end of the ice and Tilman at the other end.

The whistle goes and we take off. I've got the puck, and he's going to check me. I keep my head up because I'm not an idiot, and sure enough, he's putting on more speed than he did the first run through.

I brace for impact.

He twists at the last second, slamming up and in to try to make me go over his back in a brutal open ice hip check.

I don't go flying, so he gets tangled up around my knees and then tries to scramble away.

Fuck that.

I hook him around the neck and haul him back.

He flicks his gloves off, and I'm not backing down from that, so mine go flying too. He makes a bare knuckle run at me, but before he can connect, our teammates are between us and I'm being pushed off the ice.

"All right, all right," Marsh says, shoving me down the tunnel as I yell choice words back in Max's direction.

"He's a fucking clown," I snap angrily.

"Be louder. I don't think the entire press crew heard you," he says mildly.

I swallow whatever was about to come out next.

Whoever has Tilman takes him somewhere other than the dressing room, so I have a minute to cool down with Marsh just watching me.

But then the doors swing open and it's not Max, and it's not the coach. It's Dick Dorrian, the team's general manager. And he comes in at top volume.

"What the actual fuck was that, Rusty?"

I stare at him, thinking silence is the safest response.

Marsh clears his throat. "Emotions are running high."

"The season hasn't even fucking started yet. I didn't realize you were so fucking soft that losing two games that don't have any fucking points attached to them would be such a fucking problem." Every f-bomb is a verbal exclamation mark on his diatribe.

And I don't fucking disagree with him. "I didn't start it."

Dorrian throws his hands up. "Oh! Well, then! The rest of your unprofessional bullshit is fine!" He spins around. "Why am I only yelling at one of you?"

Max strides in behind him, shrugging off Gusty and Connor. "We collided. It happens."

"You fucking tried to table top me, asshole."

"Why the fuck would I do that?"

Dorrian holds up his hands. "Shut the fuck up, Tiller. You too, Rusty. Get changed. Then my office." He looks at our teammates. "*Emotions are as high as our expectations for the season. Nobody likes starting flat footed. We're going to figure it out. That's the message, understood?* Even better if I don't read a word of this on Twitter, but that's probably already too fucking late."

And then he stalks out.

Nobody moves.

"For the record, I said the *emotions are high* line first," Marsh says dryly.

There are a few chuckles, but Max and I aren't laughing.

"You fucking overreact to everything," he mutters, glaring at me.

Goading me.

And I have fucking had it. "Is that how you justify it to yourself? You're telling yourself that the big guy overreacted to you slamming into me? You can't not lie, can you? Even to yourself."

"Shut the fuck up."

No, I won't be doing that. "You were already mad when you gunned it. You've been mad at me for weeks now, and you can't seem to keep that under wraps, so let's do this. Let's work out these feelings where *you're* the one who over-reacts to everything. What's wrong, Tiller?" He doesn't answer, and I pace closer.

"Come on, bud," Marsh says, trying to stop me.

I swat him away. I'll apologize for that later, but it's beyond time for Max and I to have it out once and for all.

"Cat got your tongue?" I shove Tilman in the chest and lower my voice to a growl. "Teammate got your wife?"

He swings first, just like he did on the ice.

But this time, nobody is between us. I swing last, and that's all that matters.

CHAPTER 41
SHANNON

I've just gotten back to the hotel with my new dress when I get a text message that makes my blood run cold.

> **RUSS**
>
> I fucked up. I'm so sorry.

No further explanation.

It's the kind of message that doesn't invite a clear response. I'm typing my third variation of *what did you do???* when texts start rolling in from Highlander WAGs. Asking if I need a drive to the arena, to the hospital.

What. The. Fuck?

I reply to the group chat, letting them know I'm in New York, and asking what happened.

Radio silence is the only response, for what feels like ten minutes but is probably thirty seconds. And then Kiley calls me.

"Hey, babe. Sorry about the drama. First of all, everyone is okay." She sounds calm. Too calm.

I squeeze my shaking fingers into a fist and try to breathe. "Then why was Ani asking about the hospital?"

"We might have overreacted a little."

"To what?"

"There was a brawl in the dressing room."

Russ's text message flashes through my mind. Oh no. *Russell, what did you do???*

"Okay. Is, um… Who is injured?"

"Who isn't?" She sighs. "Ty thought Max was going to the hospital, but apparently he's being treated by the team doctors at the arena. It's his jaw."

"Oh my God." My heart is in my throat. "And…everyone else?"

"Cuts and scrapes, I think." She pauses for a second. "It sounds like emotions were running high at practice today since they've lost the first two preseason games."

That's a line if I've ever heard one and I think we both know it. "Okay. I'll, um, reach out to Max."

On the other end of the line, Kiley is silent. But she doesn't say goodbye.

I wince as I realize what she must be thinking. And the worst part is, she's not wrong.

Before Ty, Kiley was cheated on repeatedly by her ex. Infidelity is a sore point for her—as it should be. It's a horrible feeling to be cheated on.

It's a horrible feeling to have your friend judge you for getting between teammates, too, though.

"If you talk to Rusty, too, let me know how he's doing?" she finally says.

"I—" *There's strength in honesty.* I swallow hard. "I will. But Kiley—"

"It's okay. I love you, babe. Whatever those two dummies were fighting over, that's between them."

"I owe you a long story sometime soon."

"Is it podcast worthy?" She retracts that almost immediately. "Forget I said that. Bad instincts. But if you want to share a bottle of wine when you get back, I'm all ears."

"Thank you. I love you, too."

But when I hang up, I can't stop thinking about her first instinct. A podcast about breaking up a hockey marriage is radically different from my original idea.

It's scarier.

More raw.

More dangerous in so many ways. I don't know where it would go. I can't imagine how to craft a story that is still unfolding.

I look at Russell's text message. *I fucked up.*

But here I am, sitting in another city, secretly arranging to meet up with someone from my past to benefit someone else who I want to shove into my past, when my heart is back in Hamilton, worried about Russ blaming himself for something that was probably inevitable. Between the two of us, I'm the one who is fucking up more.

I need to reply to him.

I should also check on Max.

Need. Should.

A kernel of a podcast idea comes to me. I don't know when I'm gonna be willing to share it with the world, but just in case it ever becomes something, I want to document this time in my life.

I sink down to the hotel room floor and turn on the voice recorder on my phone. "My marriage ended yesterday. I can't tell anyone because my friends are fellow wives and girl-friends of hockey players. That's the life that I have lived for the last eight years. Where he goes, I go. Where he plays, I build us a life. In his circles, I find friends, and we knit together into supportive, wonderful networks—but the second he's traded, I have to do it all over again. Today, I'm actually in the city where he used to play, and as I record this, I realize it didn't even occur to me to reach out to those WAGs I was once tight with here. But to explain what I'm going through right now would mean unpacking a lot of the lies I used to live."

That's hard to say. I let the recorder keep running, but I have to pause for a minute to compose myself. My voice grates a bit when I resume.

"One day, they might hear this and wonder why I didn't tell them what I was going through, and I honestly hope that they never understand, because I truly believe that the only person who can understand what I feel right now is an ex-WAG. And right now, I feel very alone, but I know that I'm not. I know that this life chews people up and spits them out."

I sigh, audibly, and I don't know if my phone picked that up, but if it did, I would love to have it worked into the opening credits of the *Ex-WAG Club.*

"There are lessons to be learned when you have invested *your* entire life in *someone else's* entire life. And those lessons probably aren't just for women who marry professional athletes, but also for anyone for whom marriage is a trap."

Another audible sigh. I fist my hand and push it into my temple. Fuck.

"I have so much to say, and right now I have nobody to say it to, but in the future, if you're hearing this, it's because I realized that there *were* people who I could say this to, and that's you. Thank you for making me feel a little less alone in this very lonely moment."

I stop recording and listen back to it. It's not much, but it's a start.

And then I think about the fact that Max hasn't texted me. Why do I feel like I should make sure he's okay, when the phone works in both directions?

Only one person reached out to apologize for what happened this morning. He's the only person I need to check on right now.

SHANNON

I heard there was a fight. Are you okay?

CHAPTER 42
RUSS

I go to shift the ice pack off my right hand so I can text Shannon back, but before I can, Dorrian's door swings open.

Stony-faced, he gestures for me to come inside without saying a word.

He's not alone, either. Coach is sitting in one of the two chairs in front of his desk. The assistant general manager in charge of contracts is in the other chair, leaving nowhere for me but to stand.

Which is fine, it hurts too fucking much if I bend at the waist.

Maybe if this meeting was as he first ordered it, ten minutes after the first altercation, it would have just been the two of us. But I escalated the situation pretty badly, and both Tilman and I had to go to medical. He's still there. More than an hour has passed since Dorrian yelled at me, and now I can see he's moved on to cold indifference.

The life of a journeyman player.

I'm not surprised at the first words out of his mouth. They could be worse, actually. "We're putting you on waivers. If you aren't claimed, you'll report to our AHL affil-iate in Niagara Falls tomorrow afternoon. To say that I am disappointed in your conduct today is an understatement. We had a debate about whether I should just put you on waivers for purposes of contract termination, Russ."

That would be the worst. And it had been on the table. Fuck.

I nod. "I'll report to Niagara Falls."

"If you aren't claimed," he repeats, his eyes narrowing.

"Yes, sir."

"You put your position on this team in significant peril."

"I regret that very much."

His mouth tightens. Silence stretches. Then he exhales. "Could I have the room, please?"

I glance at the door.

"You can stay." He clears his throat. "Coach, maybe you go and find out how long it will take for Tilman to get his ass up here?"

"Will do."

The AGM follows him out. Even after the door closes again, I stay standing.

"Do you want to sit?" Dorrian asks.

"I'd rather stand, sir."

"He get you in the kidneys?"

"Aye."

"You want to tell me what the fights were really about?"

"I do not."

"Why is that?"

"It's personal."

"That's a fucking shame. Because I expect you to be professional in my dressing room and on my fucking ice."

"It won't happen again."

"It sure as fuck won't." He takes a deep breath. "Have you met my wife, Armstrong?"

Billie Dorrian is often around the arena. "Yes."

"Do you know who her ex-husband is?"

I shake my head. "I do not, sir."

His eyebrows lift in surprise. "Well, you might wish you were sitting for this story. She was once married to Jasper Pike."

I do know who Pike is. He would have played in the league at the same time as Dorrian—a fearsome former defenceman who never hesitated to throw off his gloves.

"He found out just before the All-Star Game one year that Billie and I were having an affair. You should look up the fight on YouTube. It might look familiar."

I rock back on my heels.

He shakes his head. "You can't play on the same team as Tilman anymore. And I can't trade you. I tried to offer you to Calgary today for future considerations and they passed. So it's down to the minors for you. I hope she's worth it." He pauses a beat. "Billie was."

I don't bother explaining to him that it never got as far as an affair. It doesn't fucking matter.

Because the truth is, Shannon is worth it anyway.

CHAPTER 43
SHANNON

RUSS

I'm okay

Mostly sorry that this might get out and
affect you

SHANNON

I can handle that, I'm used to blocking
online chatter

I'm in New York for a few days (long story).
Can we have coffee when I get back?

RUSS

I want to hear all about it, but I won't be
here. I'm getting sent down to the Niagara
Falls AHL team.

SHANNON

What?

RUSS

It's okay. It was worth it.

CHAPTER 44
RUSS

I clear waivers the following afternoon. After getting the call from my agent, I hit the highway and head to the Niagara Falls barn to report to my new team.

CHAPTER 45
SHANNON

The playful knock at my suite door is a hit of déjà vu that makes me feel faint.

Taking one last look at myself in the mirror, I open the door to my past.

"Francois, please come in."

He looks shockingly the same. A few more grey hairs, but I think they're deliberately allowed to be there, and others have been dyed away. The same is probably true for the slight lines at the corners of his eyes. The best work in the world, allowing him to age on his own terms.

His brows tug together in confusion. "You aren't dressed for dinner."

I take a deep breath. "I can't go with you tonight. I'm so sorry for changing my mind, and reaching out to you in the first place. It was all a mistake."

He glances at my new glossy brown hair and makeup. "But you started to get ready, yes?"

"Yes."

He holds out his arms. "My beautiful girl, it has been a long time. But we are friends, no?"

"I like to think so." But I don't go in for the offered hug. "You look…great."

"I know." He moves past me into the suite and gestures at the couch. "May I?"

"Of course. Can I get you a drink?"

"What are you having?"

"New York's finest tap water."

He laughs. "Find me a glass of wine."

I bought a bottle yesterday, one of his favourites, when I thought this would go differently. I open it and decide to pour two glasses after all.

"So, what is going on, hmm? The last I heard, you were married to a very talented hockey player."

"And the last I heard, you were looking for very talented hockey players for your new league."

"Ah. I wondered." He takes a sip of wine. "Was it your idea or his? To reach out to me?"

"His."

"He knows you are hard to resist."

I wave at my jeans and flannel shirt. "I do my best."

"A fancy gown or a country hunting outfit, it makes no difference to me. It's all very nice draped over a chair in the corner."

I blush.

"Speaking of which, I bought a hunting lodge in Scotland."

At the unexpected mention of Russell's home country, I jolt. "Why?"

"Why not?"

And I suppose for billionaires, it is just that simple. Real estate is an investment. An apartment in New York, a lodge in Scotland, a compound in the Middle East. Wherever Francois does business, he needs a place to sleep.

And fuck.

"Maybe I'll visit you there someday," I say around the lump in my throat. "With a friend?"

"Not your husband?"

I shake my head. "Not my husband."

As we drink our wine, I tell him almost everything. I leave out the most intimate details between me and Russ. The conversation on the dock. How hard it was to say goodbye when we left the cottage. The bone-deep aching pain, knowing I was leaving with the wrong person.

But in broad strokes, I confess to my old friend how I fell in love with someone, maybe for the first time.

"I don't know what comes next."

"Does he want to play in the Ice League?"

I laugh at the suggestion. "Russ? I don't know. Probably not. He wouldn't want me to ask you, anyway."

"But your husband not only wanted you to ask me, he blackmailed you into doing so." He shrugs. "Ma chérie, the choice could not be more clear."

"I really don't want to be married to him for another year."

He glances at his watch. "Then I suggest you remove yourself to the bedroom and change into something appropriate so I can introduce you to some powerful people in the American Foreign Service. I've heard they can be helpful at times."

"Helpful to billionaires, yes. Small-town girls from Michigan who want a divorce, not so much."

"Du pareil au même." He smiles. "It's all the same when you're on my arm."

———

Francois doesn't come straight out and ask anyone if they can help me get a divorce. It's much more subtle than that. He makes sure they know my name. He makes sure they know I'm an old friend. And he gets their assurance that if I run into any difficulties as an ex-pat living in Canada on a spousal visa, I can use their name with the consulate.

"The Foreign Service can grease a lot of wheels, right?" He says it over and over again, and each time I want to cry, because I was willing to spread my legs to get this man to help Max, when really I should have known that he would have helped *me* for absolutely nothing.

Kiley's point about friendship not being contingent on anything rings through my mind.

Francois is also delighted that I know Livy already, and insists I must come to France with her at some point soon.

"I won't be able to afford that soon," I point out. And I hold up my hands. "Which is how it's just going to have to be. It's time for me to learn how to be self-sufficient."

"I can't offer you a job as my muse emeritus?"

I tip my head back and laugh.

When I look at him again, still smiling, there's a spark of heat in his eyes. But it's restrained, as if he understands that there's no corresponding fire burning in my belly to take him back to The Lyle tonight.

He brushes a loose strand of hair off my cheek. "When are you flying home?"

"The day after tomorrow. I'm going to take a day to do

all of my favourite things in the city. And then I'm going to go home and find a cozy little one-bedroom apartment to move into."

He looks visibly pained at the thought of a cozy anything. "Sounds…"

"Provincial?" I fill in lightly.

"Not the word I was reaching for," he murmurs.

And I laugh again. It's a deep belly laugh, and it feels good.

Shannon Barker is back, and better than ever.

After dinner, he asks me to dance. I join him for one song, and it's very nice. But as his hand strokes my bare spine, I realize there is somewhere else I need to be.

"Would you mind if I duck out early?"

"Not at all. Do you want to use my car?"

We're down in the Bowery, not far from the East Village, but my hotel is all the way up on the Upper East Side. I wouldn't be the first girl to get on the subway in a fancy dress, though. And besides, I'm not ready to go back to the hotel just yet. "Thank you, but no. I need to find Livy."

The incoming ambassador's daughter is just across the dance floor. When I catch her eye, she twirls right over.

"Are you having fun?" she asks breathlessly.

"I had fun. Now I want to get out of here. Can you recommend any tattoo places that might do a walk-in tonight?"

CHAPTER 46
RUSS

"Hi," Shannon says softly in my ear. "I wasn't sure if you'd still be up."

"It's okay, I couldn't sleep." I walk down the budget hotel corridor, looking for a window ledge or something to sit on while we chat, because my roommate is snoring.

"How's it going?"

"Spent eight hours on a bus today for an exhibition game."

"Oh no."

"Aye." I laugh until it turns into a sigh. "It's okay. I told you it was worth it and I meant it. How are you?"

"Oh, you know. A mess of weird feelings."

"Are you still in New York?"

"Yeah. I'm heading home tomorrow. Will you be around later in the week? I can drive down to Niagara Falls. Maybe we could get coffee or something?"

I lean against the wall and close my eyes. Fuck, I want that so much.

When I don't answer, she makes this soft little wounded

sound that makes me want to rip my heart out of my chest. "Or not."

"Not this week." I rub my sternum. "I want to get back to Hamilton as soon as possible, okay? That's my goal. But to do that, I need to be on my best behaviour and the personal stuff needs to stay private."

I feel like absolute shit saying that.

"I understand."

"It won't be forever."

"Just until I'm divorced." Her voice is so small.

"Aye. Or a miracle happens and Max leaves the Highlanders for the Ice League. I wouldn't even care if he got the blockbuster contract of his fantasies if—"

"He won't." Her voice has shifted to sounding painfully resigned.

"What—"

"I'm in New York for a reason. And, um… I couldn't do it."

The pit of my stomach falls way. "You went to see Dumas?"

"Don't judge me, Russell."

"You went to get Max a deal?" My voice is raising, and I know that's not what she wants to hear right now, but it's hard to think of her doing that for him while I'm sharing a hotel room with a call-up from the ECHL. I grip the phone tighter and drag my voice back to a quiet note. "Shannon, what the fuck?"

"He promised me a quickie divorce, Russ. I thought I could do it for that. To be free." Her voice cracks. "And I couldn't. So he's not getting a sweetheart deal. And we're not getting a quickie divorce. None of the pie-in-the-sky easy fixes are coming our way, so please don't yell at me for something I didn't actually do."

She hangs up and I kick the wall behind me.

Fuck.

RUSS

I'm sorry. All of that came out wrong. I understand how stressful this is for you. We'll get through this.

SHANNON

It would be easier to talk in person

RUSS

Soon

SHANNON

I know

RUSS

I miss you

She doesn't reply to that, and I don't sleep more than a wink that whole night. But in the morning, my scratchy eyes see another text from her, sent first thing.

SHANNON

Good luck today. I've heard the Hershey team is terrible, right?

I laugh.

RUSS

Sort of the opposite.

SHANNON

No, no, I heard from a high quality source that you're the favourites to win tonight

We aren't. But we win anyway, and when we pile on the bus to drive back to Niagara Falls—no second night in a hotel room for us—there's another text waiting.

SHANNON

I told you

RUSS

We'll celebrate together real soon

———

Another week goes by. We play another exhibition pre-season game, and win it as well.

Meanwhile, the Hamilton Highlanders lose all of their remaining pre-season games.

And then the day before the NHL season opener, Max Tilman is traded to Calgary in a blockbuster deal that shocks the NHL.

"Did you see this?" One of my AHL teammates shoves his phone in front of my face, showing a screenshot of three hockey insiders tweeting the news.

FreidTheMan:
The deal is done. To Calgary: Max Tilman. To Hamilton: Alexei Artyomov, Joey Slough, and a second-round draft pick for next year. Worth noting that Tilman has a fractured jaw and is expected to be out for another six weeks. Calgary must have wanted him if they were willing to trade for him while injured.

ShaynaWritesHockey:
It sounds like Hamilton is retaining half of Tilman's

salary for the remainder of this year as well. He'll be a UFA at the end of this season and is widely rumoured to be interested in an Ice League contract, but no offer has been extended to him yet.

AaronGreen:
Hamilton is expected to assign Slough to Niagara Falls. They have the cap space to keep Artyomov on as a goalie, so expect him to be the third and maybe challenge for starts. He's been a strong backup for Calgary but they have depth in their prospects. My sources say the team will also recall Russ Armstrong, who passed through waivers in training camp, from Niagara.

I read it twice.
And then I start laughing.

CHAPTER 47
SHANNON

The first thing I did when I got back to Hamilton was pre-pay for a week in a motel room, on Max's credit card.

The second thing I did was tell Max the deal was off. We'd have to do this divorce the standard Canadian way, with a year of separation.

I need the time to be sure of who I am, anyway. I can't rush to be single, only to throw myself into the arms of another man, even if those arms are steadier and stronger than any I've known before.

In those days in the motel, I record a dozen audio clips of myself processing the breakdown of my marriage. They start to sound all the same, but it's good to get it out.

I start therapy, which is hard and awkward.

And I take myself off of Max's Instagram after unfollowing my account from his. I'll let him manage that himself.

If he notices, he doesn't say anything. We don't talk at all, and it's so peaceful I don't even care that I'm sleeping on the world's worst mattress and a lumpy, thin little pillow.

So when the trade announcement happens, it's news that

I hear not on social media, or from my estranged husband, but from my lawyer.

LAUREN

> Just heard Max has been traded to Calgary.
> I want to file an injunction that allows you to
> live in the Hamilton house for the duration
> of your separation. Can you call me?

I blink at my phone.

Yeah, I can call her. First, I go to the team's Twitter account. Sure enough, there's a trade announcement.

I read it twice, then dial Lauren's number.

"I'm in the Vancouver airport, in case it's loud," she says. "I'll be in Toronto in six hours. Can we meet tomorrow before the game? I can arrange to work with a local Hamilton attorney on this, and we can meet in their offices."

"It's happening." I sound shocked. I am shocked.

"Yep. I'm still waiting for my New York associate to get the marriage records I will need from NYC, but we can begin to establish a formal date of separation and push Max to hire his own attorney."

"I was just in New York," I say with a sigh. "I didn't know you needed those records. Maybe I could have picked them up myself."

"It's all right. This process takes a while, so we're not in a rush. My first priority right now is getting you a separation agreement that protects your right to live in that house without him."

I lurk on Max's social media until I see him post a photo at the airport, saying he's heading to Calgary and looking forward to playing in their season opener.

Then I turn my phone off, check out of the motel, and drive home.

The last time I stood in my kitchen, Max taunted me that I should remove myself from the WAG chat. Now I realize I need to do that, but for a completely different reason—not because I was kicked off for being dumped, but because I'm no longer a Highlander WAG.

And I won't be added to the Calgary group chat, either.

In a daze, I climb the stairs to my bedroom.

I appreciate Lauren's swift reaction to the news and her energy in defending my right to this house, but this no longer feels like my home.

I run myself a bath. I am going to miss this tub so much.

While it's filling, I unpack from New York and dig out my biggest suitcase. With the two suitcases open on my bed, I fill them with all my most comfortable clothes. Workout gear, PJs, cozy socks, and sweaters.

Then I have a bath. I sink under the surface over and over again, letting the heat surround me.

After, I turn my phone back on. Messages flood in. I don't read them all. I can't, not right now.

I dry my hair, but skip makeup.

And then I head out the door, because I desperately need to be somewhere that isn't here.

CHAPTER 48
RUSS

I've only been home from Niagara Falls for half an hour when there's a knock on the door.

I assume it's someone who lives in the building, but when I answer it, who I find is even better than a neighbour.

"Hi," Shannon says nervously. "I went home and then it didn't feel like home. And I didn't know where else to go."

My knees almost buckle at the sight of her. "Come here."

She folds into my chest, letting me hug her tightly. Her hair—which she's done something fancy to again, made it darker—smells so good. I never want to let her go.

"I got your text," she mumbles into my chest. "I'm glad you're back."

"Me too, beautiful. And I'm glad you're not on a plane to Calgary right now."

She laughs. And then it turns to tears.

"Okay," I murmur. "Let's…"

I step back and let her in. "I left in a hurry and just got back, so it's a bit of a mess."

I'm self-conscious as I invite her into my space for the first time.

"It's nice." She only glances around briefly, and then looks at me again with watery eyes. "It's been a long week. For both of us."

"Let's talk about it, then." I lead her to my couch.

I sit first, and she curls up right next to me. I ghost my fingertips over her shoulder and up to her silky brown waves. It feels so good to have her within touching range and mine to talk to as much as we want. "You changed your hair."

"Do you like it?"

"I always like your hair. But yes. I like it. It seems more...you."

Relief flickers across her face.

I keep touching her. I need to, maybe to convince myself she's real. "I can't believe you're here."

She smiles shyly. "Kiley gave me the door code."

"Does she know you used it today?"

"Not yet. I'll probably tell her soon." She takes a deep breath. "I know we have a lot to talk about, but I need to clear something up first."

"What's that?"

"You said you wouldn't kiss another man's wife."

"I—"

"The thing is that legally, I'm going to be married for another year. And I don't want to wait a year to kiss you. So I was hoping I could convince you to carve out an exception for me."

"An exception?"

"Based on circumstances."

"And what circumstances are those?"

"I'm in love with you."

I'm focused so closely on her, on her face and her voice and the warmth of her body next to mine, that I hear the words before I *feel* the words.

And then I'm hauling her into my arms, one hand behind her neck, the other on her hip.

I kiss her hungrily, tasting her mouth for the first time, and she's sweeter than my dreams ever imagined. I devour her, so hungry, and she kisses me back. That is, hands down, the best part.

She pants into my mouth as she wraps her arms around my neck and licks back against my tongue.

"I love you, too," I say between kisses. "Everything I said before was just self-preservation. You can have all the kisses you want."

"I want a lot of them," she whispers.

"You can kiss me as much as you fucking want."

She laughs. "I want to kiss you so fucking much."

I growl happily and cup her arse with my hands, knowing she can feel my erection against her core as she straddles me. "Swear more. Be dirty."

"I want to kiss you everywhere," she says breathlessly. "I want to kiss your fucking cock."

I groan and tip my head back, throat working.

"Please, Russell." Her voice goes soft and she slides off my lap, kneeling in front of me. "Let me make you feel good."

I manage to hold on to one final brain cell and I reach down to stop her hands as she goes to my bulge. "Sweetheart, just... If you let me have you, I'm never letting you go."

She gives me a brilliant, glittering smile I've never seen from her before. Shannon has smiled a thousand smiles over the last year that I've known her. And none of them have looked half this real. "Never let me go," she says. "Please."

And then she frees my cock.

Her fingers wrapped around my erection is the best thing I've ever felt. That's immediately replaced by the sweetness of her lips pressed against my flared crown in a gentle kiss. And then *that's* topped by a lick around the tip, teasing where my straining cock has pulled away from my foreskin.

Every step of this blow job is going to destroy me in the most incredible ways.

"What do you like?" Her voice is silky and her gaze is seductive as she strokes me slowly.

"Yes. Anything. Your mouth. I love your mouth already."

She laughs and takes me between her lips properly.

Holy fuck.

I've never felt warmth like this. It's more than just a sweet mouth, it's the whole moment. It's the zero-to-sixty energy that doesn't feel wrong, at all. It's a heat that isn't just inside her, but swirling between us. A heat that demands action.

My hips pulse and she moans around me.

"Aye?" I'm breathing hard now. "You like that? Fuck, beautiful, tell me I can push my cock into your mouth."

She nods around me, and I sink my hands into her hair, gently holding her head as I start to thrust. She's so soft and pliable, such a giving girl, it doesn't take me long to climb to a quick, powerful release.

"You want to pull off? I'm close. Oh, fuck, Shannon, I'm coming. God damn it."

She pushes deeper, taking my cock all the way to her

throat just in time for the first spurt to pulse straight to her belly.

"That's so good, sweetheart. Fuck." I snap my hips up, fucking her mouth again, riding the vision-darkening orgasm instinctively.

She holds me in her mouth until I stop throbbing, and then she licks up the last drops of my seed as she lets my cock go.

I drag her back into my lap. "That's so sexy," I say, my words slurred, my head spinning. Then I slant my mouth over hers and taste myself on her tongue.

"I might need to retire from hockey tomorrow," I mumble.

She laughs. "Why?"

"I'm afraid I might not be able to let you out of my arms for even a second." I press my forehead against hers. "I've missed you, Shannon. I know that's a weird thing to say because you weren't mine, but—"

"I've missed you, too. I think on some level I was yours. I should have been yours." She kisses me softly. "I taste like you."

"You taste incredible." I exhale happily. "My orgasms have been so fucking lonely. This was the opposite of that. I can't believe you're here. I can't believe you're mine."

She touches her fingers to her own lips. "I'm glad I got a chance to do that. It felt like I owed you that to close a loop. I've felt bad since that night that you didn't get a chance to come with me."

I glide my thumb along her lower lip, swollen from her efforts and the way I lost control at the end. "We don't need to keep score. I'm going to give you so many orgasms."

A little cloud passes through her gaze, and she presses her hand to my chest. "It's not always easy for me. I don't… orgasms aren't always the goal, you know?"

"Okay. That's okay." I catch her wrist and lift her hand so I can nip at her fingertips. "But you got there with my mouth, right? That works?"

"That might have been helped by the danger of the situation."

That's fucking hot. "You think?"

"I don't know." She relaxes against my chest, tucking her face into my neck.

"We'll figure it out together." I rub her back. "Can I tell you something?"

"Anything."

"The memory of you moaning to being called a slut haunts me in the best way. It feels like I haven't slept a full night since. I wake up in the middle of the night, desperate to get my hands on a ghost. To pin you down and make you moan like that again."

Her breathing changes. She inhales shakily, then holds it before slowly letting it out. "Really?"

"I'll never lie to you."

She slowly lifts her head.

"I'm not a good girl," she says softly. Her gaze is steady, but part of it is far away. "Never have been. Not really. I made a choice to be more like that when I married Max, and I came to regret it, because it's not really me. Deep down, I'm afraid that I'm the dirty slut Max sees me as."

Frustration burns inside me as I hear her voice hitch. "The way I see it, there's no conflict between being a dirty slut and being a good girl. What if I want you to be that dirty girl for me? Be *my* slut? If you can do that for me, then that's a very good girl indeed."

Tears fill her eyes again.

I tangle our fingers together. "I want to know the real you."

"Do you?"

"Yes. And anyone worthy of you would say the same thing."

"Nobody ever has."

"That's their loss. But I love you. And I want you, exactly as you are. Slutty, horny, funny, smart, soft." I wipe away the tears that have slipped out of her shimmering eyes. "If we're sharing secrets, then you should know Emery and I were never like that, ye ken?"

Her eyes flare at the thickening of my usually mild Scottish accent. "Never?"

I shake my head. "It was part of a silly plan. I was supposed to get over you."

"How'd that work out?"

"Turns out, it's impossible."

"And Emery was that rebound plan?"

I laugh. "Oh God, looking back that was fucking dafty. The cottage was the first step in that plan, and then Max invited everyone and Emery was an emergency stop gap. There was never anything between us." I trace the curve of Shannon's breast. "She wanted to play matchmaker so badly."

"I did think it was odd how she underlined that she wasn't jealous. She even made it sound like you had an open relationship."

"That's funny. I, on the other hand, am a deeply territorial man who does not want to share what's mine."

"What's yours?"

"Or in this case, who is mine."

"And who is yours?"

"You are. You're mine. My beautiful woman." I roll her onto back and crawl on top of her. "My slut, too."

CHAPTER 49
SHANNON

I can't believe how easily he says it, but it doesn't sound cruel at all. It sounds like the sweetest endearment.

Of course it does, because Russ is the sweetest guy in the world.

I smile up at him. "You don't have to call me that if it isn't your thing. I will love whatever we do in bed, I promise."

He grins down at me. "What does that mean?"

I bite my lip.

Russ climbs off me and tucks his cock away, then offers me his hand. "Are you hungry? Thirsty? Can I make you some tea?"

"Tea?"

"My Nan always said a tassie makes everything better."

"Well, then. Tea. Yes, please."

He leads me into his kitchen and fills an electric kettle. Then he gets out two oversized mugs. "What kind of tea? I've got regular Scottish breakfast, green tea that isn't really my thing but I tried it for a while, and a couple of herbal blends. This ginger peach one is nice."

"What are you having?"

"Proper Scottish breakfast."

"I'll have that, too."

He pops a tea bag in each mug, then backs me up against the counter and braces his arms next to my hips. "Now, where were we? You were trying to steer me away from calling you a slut. Did I not do it right?"

I tip my head back and laugh.

He kisses my throat, his beard lighting up my nerve endings. "Should I be meaner?"

I shiver. "Maybe."

"I can do that. Maybe not right in this moment when I'm filled with joy, but give me a hot second and I'll figure it out. I'm a quick study."

He works his hands under my shirt. More electric sparks sizzle along my skin at his touch.

"I just want you, first." I don't know why this is so hard. Once upon a time, I had no problem talking about sex. Likes, dislikes. Green lights and hard limits.

But with those men, it was purely transactional.

With Russ, my entire future is on the line. I love him, and that makes this scary.

"Okay. We'll go slow, but I want to get to all the dirty raunchy stuff my woman likes."

I whimper. "Call me that more. That does it for me in a big way."

"My woman." He kisses me right below my ear. "Can I take your shirt off? I want to see your tits."

"Mmhmm." I lift my arms for him and he bares my torso. His mouth finds mine and we kiss again, slow and deep this time. I lose myself in it, letting him consume me, that I forget about—

His hands stop their slide up my back when they reach the curling piece of second skin that's plastered over the tattoo.

"What's that?"

"Actually, you could, um, take that off for me?"

I turn around, and hold my breath.

He traces over the bandage first, his fingertip so gentle. "My turn."

"Do you remember?"

His finger reaches the tiny crown at the top of the scrawled words. "Oh, I remember, my queen."

He turns me around, his hands on my hips.

"My *queen*," he growls, crushing his mouth to mine.

As we kiss, fire mounting, he unzips my jeans and shoves them down my hips.

The kettle finishes boiling and he doesn't stop touching me.

"About sex…" I manage to pant. "Some of the things I like are…"

He unsnaps my bra. "Shameful?"

"Yes."

"Says who?" He groans happily as he fills his hands with my tits. "If it feels good, it feels good. Simple as that."

"Nothing about sex has ever been simple for me."

"Then we should see if we can change that." He leans in and sucks at one of my nipples, his gaze on my face the whole time.

My eyelids flutter half-shut, hooding my gaze as the sensation of being this seen in my desires overwhelms me.

He rakes that nipple through his teeth, then repeats the attention on the other side.

And then he kneels in front of me.

"My queen," he murmurs, lifting one leg and kissing my kneecap before he hooks that thigh over his shoulder.

Then he tugs my panties to the side and presses a deep, pulling kiss right to my core. His tongue flicks up to my clit, over and over again, until I'm rocking against his face, getting his beard wet.

His tongue feels so good, but it's not what I want inside me right now.

"Russ," I beg. "*Russell.*"

He immediately looks up.

"Can you be inside me?"

He leaps to his feet and kisses me.

"You taste like me," I whisper, echoing earlier. "You taste good."

"I sure fucking do." He's breathing hard. "Stay here. Don't move. I'll get a condom. Or wait. We should go to my bed, right? I don't think it's made. Please don't stop loving me over that."

I laugh and throw my arms around him. "Here is fine. An unmade bed sounds amazing, too." And I take a deep breath. "You don't need the condom, though. Unless you want it. I have an IUD."

"But Tiller—"

I press my fingers to Russ's lips. "Is a paranoid asshole who cheats a lot. He didn't want kids, and I don't think he trusted my IUD, either." I wrinkle my nose. "Let that be the last time we talk about him while we're mostly naked."

He pulls off his own shirt. "I'm not naked enough."

Then he scoops me in his arms.

I wrap my legs around his waist and he carries me to a very nice bedroom that really isn't that messy at all.

And the unmade bed is seriously inviting.

He lays me down and I watch as he strips. All those freckled muscles are mine now. All that lovely golden red hair leading down to that incredible cock, thick and proud… mine.

The same hungry, possessive feelings racing through me are reflected in Russ's expression as he crawls on top of me and peels off my panties.

He inhales lustily as he caresses me, moving me beneath him to open up. "I don't deserve how fucking hot you are."

"Stole the words from my mouth," I say.

"How about, I'm never letting you go?"

"Never ever," I promise.

He pauses with his cock just at my entrance and looks down at me. "I've got no expectations of you, all right? If you come like this, that's amazing. If you can't, we'll try something else. I just want to be inside you."

"I need it, too." I pull him down on top of me and he rolls his hips, sliding his cock home in a breathtaking thrust.

I gasp, crying out, and he cradles me in his arms. I'm perfectly full. He's buried in me, all the way to the root, and everywhere he can be touching me, he is.

When he starts moving, it's like an earthquake, heavy and profound, and I know this man is going to fundamentally reshape me body and soul.

He already has.

He cups my face, holding my gaze. "Tell me you're with me, Shannon."

"I'm with you." Three words have never meant so much. They're as much a promise as *I love you.*

This big, mighty giant looks down at me with so much vulnerability it makes my heart hurt. It's as if he needs to know it's him I want. So I give him the eye contact, and I say his name over and over again.

Russell, Russell, Russell.

As my body melts around his, getting warmer and slicker and softer, the vulnerability in his gaze brightens into quiet confidence. "That's my girl. You're taking me so well."

The praise steals my breath, and he notices. That confidence grows.

"I love you like this," he murmurs as he moves inside me. "Beneath me. Taking my cock bare. Nothing between us."

I shiver at the reminder of how intimate this is, even for our first time.

His eyes spark at that reaction, too.

I've never been so aware of every moment of a first time like this. It's like everything is heightened and special, lodging itself in a different part of my memory. The forever part.

His voice goes rough. "I love you on your knees for me, too."

I nod, my mouth watering at the reminder.

His thumb traces the corner of my lips. "Open for me. Show me where I'm going to be coming for the rest of my life."

The unexpected dirty talk makes me moan.

"There's my slut," he growls. Low and resonant. Animalistic.

And that's… oh my God. That's perfect.

"Yes," I moan.

"Wider," he demands. I arch my back as he fucks into me faster now, my mouth pulling open.

I wish he could fuck me and I could suck him at the same time. Filled by Russ from all directions.

He pulls my face back to look at him, his attention on my wide open mouth now. His pupils dilate.

"Whose mouth is this?"

"Yours," I pant before opening wide again.

"Good girl." His nostrils flare, and then he spits onto my tongue. "Swallow it."

I gulp, desperate for him now. Every small part of him.

He wraps my hair in his hand and tugs my head to the side.

"I love you," he whispers against my ear. His hips snap, his thrusts slowing but getting harder.

My head goes fuzzy.

"I'll love you forever, my dirty girl." And he thrusts again, shoving me into a release I didn't see coming.

I sob through it, clutching at him, and he follows, filling me up.

He stays inside me until all the aftershocks have rippled through to my extremities, and then he curls me up in his arms and covers us both with a blanket.

"You're beautiful," he says, kissing my temple.

And for the first time in forever, I believe it.

CHAPTER 50
RUSS

"We never made tea."

The sweetly drowsy note in Shannon's voice is headier than a come-from-behind victory on the ice. I did that to her. I found a way to give her what she needs.

Now that I know what her purest, happiest smile looks like, I'm never going to put our relationship on pause, ever again.

I can't believe I asked her to wait indefinitely for hockey reasons.

Fuck that.

I love my job, but on the orders of magnitude of love that I feel, it's a fraction of what I feel for Shannon.

I can love her *and* give my all to my fractured team at the same time. I mean, I have to.

But first things first—my woman needs a proper cup of tea.

"It won't take long to boil the kettle again."

"I mean…it took long enough we got distracted," she says with a giggle.

"This wouldn't happen in Scotland," I mutter.

She laughs harder. "Why not?"

"We have proper electricity and water boils quickly."

"What?"

"Scotland, and the rest of the world, has 220-240 volt power. North America has 120 volts."

She watches as I swing my legs out of bed and search for my underwear. "You're kidding."

"Why, in this moment of absolute perfection, would I joke about electricity voltage?" My breath catches in my chest as she pushes the blanket off and stands as well.

It's not like I didn't already know what her body looked like. There are a lot of photos of her on the internet, and she spent days in a bikini at my cottage a month ago. And then there were the too-brief moments of closer intimacy.

But this is different.

This is my first chance to just look at her without feeling like a fucking pervert about it.

"Do you have a shirt I can wear? I have your jersey but it's in the car, and—"

"No shirt needed. No underwear either. You're perfect exactly like this. I'd keep you naked all the time if I could. Look at you. *Look at you*. Would you like me to turn up the temperature?"

She laughs, making her round, full breasts jiggle, and my brain flatlines.

"I'm not kidding," I rasp. "You're beautiful."

She presses her lips together, a gorgeous pink blooming across her chest and up her neck.

"Why are you blushing?"

"Because the way you're looking at me is…" She shifts, and there's more jiggling. "Very intimate. And I like it."

My cock throbs. I haven't even started the kettle yet and our second attempt at a cup of tea seems doomed.

I circle around her, trailing my fingers up her long, elegant arms, then over the tattoo on her back. I want to ask her for so much already, but the black ink is a reminder that she's reconsidering everything in her life, not just who she lets inside her body. Who she might call her lover, her boyfriend, her husband. I press a kiss to her other shoulder, then step back and look my fill of her again.

"This is just the start of us, beautiful. And I want us to start right."

She rolls her shoulders back, lifting her tits. Her nipples are this perfect shade between pink and brown, plump little berries that tighten into eraser tips as I stare at them. "What does *right* mean? Honest?"

"Honest. Real. Raw. Fearless."

She nods. "Can I ask what might sound like a strange question?"

"Yes. Always yes. We have a lot to learn about each other. We might as well start with the weird stuff."

"What would you do if someone sent you naked pictures of your girlfriend?"

"Like revenge porn? I'd fuck 'em up."

"Not like revenge porn." She takes another a deep breath. "Published photos. Like…if you dated a Playboy Bunny, for example."

Ah. I see where she's going with this. My chest burns at the thought that she thinks this is weird or bad, but I'll humour her hypothetical framework for now. "Photos that she posed for willingly?"

"Yes."

"How does she feel about the pictures? Hypothetically."

"She wouldn't like them upsetting you."

"They wouldn't upset me."

"No, but really."

"Really." I hold out my hand. "Come with me."

"No shirt?"

I smile. "No shirt. No underwear, either. Come be my naked woman so I can ogle you as I try to make tea before falling on your naked form."

She laughs. "That sounds vaguely competitive."

"Professional competitor here. Hard to not gamify life." I squeeze her fingers as I lead her into my living room.

There's a stack of magazines on my coffee table. I dig through to the middle for a men's magazine with a woman on the cover. "Are we talking photos like this?"

She shrugs. "Fewer clothes than that."

I flip to an ad in the middle. "Like this? Hypothetically, I'm dating this smokeshow?"

A little flare of possessive jealousy lights up her gaze and makes her stand a little taller. Good. That's my girl. But I think this photo is exactly the type she's talking about. A lot of flesh on display, but the most private bits are disguised.

After a long beat of hesitation, she nods. "Yes, like that." And then she closes the magazine and gestures at herself. "Like this, but with hands..." She takes my hands and covers her chest. "Here." She drags one hand down her belly to cover her naked mound. "And here."

"Who is going to show me these photos of you?"

She licks her lips, her gaze guarded but unwavering. "People online. They'll tag you in them."

"When you posed for those photos, was it a good gig? Were you exploited in any way?"

"It was a big ad campaign. I was thrilled to be hired for it."

"All right. Then I'd be irritated at the troll behaviour and I'd block them. They don't get my time and energy. And ideally, I'd be able to block them from your accounts, too, so you never know they tried to be an asshole about something that's no big deal."

She stares at me.

"Is that not the right answer? I mean, that's my honest answer. But if you'd prefer that I handle it differently. I will. Your history, your body, your choice."

"Oh, Russell." She throws her arms around my neck and squeezes. "I've been such a fool. Yes, that's the right answer."

She's already told me that I can't talk about Tiller while we're naked or nearly naked, which I think is fucking smart, so I'm not going to ask her right now how he dealt with it. I can probably guess that he made her feel ashamed about her past, and that's going to be something that we untangle for a while.

Especially for someone who, when everything is just right, likes to have that shame button pushed. Having your person, your spouse, your supposed lover pushing that same button without consent? That would be the worst kind of mind fuck.

I wish I'd done more than just fracture his jaw.

I cup her arse and lift her against me. She reacts immediately, hungry and sweet. My dream come true. The woman I craved from afar, but so much better, because she's in my arms now.

"What about the tea?" she whispers as I shove my underwear off.

"Third time's the charm. We'll have it soon."

I bend my knees enough to line us up, then I push up and into her, fucking her standing up. It's a little awkward at first, more clinging and kissing than actual fucking. But it's real and raw. Intimate.

I fucking love that word now.

I will bare my soul for this woman. Give her all the intimacy she needs.

She pulls herself up me like she's climbing a tree, sinking down on my cock with each pause. Up, up, up. Until she's just bouncing on my tip and kissing me, making love to me with her tongue and her breath and the sweet, sweet kiss of her pussy on the crown of my cock.

"What do you need to come like this?" My voice sounds fucking strained already, that's how unbelievable this feels.

"Mmm..." She shakes her head, her voice breathy and shaky too. "I just want you to fill me up. I want to make you come."

Fuck.

I let her take me there without trying to make it about her first. It's going to be about her next, and forever. No pressure.

Just love.

CHAPTER 51
SHANNON

As Russ shouts and groans his way through a climax I milked from him with shocking ease, I think… this must be what it feels like to cling to an oak tree in an earthquake.

I feel like a goddess, that he let me do that to him. Rolling my hips, his tip just barely inside me, as he holds me up—wild.

Perfect.

He takes a swaying step back.

"Are you going to drop me?"

He laughs. Ragged, but still a laugh. "No."

"Because you just made a big mess in me, and we might have to coordinate how, um, we get out of this situation."

He sucks in a shocked breath, then laughs again. "Jesus. Okay." He turns, cock still wedged in my pussy, and carries me back to his bedroom and the attached bathroom.

Carefully, he sets me on the vanity and then he sags against me.

I stroke his big, beautiful shoulders. "You *are* a good boy, Russell."

He growls.

"Shhh…" I whisper, laughing with him now. "Good boys don't growl."

He roars and lifts his head, kissing me with such fierceness that it takes my breath away.

"This one does." His eyes glitter at me as he sinks to his knees and pushes my thighs open in one fluid motion.

"Russ…" My cheeks flame.

"You're beautiful when you blush." He kisses the inside of my knee. "Lemme see the mess I made."

I close my eyes and tip my head back, leaning against the mirror.

His beard brushes against my inner thigh.

His hands press my legs wider.

Heat coils low in my belly, and then I feel my clit pulse.

He doesn't say anything.

Silence stretches, and I squirm, my thighs wanting to pull together.

"Shhh. Be good for me."

"You're just looking."

"I know. It's amazing."

I whimper and my clit throbs again. I can feel his gaze, even though my eyes are squeezed shut. His hot inspection, and the humiliating slide of his seed out of my greedy cunt.

And I freeze.

"Shannon."

I feel him moving, standing, leaning into me, and I still don't open my eyes.

His arms scoop around me, the tightest of hugs. Just… breathing with me. Big chest, big shoulders, big body. Inhaling. Exhaling.

"I've got you," he murmurs.

I nod tightly.

"Did I lose you there?"

No. I shake my head.

He kisses the side of my head.

More breathing.

Then an exhale that catches on, and drags my own breath out of me in a deeper, slower way.

"That's it," he says. "That's it."

When I relax, he lets go of me long enough to start the shower.

I shift my hips forward and slide off the vanity as he returns.

His gaze is cautious, but not judging.

"One of the many weird things you'll need to learn about me," I say softly, trying to brush it off.

He follows me into the steam. "Get to learn, you mean."

The water feels good, sharp and hot. I reach for him, wanting another hug, and he gives it to me so readily I want to cry.

I glance at the shower head. It's detachable.

"At your cottage," I whisper, my confession almost muted by the spray of water. "I got myself off in the shower more than once. With the shower head."

He stares down at me, water droplets clinging to his beard and hair.

Then he takes the shower head down and holds it out, the spray arcing wildly between us. "Show me."

I catch his wrist and pull his hand lower. "Can you do it? I want you to…"

"Yeah, baby. Come here." He turns me around, spreading his legs wide to come down closer to my height. He cradles me, my back against his front, as he brings the water to between my legs.

"What did you think about when you were in my shower? When you rocked this sweet pussy against my shower head and got yourself off in secret?"

Heat rolls through me at the memory. "I tried not to think about you."

He rumbles a happy sound from behind me. "Tried and failed, I hope."

"Eventually. At first, it was generic dirty talk. That's where my brain goes." My pulse is pounding so fast. I've never told anyone this, but nobody has ever made my pleasure the point, either. "That's where it went now, and with you looking at me, I just froze."

"Think about that again now. Think those filthy words."

Greedy cunt.

Dirty girl, spread wide for inspection. Seed spilling out of me...

Humiliating perusal.

Clit moving right in front of his face, betraying my true nature.

The water licks relentlessly at my clit as the words play on a loop in my brain.

Arousal takes over, clouding out all other thoughts.

Shame rolls through me at how quickly I got on my knees and took his cock in my mouth.

How desperately I took his spit without flinching.

My pussy clenches around nothing, and then I'm crashing into a climax.

Russ lets the shower head tumble to the floor as he holds me and murmurs nice things. I twist around, burying myself in his warm, wet chest.

His care promises that one day soon, I'll be able to say more of that out loud.

————

"This might be the most perfect moment in my entire life."

Russ smiles, his eyes closed. "Same."

I'm curled up in the corner of his L-shaped couch, wearing this incredible oversized terry robe of his that I could get lost in, and he finally did make me tea.

It's delicious.

He's sprawled out beside me, wearing just a towel. Barely.

That is also delicious.

He's worked his hand into the open collar of my robe, his robe, and his fingers are curved possessively around my shoulder.

His own cup of tea is sitting on the coffee table, half-drunk. But as we snuggled in, he set it aside and tipped his head back.

We're finally, temporarily, sated from the feverish hunger for each other that was unleashed when I came over.

I draw a lazy circle on the heavy slabs of his torso.

"I love you," I whisper.

I need to say it when we aren't in the throes of passion. I need to say it softly, in the quiet, and name it as the underlying reason for this moment's perfection.

His throat works, and he takes a deep breath, before catching my hand. He turns his head and looks at me as he kisses my fingertips one by one.

"I worried for a long time that what I felt for you wasn't love. I've wanted you so much, from the moment I laid eyes on you, that I convinced myself it had to be something else. Lust, maybe. Or lunacy. Because at times I thought I must be mad, dreaming of soft moments with another man's wife. And I think, in hindsight, I leaned into the lust even harder to try to convince myself it was just a captivation of my base animal need. Because you are so fucking beautiful, and sexy. Any man would be forgiven for wanting..."

I set my tea on the console table just behind me so I can touch him with both hands. "What kind of soft moments did you dream about?"

He laughs under his breath. "All of them. Movie nights. Cooking together. Getting a dog. Holding you on the ice at family skate days. Having—" He cuts himself off, but he doesn't look away.

My pulse takes flight.

His gaze has always been so direct, even when he's holding himself back.

He doesn't need to show restraint anymore, though.

"Having kids?" God, I hope that's what he was going to say.

It's like waiting for cold molasses to pour as I hold my breath for his response.

"Aye," he finally says. His voice has dipped low, to the roughest of sandpaper. "I dreamed of that."

Hot tears threaten behind my eyelids, but I will not cry again today. So I try to smile instead.

"Not mentioning your ex," he says carefully. "Since we're barely wearing any clothes still."

I laugh. "This robe feels pretty protective. We can talk about him if you want."

"I want to talk about you. But sometimes that means

talking about your marriage, too." He strokes my cheek. "How do you feel about children?"

"They're lovely. I always thought I would have a family some day. I pushed Max to choose a house with more bedrooms, because I thought…"

"But he never agreed?"

I make a face. "When we got married, he wanted babies and I wasn't ready. And then by the time I was ready, he'd changed his mind. Just one of the many reasons why we weren't suited to each other."

"And you have an IUD?"

"It's easier than the pill. I got it before we left New York, because I liked my gynaecologist there and she said it would be good for at least five years, but I could have it taken out at any time and my fertility would return pretty quickly."

He grins. "Good to know."

I push at him. He doesn't move. I push again, and he leans in, kissing me softly. He tastes like sex and tea and everything I've ever wanted. Like a future filled with loud little redheaded tykes, and a dog we can take to the rink.

"I was wrong, by the way. About all of it. How I felt about you when I met you. It wasn't love, not yet. It wasn't lust, not exactly. And it wasn't lunacy on any level. It was simpler than all of that. I met you, and I was yours. And I didn't have the words for that, so I couldn't be a better friend. I wish I'd known earlier how awful Max was to you."

"I didn't know, either," I say quickly. "It wasn't until this summer that I could see my marriage in comparison to others around me. You couldn't have helped me any sooner." I search his face. "Do you know how the trade to Calgary happened?"

He blinks in surprise. "No. No clue, why?"

"It just seemed very out of the blue."

"Something Dorrian said to me when he was reading me the riot act before sending me down to Niagara Falls might have something to do with it. He said that he knew from watching Max and I fight on the ice that it was over you. He, uh, married the wife of another player."

"Oh." My face heats up. "If he figured that out, it won't be long before the online gossip trolls put all of that together."

"Let them talk. The Dorrians are happy, years later. And most people have forgotten about that drama." He touches my embarrassed cheeks. "I need to say this. About your question earlier, and the photos from your past. I've Googled you. More than once. I've probably seen them all."

"Oh."

"They're hot."

Max hates them, I almost say.

But Russ knows that, and we've had too many conversations about my ex-husband already. So I cling to something else I haven't felt comfortable saying in a long time. "I think so, too."

He smiles softly. "Good. Now that I've had the repeated pleasure of being intimate with you, I can confidently say that seeing a naked or near naked picture of you isn't the same thing. They aren't in the same universe. Ever since that night on the terrace, I haven't been able to forget the way you look when you come. Which isn't anything like a fancy New York City model, by the way. It's like a desperate, eager small-town girl from Michigan. A girl with big hopes and dreams, excited that they're coming true."

I stare at him in shock.

"I imagine it's a very exclusive club, the number of

people who know how real you look in that moment. How very down to earth and sexy and relatable you are. Because when I'm that close, I'm pretty fucking desperate and eager myself. A kid from Scotland who thinks he's all that and nothing will stop him."

When I still don't say anything, he rolls his eyes at himself. "Or maybe I'm trying to make sense of two separate things—"

"No," I say in a rush. "No, you're right. Sex with you feels like I'm being stripped back to my most real self." I lick my lower lip nervously. "Max doesn't know what I look like in that moment. I mean, he does now…because he watched me fall apart because of you. But before that…"

Russ frowns. "Never?"

I shake my head. "No. Never. I faked it a lot, but… he didn't care if I got off once I told him it was hard."

"Jesus Fuck. But at the same time, he got all twisted over photos from your past? I know you know this now, beautiful, but it's really fucked up that your husband was more possessive over public images of you than he was of the actual flesh and blood you. And among a myriad of other things I'll never forgive him for, the fact he left you untaken care of in that way for eight years is disgusting."

"My fierce protector."

A growl emanates from deep within him. "Always. And your fierce provider. Of orgasms and tea. Centre of palm kisses and biscuits at midnight."

"And babies?"

"Aye. And babies as soon as you want them."

CHAPTER 52
RUSS

The next morning, as I'm getting ready to go over to the arena for morning skate before our evening season opener, I get an email from the team at BioPunk.

The subject line reads, **Guess who our top brand ambassador for Q3 was?**

If the answer isn't Russell Fucking Armstrong, I'll be an idiot for clicking into this email on an important game day. But since Shannon slept in my arms last night, I'm feeling lucky.

"What are you reading with that smile on our face?" Shannon asks as she strides back to bed from the washroom, naked and perfect.

"It's another offer from BioPunk. They're happy with me."

"More commercials?"

I groan as I read the email further. "A new product."

I hand her the phone. She skims the message, and starts laughing when she gets to the good part. Or bad part, depending on how much I care about what Scottish TikTok thinks of me.

"You have to do it," she says, handing it back. Her eyes are dancing. "It's perfect."

"I cannae."

"No?"

"I'l be the laughingstock of the entire hockey world. Not to mention Scotland."

"But what if they're laughing *with* you?" She winds her arms around my neck. "Russell Armstrong proudly drinks—"

"Don't say it."

She's already memorized the tag line. "A sweet and tangy complete meal drink, from the makers of BioPunk."

Her voice is a husky purr in my ear, and I have to admit, I'd watch that TikTok on repeat a thousand times. "Aye. When you say it like that, I'd order a caseload."

"Say it," she whispers.

I'm laughing. "A sweet and tangy meal—"

"A sweet and tangy complete meal drink—"

"A sweet and tangy complete meal drink, from the makers of BioPunk." I sigh. "SPUNK makes all the difference."

She tips her head back and lets out a throaty, perfect laugh.

I guess I'll be taking the contract after all.

"All right. I'll email them back after morning skate. Will you be here for my afternoon nap?"

"Would you actually nap if I were?" She kisses my cheek. "I'm going to pack and find an apartment this afternoon."

"You can stay here as long as you want."

"That's so tempting, and my answer would be forever."

She takes a deep breath. "But I've never lived on my own. And probably, after this—I mean hopefully!—I won't again. I need to have my own space for a bit while I go through my divorce and do some therapy."

How can I argue with that? "Maybe there's an empty apartment elsewhere in this building."

"I'll look close by. Not that close, though."

I lean back against the headboard and watch as she dresses again in the clothes she wore here yesterday.

Once she's ready to go, I leave with her. At my apartment door, just before we head downstairs, I hook my fingers into the back pocket of her jeans and yank her towards me. The thread protests, threatening to pop, but she thuds into my side before the pocket rips off.

"Careful," she teases.

"I'm going to miss you tonight."

She tips her face up to kiss me. "Have a great game."

"I want you in the stands. I want you in my number, cheering me on."

"I know." But she can't cheer me on from the WAG suite, not yet. "Not tonight. Soon. But not opening night. Not your first game back from being sent down. Come on."

"Stop being reasonable. I don't want you to be reasonable. You're mine and I want everyone to know it."

She beams at me. "I love you. Go win a hockey game."

"The big guy is back!"

I clap hands with Malik and give him a wink. "I had to go win some games somewhere else to bring the right energy tonight."

"Man, while you were gone, the locker room vibe was *not* it. So grateful you're back and—" He glances around. "The former captain is *gone*."

I grin. "It's only going to get better from here, I promise."

"Boys!" Ty strides towards us, his arms out. "The crew is back together. Have you seen the line up on the board?"

Zondi nods. "I was just about to tell Rusty I'm on his line today."

"Fuck yeah." I pump my fist. "We'll smash 'em good."

Before we go on the ice, we have a team meeting to go over the scouting report on Florida.

One of the assistant coaches leads us through a few video clips, and then summarizes at the end. "They forecheck hard. They're very good at breaking up plays out of our D-zone. Watch their sticks! They're going to get in your grill and make it hard to make space. Stay calm and reset as needed. Focus on hitting the net and creating rebounds that disrupt their systems. That's the plan. Run through some of that in your skate this morning, and then get a good rest. We'll see you back here at five for the evening team meeting."

Out on the ice, I run through some of those disrupting plays with Malik.

"The most important thing to remember is that you're a big kid. Their scouting report on you is going to be to try to make you second guess yourself. Play big."

"Play big," he repeats. "Got it."

He heads off in search of food next.

"Remember when you were still growing?" Marsh asks as he skates up. "I swear that kid eats eleven meals a day and he's still always hungry."

"What do you want to bet he ends up at six-five and two-fifty?"

"Ooof. I just hope he's either still on my team, or I'm retired, by the time that happens." Kieran hooks his arm over my shoulder. "Speaking of guys I'm glad are on my team, welcome back. How was your brief stay in the AHL?"

"Humbling. We drove to Pennsylvania on a fucking bus."

He laughs harder than he should. "You did break the guy's jaw."

"He had it coming."

"Definitely won't be missed." Marsh shakes his head. "It's too bad, though. Shannon is the top fundraiser for the team foundation, did you know that? I just saw something for the Highlanders Ball—they were going to give her an award."

"She's not moving—" I cut myself off.

He narrows his eyes and grins.

"Was that a trap?" I skate away from him, flipping him the bird. "Fuck you, Marshie."

"Missed ya, bud!" he calls back cheerfully. "Hey, go check out the new goalie. Apparently he's starting tonight."

CHAPTER 53
SHANNON

For the second time in two days, I turn on my phone to a flood of text messages.

Yesterday, the only one I looked for was from Russ.

Today, I know I owe my friends some responses.

Removing myself from the WAG group chat is one of the things I talked with my new therapist about in my first session. She didn't fully understand why I was so emotional about having to do it, or why I would have to.

"It's hard to explain," I told her.

But as I stare at my phone now, I realize it's tied up in all of the voice notes I've recorded for the podcast—these women are my friends, and I'm supposed to remove myself from their space because my husband moved on from his job.

And I just…did that, no problem, when I left New York.

All of the stupid rules I just accepted that kept me tightly confined in a life defined by the choices of a man. And not just any man, but an asshole.

A wave of furious, righteous anger rolls through me, and I start typing.

SHANNON

I'm so sorry I didn't reply sooner. I turned my phone off yesterday because it was just all too much.

I know the ritual here is that I remove myself from this chat but I don't want to. Can you make a new WAG chat loop for team stuff and we can keep this one going for everything else?

KILEY

BABE! Are you okay?

HARPER

Have you left for Calgary yet? Or are you still at home? I drove by last night but didn't see any lights on.

ANI

I came by and pounded on your door, so if you were home and you ignored me...well, I get it. How are you feeling????

Lauren, who rarely participates in the group chats anyway, but also in this case knows that I'm not going to Calgary, just drops a heart on my second message.

BECCA

You can't abandon us, even if you move! This group chat is for life. You and Ani were my first WAG sisters.

ANI

Sister WAGs would be such a good show

KILEY

I read a horny fanfic like that earlier this year

HARPER

Inside voice, babe

KILEY

What? Maybe they want to read it, too?

I wipe my eyes. I'm laughing with them, but I'm just straight up crying, too.

Then Kiley sends me a text separate from the group chat.

KILEY

In case you didn't see my earlier messages,
if you need anything at all...I bet this trade
is making everything more complicated.

SHANNON

Actually, in some ways it makes it easier.
But if you have the name of your landlord to
share...I'm in the market for an apartment.

KILEY

You aren't moving?

SHANNON

Not out of the city, if that's what you mean

KILEY

Holy shit. Where are you?

SHANNON

I'm going back to the house to pack

KILEY

Where were you last night?

I take a deep breath.

SHANNON

I stayed with Russ for the first time

KILEY

BABE

SHANNON

We're going to take things slow

KILEY

Shut up, no you aren't. That man loves you.

It takes my breath away that the truth was so obvious. *I know. And I love him, too.*

SHANNON

I still need my own place for a bit

KILEY

Okay, I'll talk to my landlord and see if you can do month to month

Holy shit

In hindsight, maybe we should have seen this coming

I'm happy for you

I let out a sigh of relief.

Okay. Now it's time to find some cardboard boxes.

———

I watch the game that night while I pack up my house. After starting this afternoon, I was shocked to realize it wouldn't take me that long, and I decided to keep powering through until every personal trace of Shannon Barker was removed from the Tilman residence.

It is shocking how little is actually mine. I spent a lot of Max's money over the years on furniture for *us*, furniture for *his* life. But none of it is solely *mine*. When I met him, I had a lot of expensive clothes and some jewelry, and other than a growing book collection, that is still pretty much all I have at the end of my marriage, too. Over the years, Max added to that jewelry collection, and I'm conflicted about taking those pieces, but Lauren is clear that they were gifts and they are solely mine. Also, I might have to sell some or all of it to support myself over the next year.

The goalie they got in the trade to Calgary is in net tonight, because their regular goalie and their back up are both out with a stomach bug. And the big Russian looks… good. Very good. It's all the announcers can talk about.

In front of him, the team is playing with joy. The first period is scoreless, but it's not joyless, and when they come back for the second period, Hayden Calhoun scores forty-three seconds in. As he skates onto the bench, Russ's line comes onto the ice. They look big and imposing, and every time Florida tries to take control of the game, either Russ or Malik Zondi delivers a middle of the ice hit that I can hear all the way at home.

Their shift is almost two minutes of bone-crunching pain, and when the next line change happens, Florida looks broken.

I bite my fist with excitement. They're doing it. First game of the season, and they've *gelled*. It's beautiful.

My packing slows down.

By the third period, I'm kneeling on my bed, yelling at the TV.

When the Highlanders win, I'm crying. I wish I was there to hug my girls and blow kisses to Russ. The team circles around the goalie as the arena turns thunderous for him, cheering Arty Arty He's All Right.

"Welcome to Hamilton, Alexei," I murmur as I climb off the bed and get back to packing.

I put what I can into my car, and stack some boxes near the front door to be picked up once I have an apartment arranged.

I've just come back in from outside when my phone rings.

The joy that I feel when I see Russ's name on the screen is unparalleled. "Hey, you."

"How's my girl?"

"Better now."

"I thought about you all night."

"Even when you were being a brick wall on the ice? It was a good game."

"I'm motivated to multitask now."

I laugh. "Please pay full attention to the game."

"You get every other minute of the day."

"Fair deal."

"What is my love doing right now?"

I sigh. "Packing. I've done everything except my main closet, so I'm almost done."

"Do you want help?"

"Would that be weird?"

"I've been to your house before. And I'm a grown-up. Unless it's too weird for you."

"No, not at all. Come on over."

"I'm already on my way."

It doesn't take him long, and before I know it he's

bounding up the front walk and sweeping me into his arms as I push the front door shut behind him.

"Missed you," he says between kisses.

His hair is still wet from the shower. "You sped through your stuff after the game."

"Wanted to get to my girl."

"Be still my heart."

He ducks his head and kisses the top curve of my cleavage. "Don't be still, little heart."

From somewhere upstairs, my phone rings, interrupting our flirting. I ignore it, but when it starts again, I sigh.

"I should go see who that is. It might be the girls spying on us from outside."

He chuckles as he follows me up the stairs.

"I told Kiley I spent last night at your place," I say over my shoulder.

"Good."

I grab my phone off the top of the box where I left it when Russ arrived, and look at the screen. "Ugh. It's Max."

"Can I take it for you?" Russ's eyes lights up.

"No." I hold my finger to my mouth. "Shh. I'll be quick."

I tap the answer button, then put Max on speaker phone.

He immediately lights into me. "That didn't take you fucking long, did it?"

I roll my eyes. "What are you talking about?"

"Did you forget about the Ring cam?"

I wince at Russ. Yes, I had. "Okay, so?"

Russ just shrugs, unaffected.

"I want him out of my fucking house," Max snarls.

"He's helping me pack."

"I. Saw. Him. Kiss—"

Russ pushes my phone of my hand. It tumbles onto the

bed as he covers my mouth with his, his tongue possessively pushing between my lips.

Hot, fierce arousal climbs inside me. This need was stoked all evening by watching him play so magnificently and then his immediate desire to see me post-game.

In the distance, there's some swearing and a demand to know if I'm still listening.

No, no I am not.

Russ circles my throat loosely with his hand, his thumb stroking against my pulse point at the base as he deepens the kiss, making my thighs shake.

When he pulls back, I'm out of breath. He turns me around and bends me over the bend, pulling down my yoga pants. Just to my knees, making it impossible to spread my thighs.

"Aye," he growls loudly. "I kissed your wife. And she liked it." He cups my sex from behind. "Fuck, Shannon, you're soaking wet for me, aren't you?"

I moan shamelessly.

He ruthlessly finds the core of my slickness and shoves two fingers into my achingly empty pussy.

"Hear that, Max? I'm helping her pack. You can hang up at any point, bud. We're busy over here."

CHAPTER 54
RUSS

Fuck, this is dangerous. But as Shannon twists her head back to stare at me, she looks *alive*, and that's worth every risk.

"*No?*" I ask her silently, mouthing the word.

She squirms on my fingers, humping her hips back against my touch.

Not *no*, then.

And I don't have to fully glance at the phone to see the line is still engaged.

That makes me so fucking hard. Just as it did that night on the terrace, knowing that Max is reduced to nothing but an observer as I claim his wife again is a fucking rush.

He underestimated both of us.

I push her yoga pants lower, off her legs. "I need to be inside you. Can I use you? Can you be a good little hole for me?"

She moans and nods.

"Spread your legs. Show me where you need this big cock."

Her hips tilt up, revealing her glistening core. So fucking pretty.

I shove my own clothes to the floor and climb on top of her, mounting her from behind, my erection slapping against her wet cunt. With the fingers I shoved inside her, I now trail my touch up her back and around her throat, circling her neck before I grip her jaw as I drag my cock against her pussy.

She's liquid for me now, my dirty girl. My perfect slut.

But he's not going to hear me use that word out loud for her. He's only going to hear someone treating her like the princess she could have been for him—if he'd been someone entirely different. If he'd been worthy.

"My pretty girl. You're all mine, aren't you?"

"Yes," she breathes.

"This is the only time I'm going to fuck you on this bed. We'll pack up these sheets smelling like sex, won't we?"

"Russ…" She rocks her hips up, trying to capture the tip of my cock with her wet little hole. "Please. I need you."

"Aye, you do. Just like I need you. Waited too long for you. Need to…" I groan as her wiggles finally work and she impales herself on my shaft. "God *damn*, Shannon. You're so fucking tight for me."

"Use me, Russ," she pants. "Take me as rough as you can."

"You want more? Of course you do. Fuck, you're so sexy." I rear up, ignoring the twinges along my ribs and down the back of my thighs from the game.

Being inside her is already making me feel better.

I slap my hips against her arse, groaning with each thrust.

And this view…fuck.

Her bottom is perfect, tight and round, and between her cheeks I have a perfect view of her arsehole clenching against nothing and her slick little pussy lips wrapped around my wet cock.

"You're so tight for me." I shove balls deep and moan as she squeezes my entire length. "Taking my cock like a good girl, aren't you? A good little bad girl."

She slaps at the bed, writhing as my cock throbs deep in her belly.

"Harder?"

"Yes!"

"Tell me you're my good girl."

"I'm…" She sobs. "Russ!"

"Tell. Me." I snap my hips, thrusting for emphasis.

"I'm your good girl," she moans.

"What else?"

"I'm your dirty girl."

"Aye. Fucking right. Mine. Only mine."

"Only yours." She's shaking now.

I put my thumb to her back hole and rub a slow circle, loving how that steady touch makes her thighs shake against mine. "Are you going to come for me, dirty girl?"

"Yes!"

"Come on my cock, baby. I love feeling you come. Make me feel like the luckiest man in the world and—" Her pussy clamps down on me, and my words turn into a feral grunt.

"Fuck." My balls jolt, my arse pulling tight. "That's it. Milk my cock."

She moans my name and I thunder into her, falling on top of her as I fuck her with a ragged, desperate energy, pumping her full of my seed.

The edges of my vision turn dark and blood roars in my ears.

I wrap myself around her shaking form and press my mouth against her temple.

"I love my dirty little slut," I whisper for her ears only.

"I love you, too," she murmurs back, dreamily.

I climb off her and slap her arse lightly when I see the phone has gone dark. "I think he hung up."

She rolls over and grabs it. "Yep." She laughs and shoots me a look that's part cringe, part unabashed amusement. "Should I check and see how long he listened for?"

I take the phone from her and stretch out beside her, wet cock twitching against her soft little belly. "Nope. All that matters is he knows that if he calls you again, I'll be right there to remind him that someone else always has your back."

She squirms against me. "And my ass."

I cup her bottom and pull her against me. "And your arse, yes."

She kisses me softly. "Thank you."

"Don't thank me until we've finished packing."

"Aren't you tired?"

"Fuck, no. I won a game tonight and just had incredible sex with my girlfriend. I'll be wired for a few hours yet."

She giggles. "Mmm, I like the sound of being your girlfriend."

She's more than that already, but it's as good a place as any to start.

"Speaking of that, a little birdie told me that you're supposed to get an award at the Highlanders Ball for being the top fundraiser."

She groans. "Oh."

"What?"

"Nothing."

"Hey, we don't do that, right? No hiding."

"It's not *hiding*, it's just that…"

I lift her chin and give her a stern look. "Baby, have I not shown you enough yet that I don't care about mess?"

"I don't really want to get an award for raising money as Max's wife."

"It's not for two more months. I bet we can ask discreetly for that to be revised to your maiden name."

She doesn't look convinced. "The only reason I'm getting it is because I was a WAG."

"You *are* a WAG. It's right there in the acronym. *Girlfriend.*"

"I think the rest of the world needs a breather for a hot second before I go from *Wife* to *Girlfriend* on the team's social media account, you know?"

I don't know. I don't give two flying fucks about social media. But I know she does, so I move past that, because I have full confidence Mabel can delicately figure it out.

I kiss her softly. "Let me worry about it. But I'm taking you to that gala as my girlfriend. You're going to hold your head high. We're going to dance all night, and you're going to be recognized for your fucking hard work. Understand?"

She exhales against my lips. "Yes, I understand."

"Good girl."

CHAPTER 55
SHANNON

The next day, I get the keys to Kiley's old apartment, because the landlord hadn't rented it out yet, and Russ paid cash up front for three months' rent.

"I can pay my own rent," I protested.

He kissed me and told me not to be silly. If I find a job and still want to rent the apartment in the new year, I can do that, but he wants me taken care of right now—and he's not making any bones about the fact that by the new year, he wants me to move in with him.

I have a stupidly long list of things to do, including hiring movers, because I am not carrying boxes and a bed up the three storeys of the walk-up apartment building. But at the top of the list is finding time to reconnect with my friends.

"Guess where I am?" I say when Kiley answers her phone.

"Paris," she says readily.

"What? No. I'm in your old place." I laugh. "Why Paris?"

"I dunno. It just seemed like a Shannon thing to do, a quick jaunt across the Atlantic."

"That's the old Shannon. The new Shannon is all about the budget do-it-yourself mani-pedi."

"Oooh, I love it."

"Girls' night?"

"Absolutely. At your new apartment?"

I look around the empty space. "Umm, no. Can you host?"

"Of course. I'll send out the bat signal."

———

It's nice to kiss Russ goodnight—until I get back—and head up the elevator to Kiley's new apartment. Not that different from walking over to Ani's house…but I know I won't feel nearly as lonely on the short trip back to Russ at the end of the night.

I'm nervous knocking on the door. I deliberately waited until I was sure that the girls driving down from the Mountain would be here, so I only have to explain about the darker hair and boyfriend downstairs once.

But now that means they're all on the other side of the door, waiting.

Maybe I should have done this via text.

Kiley swings the door open. "You're here— *Your hair!*"

Which gets everyone's attention, I'm sure.

"Hi," I say, stepping inside.

Everyone calls out my name, and then I'm in the middle of a hug tackle.

"Where have you been?" Ani searches my face. "I keep looking for signs of life at your house."

"Well…"

"Let's give her room to breathe," Kiley says. "Wine?"

"Wine," I say affirmatively.

She pours a glass for Becca, herself, and me. Harper and Ani both get glasses of sparkling water, which I don't miss.

I take a deep breath. "Max moved to Calgary by himself. We've been separated since the end of the summer, really. And our marriage has been failing for longer than that."

The silence that follows is…complicated. Kiley already knew, and looks supportive. Ani and Harper probably picked up on something on some level, I'm guessing from their careful expressions. Becca, though, bless her sweet little heart, looks genuinely confused. "But…why? You're the perfect wife."

"Oh, sweetie. I really wasn't. And Max wasn't the perfect husband for me, either."

"Are you staying here?"

"Yeah, I am." I give her a warm smile. "I actually moved into Kiley's old apartment today. And I wanted to tell you guys before Ani and Harper notice moving trucks and a for sale sign at my old place. And that's why I asked Kiley to host a more low-key girls' night tonight. I'm not in the pampering income bracket anymore."

There's another knock at the door. From down the hall, Ty hollers out that he'll get it.

"About that," Kiley says. She bites her lower lip, but she doesn't actually look sorry for whatever she's about to confess. "You have spoiled all of us so many times. I think it's time for us to repay the kindness."

A familiar squad of aestheticians parades in.

My chest squeezes tight. "Guys, this is…"

"Shush," Harper says. "You deserve it."

"I haven't told you the rest of the story, though." A lump forms in my throat. "I didn't come from your old apartment building just now. I was downstairs in Russ's apartment."

They all stare at me, waiting for the punch line.

I swallow hard. "Because I'm seeing him now. He's my boyfriend."

This silence is definitely stunned. Even Kiley, who already knew I'd slept over once, looks shocked at the ease with which I said that.

I smile and laugh in delight. "Russell Armstrong is my boyfriend."

"Holy shit," Ani says.

"Finally," Harper says.

Becca is the last to react. Her eyes are big and she's covered her hand with her mouth. "Wait," she whispers. "This means you're still a WAG!"

———

"So they were all very supportive," I report to Russ.

When I came back to his apartment, I found him sprawled in bed, reading after a shower—wearing nothing but a towel slung loosely around his heavy body.

He looks so good I have to pause in the doorway and just look at him for a minute.

He slowly puts his book down. "That's good."

"And they spoiled me."

"They love you a lot." He pats the bed. "Come here. Tell me everything."

I curl up in the crook of his arm. As I think about where to start, I run my fingers up his thigh. The muscles bunch beneath my touch, and his thumb strokes an encouraging circle on my shoulder, but he doesn't otherwise move.

It's such a quiet, subtle shift from relaxing to something more intimate, and I'm not even sure if I'd call it sex at first. It's just…touching. Appreciating his magnificent body.

But then he exhales, and it's loaded with tension, and *that* feels like sex. Electricity zaps through my core at being able to affect him with just a little light touch.

"Do you like touching me?"

I squeak at the unexpectedly direct question. "Yes." I sound breathless. Girlish. My face flames. "You're sexy."

"You touching me is sexy." He tugs his towel out of the way, baring his cock and balls. "Go on, then. You can play with it."

Heat pools low in my belly as my fingers move as if on their own, going straight to the tight dark brown curls at the base of his shaft. His cock thickens, rising up off his sac, and I slide my touch there next. More deliberate now.

You can play with it.

Explicit permission to do what I want.

I curl my fingers around his balls, cupping the warm, silky weight of them.

"Do you still want to tell me about your night?" he asks thickly..

"Maybe later," I murmur.

"We have time." He strokes his fingers through my hair. "We have all the time in the world."

I'm leaning in to flutter kisses up his shaft when my phone goes off in my back pocket.

I sigh against his cock, then reach back and grab it. Without looking at it, I hand it to him. "Can you put this on the bedside table?"

He glances at the screen and stops his arm halfway to setting it down. "Hang on, you might want to read this."

I sit up and take it back.

LAUREN

Please call me, it's urgent

Frowning, I tap the phone button on the screen.

"Hey Shannon." She sounds out of breath. "Are you alone?"

"I'm with Russ. You're on speaker phone."

She hesitates a beat.

He gestures for me to go to the living room.

"Hang on." I take her off speaker and go out, closing the door behind me. "Okay, I'm alone. What's up?"

"Boy, do I have some news for you."

CHAPTER 56
RUSS

I wait fifteen minutes, but Shannon doesn't return to my bedroom. So I put on some sweatpants and a t-shirt, and I go to find her.

She's curled up on the couch. Not on the phone anymore.

"Hey," I say softly, rounding it and sitting at her feet.

She looks up at me, her face blank. "Hi."

"You didn't come back."

"I'm just…" She shakes her head. "Ummm…"

"What is it?"

"I'm not married to Max. I never was, apparently. They had trouble getting our New York marriage certificate, because it turns out that it was issued by a clerk who didn't do their job—I'm not clear on the details—and at some point, that mess was quietly cleaned up by someone who didn't want it to come out. Long story short, Max has another marriage certificate from the State of Nevada from when he was eighteen."

"He married someone in Vegas." I can't believe it. Now I

know why she didn't come back to find me. I feel just as stunned as she looks.

"I, umm… I'm here on a spousal visa that now my lawyer knows is invalid. The team needs to be notified, since they did our immigration paperwork. And Max is exposed to huge legal ramifications. She asked me if I think he's a bigamist." She laughs, but it sounds hollow. "Can you imagine Max trying to keep up with two wives? There's no way."

"You think he forgot about the first wedding?"

"Drunk eighteen-year-old? Probably." She shivers. "I don't know. But I'm not sure how I can stay here now."

"Oh, baby." I pull her into my lap. She's still and unyielding, but I just rub her back and hold her against me until she finally softens. "Look, I'm not a hot shot superstar of the league or anything, but I'm a Canadian citizen. We can get married. Or I think there's a fiancée visa we can apply for. Or we'll find out how long you can stay on a visitor's visa, and you'll just cross the border regularly. People do this. It's okay. And that's a problem for the lawyers to sort out. Which they will, because they all fucked up if nobody else found this before your divorce attorneys."

She laughs. "I guess I don't need to use Lauren for my divorce anymore. Now I just need her as an immigration attorney."

I chuckle. "That's the spirit."

"I had resigned myself to a year-long separation." She sucks in a breath. "Oh my God. I'm not married."

"You aren't married."

"Fuck, that's a…" She shakes her head.

I shift my body weight to the edge of the couch, then lift her in my arms.

"Russ!"

"I'm taking you to bed. To sleep. Everything will seem simpler in the morning."

She wraps her arms around my neck and rests her head on my shoulder. "You promise?"

I'm already thinking about the calls I'm going to make once she's asleep. "I promise, beautiful."

CHAPTER 57
SHANNON

"I might need to move to Hamilton sooner than later with all of this excitement," Lauren says when she meets me at the law office she's working out of on my behalf.

I still can't believe the news she told me last night. At some point today, Max was notified by someone who works with Lauren. There's no point in keeping this information from him, she says, and our effort to communicate the discovery at the earliest opportunity was presented as a sign of good faith.

"Good faith?" I snort. "What did he say about that?"

She keeps her expression straight. "He said something about you making this up to cover up the fact that you were flaunting your infidelity through a phone call to him?"

"It can't be infidelity if we weren't ever married," I say tartly. "But anything he might have accidentally overheard was very recent, post-separation."

"It's fine. Let us handle that. If he contacts you again, you can just ignore him. If he persists, we'll get a restraining order."

It's surreal, the power he thinks he still has over me when he exposed himself to this insane level of legal risk. But that's a problem for his lawyer to explain to him. I'm done with this man.

I change the subject slightly and ask her to explain to me again how she thinks this happened, and what it means for me.

"You aren't married to Max Tilman. Legally, you never were."

"But we had a marriage license. Didn't we have to present it when we moved to Canada? I have a spousal visa! Did I lie to a foreign government?"

"Let's take this step by step. First of all, you bought a house with Max, under the good faith belief that he was your husband. Our first step will be to file in family court and hope they can deal with the division of marital assets in the same way they would in a divorce. But crucially, Max's attorney will not be able to use your prenup against you. He signed that in bad faith."

"There's no way Max had another family."

"No, I don't think he did. He got married in Vegas when he was eighteen. That first wife was easy to track down, and I spoke to her last night. She hasn't heard from him since that weekend. But she is his legal wife. So the prenup and marital contract he made you sign definitely aren't legal, and the dissolution of your relationship is like a civil union. You didn't sign an agreement for that."

"I don't want his money."

"Fair. We won't go for support. But your name is on the deed to that house. You decorated it. You spent equal time, probably more time, in it than he did. You made it a home.

You deserve, if nothing else, half of the proceeds of its sale. And we'll ask him to cover legal costs, as well."

"What does this mean for my visa to stay in Canada?"

She takes a deep breath. "That's more complicated."

———

Two days later, I'm ushered into a nondescript meeting room in the Highlanders head office, with Lauren at my side.

"Have a seat, Ms. Barker," the receptionist says.

She's the third person to use my maiden name since we arrived at the arena. It's like a team-wide memo was issued to ignore the fact that I had been the team's captain for a year.

That's Russ's doing. I haven't slept much since Lauren broke the news to me, and I've heard him slip out of bed to have hushed conversations, only to crawl back into bed soon after and hold me tighter than before.

We've only been sitting for thirty seconds when the door opens behind us.

A trio of lawyers I've never seen before file in. They exchange pleasantries with Lauren, and then they begin discussing a lot of preliminary details that go over my head.

There's a closed caption TV in the corner. I watch the feed of the morning skate—today it's a visiting team having a light practice before tonight's game.

Lauren touches my hand, and I refocus on the conversation. "We're asking for time to sort out this very unexpected legal upset that my client had no part in. She owns a home with your player—"

"He no longer plays for our team—"

"But you were the sponsoring organization for his work visa," she says pleasantly. "And while that will transfer—"

"What we're saying is—"

"I don't want to embarrass the team," I interrupt. "Look, I don't know about the legal stuff. That's for you to work out with Lauren. But I think it's reasonable to ask for a bit of support from the team to avoid mutual disruptions, right?"

They glance at each other. "We understand and appreciate that perspective, Ms. Barker. Legally, however, our hands are tied. We can't extend your visa. We have tried to look at this creatively. However..."

Creative legal solutions are not my forte.

I look back at the TV. It's flipped to an empty hallway. Back in New York, they had a similar set up, but when they weren't showing a live feed from the ice, they re-ran old games and other team-owned media material.

Team-owned media.

"Offer me a job," I say suddenly.

Lauren looks at me in alarm. We haven't discussed this. I don't even know if it's viable.

"You don't need to pay me much. But surely there's a work visa you can give me until the end of the hockey season." At that point, Russ and I will know what our next step will be. I just need a bit of breathing time. "I have television experience in New York. And I'm starting a podcast."

I force myself to finish the end of that sentence, to have pride in myself, despite feeling like an absolute faker pretending I'm worthy of this gig.

Nobody replies.

A phone vibrates on the table, and it's so loud in the silence. One of the lawyers picks it up, then passes it down their line, and then they all look expectantly to the door.

"It's a good idea," Lauren whispers to me. "We can discuss more—"

The door swings open and a handsome man in his late forties, maybe early fifties, sweeps in. "Please don't get up. Jack Benton. Shannon, I think we met at the expansion draft announcement, yes?"

I nod, surprised to see the team owner. "Yes, sir."

"Oh, let's not be like that. Call me Jack. And Ms. Point is your lawyer?"

"Call me Lauren," she says confidently, holding out her hand for him to shake.

"You have a lot of people rooting for you, Shannon." Jack sits down at the head of the table. "The team General Manager in particular, but also one of our founding players, I understand."

"Yes." I press my lips together to keep from grinning at the reference to Russ.

"Tell me about your podcast."

My mouth goes dry. "Um… Well…"

His eyebrows curve up.

I swallow hard. "It's called the Ex-WAGs Club. I mean, that's the current idea. But—"

"Go on."

"It's a raw look at what it's like to have a marriage fall apart. Probably not team-sponsored content, but I'm confident in its storytelling value. Rediscovering oneself after a relationship ends is hard. Doing it in a foreign country or across the continent from your entire support network is a whole other thing."

"That's not something we can put the team's branding on."

"No, sir. I get that. But there's a lot of value in native

advertising and authentic brand development that is separate from the corporate space. I would be happy to develop another podcast at the same time for the team."

"Interesting." He flicks a gaze at the legal team. "Make it happen. A three-month visa to start. And then if it works out, we can extend her for a year."

My mouth falls open.

He stands.

I stand, and the lawyers stand.

"Thank you," I whisper.

"Welcome to the team on your own merits, Ms. Barker." He holds out his hand to me, and I shake it. "Good luck."

CHAPTER 58
RUSS

The next day, I have to leave on a four-game road trip. And for the first time in my sixteen-year career, I don't want to pile onto the bus to the airport.

"I'm fine," Shannon says as I reluctantly pack.

Is she? How can she be? I'm not fine, and it wasn't my fucked-up marriage that evaporated into a dark version of Never Never Land. "Stay here while I'm gone."

"I need to stay at my own apartment."

It doesn't even have a bed yet. That's being moved later today, along with more boxes that she probably won't even unpack until I can talk her into moving in with me.

But she needs this process. She needs to go through the steps, and trying to take over and boss her around won't help. "Ach, go on then. But I'll worry about you."

She puts on a bright face. "We'll talk every night."

I fold her in against my body and breathe in the scent of her hair. "And every morning, too."

———

That night, she FaceTimes me from her apartment. We chat as she makes her bed and crawls into it, and then I say goodnight.

But I don't end our call.

"I don't want to hang up," I confess.

"Me, either."

"Then we won't." I stretch out on my hotel bed.

She closes her eyes. "Are you just going to watch me sleep?"

"No."

She opens one eyelid. "Yes, you are."

"You aren't even sleeping yet. I'm watching you pretend to sleep, actually."

"Same thing."

"Very much not."

Both of her eyes are open now. "Want to have phone sex?"

I hesitate. "Yes."

"But?"

"But I don't want you to think that all I love you for is your sex appeal."

"Of course not. I'm a complete package. Sex appeal, legal quagmires, dubious employment contract—"

"Thoughtful, smart, funny—"

"I'm not that funny."

"This conversation would suggest otherwise. Sex appeal, legal quagmires, dubious job? That's objectively funny. Dark, yes, but a banger."

Her expression goes soft. "You think I'm funny?"

"I really, really do."

"Now we definitely need to have phone sex."

"Shan—"

"Russ, I know you want to make this better for me."

"I do. I don't like you being alone right now. Even as you're handling capably. It's still a lot of stress."

"I know. I just need to get through it." She pauses and makes a face. Then she licks her lips, her eyelids fluttering. Instantly, there's a vibe shift. A clearly communicated push on a conversation-reset button. "But nice words won't help."

Ah, fuck me, I'm a goner. "What will?"

She flicks an innocent gaze at the camera. "I don't know."

That's all right. "I do. Even though I'm not home, that's not going to stop me from giving you the sloppy, desperate sex you deserve. You think I want to make this better? I want to make it worse. I want to show you that no matter how messy and bad life gets, you're still a queen to me. Don't you think the best way to do that is to make *you* messy and bad?"

Her cheeks flush and she makes an indistinct sound in the back of her throat.

I've been thinking about pushing these buttons with her. Had planned to do it at home, but here we are, and she seems to like it.

"Right now, the only thing I want to hear out of your soft little mouth is yes and no and stop and more. And if you want me to *actually* stop, you can say a safe word."

"Cottage," she whispers softly.

"Cottage," I repeat. Fuck, I'm glad that's safe for her. "I like it."

"Me, too."

"Good girl. Now get on your back for me."

She rolls over, holding her phone above her.

I do the same, putting my phone on the bed and looming

above her. "You're so soft and pretty. Love your mouth. Open for me." Her lips part and her tongue peeks out. God, to lay my cock right there, right now. I drag in a breath. "That's it. Wider. Show me how needy you are for something in your mouth."

She moans and strains beneath me.

"Where's your other hand?"

She gives me a guilty look. "I was just—"

"Mouth open. No talking. Show me your fingers."

She brings them into view. They're glistening.

Fuck.

"Suck them for me. Show me how that naughty fucking mouth can be useful. Don't hesitate. Don't think about it. Just be messy for me. Be slutty for me. Lose yourself in how right it feels to be bad, because fuck, it looks good from here."

I'm hard, my cock pinned between me and the bed. And as she pushes her fingers into her mouth, her lips closing around them, my balls squeeze tight.

Good doesn't touch how fuckable and perfect she looks.

"Do you want to touch your slick clit again?"

"Yes."

"Do you think you deserve to come?"

"No."

"What if I want you to come anyway, for me?"

Heat slashes across her cheeks.

Yes, she'd like that.

"Touch yourself, beautiful. I want to see you come."

"I—" She cuts herself off. I told her to only say *yes* and *no* and *stop* and *more*, and I can practically see her thoughts process that.

I don't care which she picks. She doesn't need to be bad

for me, but if she wants to be bad for herself, I can play that game.

But pinned beneath me, even with a thousand kilometres between us, Shannon's desire to please me wins out over her self-doubt.

Coming for me is exactly the distraction she needs.

She lifts the camera and tilts it to follow her hand as she pushes her fingers down to her panties.

My vision narrows as her hand disappears under the stretchy cotton. It's the best and worst kind of tease, where I can't actually see much, but what I can see (glimpses of bare skin) and hear (soft, slick sounds) is everything.

"Fuck, I can hear how wet that messy cunt already is," I growl.

She whimpers and rubs faster.

"Now you want to come, don't you? Dirty girl."

"I need it," she confesses, breaking.

"So fucking horny once you get going. I bet you can come twice."

"No…" Except now her face is flaming.

Yes she fucking can.

"You're not going to stop rubbing."

She's panting hard now.

"Even after you come. Your fingers will keep circling that needy clit."

I don't know if I'm issuing orders or just stating the obvious.

She nods and shakes her head at the same time. Yes. No. *Yes.*

I push up on my knees, giving myself enough space to fist my cock as I watch her get closer and closer to her first orgasm.

"Russ," she begs.

"Keep rubbing."

"I need—"

"I know. Keep going. I'm so hard for you."

She lets out a ragged moan, her hips lifting and her hand holding the camera wavering.

I squeeze the tip of my cock roughly, stopping myself from joining her in her release.

She's not done yet.

I'm not done with her yet.

"Keep going," I growl. "Give me another."

"No…" She laughs and keeps rubbing. "You're mean."

"You like it."

"So much." Her breath hitches. "Are you going to come with me?"

"Maybe on your fourth orgasm," I lie.

I'm not going to make it through three more pretty displays like that. When we're home together, though…

I have plans.

"Don't make me use cottage," she whispers. "I want to hear you let go."

"Together, then." My cock thrusts through my fist. "If I see you let go again, I'll follow. I promise."

"You promise?" Her voice is shaking already.

"I'll follow you everywhere," I swear. "But especially into bliss."

She gasps and holds her breath, her eyelids fluttering shut.

My own breath seizes in my chest until she shudders her exhale, and then I come with a roar.

"Yes, yes, yes," she breathes, her eyes wide as she stares up at me.

I thrust into my hand, flooding it and filling my shorts.

"Fuck. Made a mess."

She grins. "Sloppy and desperate?"

I give her a crooked smile right back. "I guess we both needed that."

CHAPTER 59
RUSS

Two months later

Even though Shannon spends a lot of nights at my place, on the evening of the Highlanders Ball, she gets ready at her little apartment on the edge of downtown.

I'm expecting that we might both drink a fair bit tonight, so instead of driving myself, I've arranged for town cars to take us there and back again.

Tonight is my girl's celebration.

I let myself to the apartment building and jog up the stairs two at a time.

It's her night, but I'm excited.

I double knock on the door and she answers immediately.

"Hello, sexy," she says, taking in my black tuxedo. "I'm almost ready to go, I just need to grab my purse."

She's wearing a short red dress with puffy little sleeves and a square neckline that leads to a lot of touchable fabric that flares out around her body when she turns.

It's equally sweet and sexy, very playful, and unexpected for an event that will have a lot of long evening gowns.

But the fabric up close is expensive and glittery, and she shines in it.

As she twists away, I catch a glimpse of her tattoo, but her long swishing ponytail obscures it. Another perfectly Shannon touch, wanting to frame and show up her symbol of reclaiming herself.

I prowl after her, letting the door shut behind me.

The hired car can wait.

The gala…well, the gala can't wait forever. But I can take a few minutes to make sure my girl knows she's loved before we hit the red carpet.

EPILOGUE

SHANNON

April

For the second year in a row, I'm wearing a WAG jacket for the playoffs. Different number on my sequined back, but the same joyous crew of girls in the box with me as we cheer on the Highlanders for their first game.

Nothing about this season went to plan. When Max ordered half the team to gather at Russ's cottage last August, they thought they knew what they had to do to win—and then the team fell apart.

They lost more games than they won at the start of the season. By the time of the Highlanders Ball, everyone had counted us out of the playoffs.

But soon after that, Dorrian made a big coaching change.

They went on a heater.

In January, the team named a new captain. The C looks better on Jenson Hale. It looks right.

And they rallied.

Ty had as many games with hat tricks (four) in the next month as he'd had in his career to date. Kieran led the league in assists for the last thirty games of the regular season.

Russ led the league in hits *and* shots blocked by a forward, and he's going into these playoffs with the bruises to prove it.

The team finished third in our division.

Now we're in Florida for the start of the first round series.

I know it's going to be hard for them. That's the game.

But as we ease into the final chapter of this season, I don't think this is Russ's last chance at the Cup. He doesn't seem done yet.

Provided he can avoid real injury, I think he has another ninety-eight games in him for next year.

And as he jokes, his wedding schedule this summer is pretty light. Two of his teammates are getting hitched, Ty and Hayden.

And then in August, on the anniversary of that fateful team retreat, we're going to exchange our own vows.

It wasn't how I thought my WAG journey would go, but I can't think of a more magical ending—and the start of an even better next chapter as Russell Armstrong's wife.

THE END

Do you want a bit more of Russ and Shannon? Click here

to get a five-years-in-the-future look forward for our Queen WAG and her forever HEA: https://geni.us/Russ-and-Shannon-4ever

ABOUT THE AUTHOR

Ainsley Booth is a three-time *USA Today* bestselling author of erotic romance. Between her two pen names (she also writes contemporary romance as two-time *New York Times* bestseller Zoe York), she has published more than seventy books since 2013. Notable hits include *Prime Minister* and *Hate F*@k*.

facebook.com/ainsleyboothwrites

instagram.com/ainsleyboothwrites

tiktok.com/@ainsleyboothwrites

patreon.com/zoeyorkwrites

9 781998 523030